Everything but the Earl

The Night Fire Club
Book 2

KATE MCMURRAY

ARE YOU SIGNED UP FOR DRAGONBLADE'S BLOG?

You'll get the latest news and information on exclusive giveaways, exclusive excerpts, coming releases, sales, free books, cover reveals and more.

Check out our complete list of authors, too!

No spam, no junk. That's a promise!

Sign Up Here

www.dragonbladepublishing.com

Dearest Reader;

Thank you for your support of a small press. At Dragonblade Publishing, we strive to bring you the highest quality Historical Romance from some of the best authors in the business. Without your support, there is no 'us', so we sincerely hope you adore these stories and find some new favorite authors along the way.

Happy Reading!

CEO, Dragonblade Publishing

Additional Dragonblade books by Author Kate McMurray

The Night Fire Club

I Never Forget a Duke (Book 1)
Everything but the Earl (Book 2)

Chapter One

London, 1817

GRACE MIDWOOD STOOD just inside the Rutherford ballroom, trying to process what she had just seen.

The man she'd been betrothed to since their youth had been kissing—

"Grace!"

She looked up and saw that her dear friend Penelope Thistledown was approaching.

"You look stricken," said Penny. "Are you all right?"

Something about Penny's tone helped Grace snap out of her stupor. "I must speak with you quietly. Perhaps we can go out into the hall. To, er, get some air."

The Rutherford ball was in full swing. It was one of the largest crushes of the Season. Dozens of couples danced, a few hundred other people milled about in the ballroom, and mamas were throwing their daughters at all of the eligible bachelors. The room was hot and oppressive, the sort of space that made it hard for the ladies laced tightly into their stays to breathe properly.

Grace led Penny into the hallway outside the ballroom, where several other small groups of people lingered, having hushed conversations.

"My mother intends for me to marry the Marquess of Beresford," Grace whispered.

"I thought that was common knowledge."

"I do not wish to marry Beresford. Nor do I believe he wishes to marry me."

"Fiddlesticks. Who would not want to marry you? Why, Grace, you are beautiful and intelligent and—"

"I just spotted him kissing another." Grace opted to leave out the part where she had spotted him kissing the Earl of Waring. That was too much of a scandal to even say aloud.

"That is damning evidence," said Penny. "Well, that's simple enough. Tell your father that you and Beresford do not suit and therefore you do not wish to marry him."

"Beresford may be easily dispatched, but Father will insist I marry *someone*. Both of my parents have repeated that this will be my last Season."

Penny nodded. She was fully aware that Grace's main issue was that she did not wish to marry at all. She had no interest in becoming the property of any man. Her own parents had a dreadful marriage, in which her mother often quashed her own misery to defer to her husband, and expected Grace to do the same. On top of that, Grace loathed the city, loathed the Season, and wanted mostly to have a nice home in the country that she could manage as she saw fit. She wanted a place her friends could visit and space to work on her pottery.

One of her pieces, a large ceramic vase, sat on a pedestal in this very hallway. She recognized it, and so did not need to see the maker's mark on the base, a stylized GM for "Grace Midwood," though the world thought the sculptor was a man named Gerard Makepeace. The only people in the world who knew Grace's hands had molded that clay were Penny and her dealer, Mr. Rhodes.

"Maybe you should marry Beresford and let him carry on with whatever chit he is so enamored with, and then establish your studio in the country somewhere. He's likely got a country estate he'd let you run."

Anthony Pearson, the Marquess of Beresford, a tall, willowy man with loose, curly hair that fell to his shoulders, rounded the corner and strolled toward the ballroom beside Larkin Woodville, the Earl of Waring, a dark-haired gentleman who, if Grace was not mistaken, was heir to a dukedom. Their heads were bent close together as they walked, clearly engaged in a serious conversation. Then Beresford looked up and met Grace's gaze.

"Ah, Lady Grace," he said. "'Tis a pleasure to see you."

"My lord, may I have a word?"

Beresford glanced at Waring, who raised an eyebrow at him. "Of course. Please excuse me, Waring."

"I shall escort Lady Penelope back to the ballroom. Perhaps I will seek out the Duchess of Swynford and ask her to dance."

"The duke may not appreciate you dancing with his wife," Beresford said.

"Yes, but she is a much better dancer than he is. Unless Lady Penelope would like to dance." Waring winked and offered his arm to Penelope.

"I should be delighted, my lord."

They disappeared back into the ballroom, leaving Grace and Beresford alone.

"My lord," she began, not entirely sure what to say. "I believe we have reached something of an impasse."

Beresford frowned.

They had known each other since childhood but were hardly intimate friends. Their fathers had been close friends, and Beresford and Grace had played together a bit as children, but once they came of age, they'd necessarily moved in separate spheres. She'd liked the boy Beresford—Anthony—had been, but she did not know the man who stood before her now, especially not after what she had just seen.

Oh, he was handsome, all right, in a way that made one forget one's name, with a beautiful face and perpetually insouciant expression. But Grace just couldn't picture them sharing a home. She liked him but could not fathom him as her husband.

And yet, at the beginning of the Season, Grace's parents had more or less announced this betrothal. It had seemed to have taken Beresford off-guard as well.

"I'd like you to know," he said now, "and I say this with deep regret and the requisite apology, that I had completely forgotten about the betrothal until a month ago when my mother reminded me, mere days before it showed up in the papers."

"Yes."

"And I'm a right cad for not properly courting you once I did find out, but, well, the habits and goings on of a bachelor and so on."

Beresford had always been colorful. Grace didn't have much patience for Beresford's rambling speeches right now, especially since she did not know how long they had to speak with each other alone. "I shall cut to the chase then, shall I?"

As if he didn't hear her, he replied. "You were, what, six years old when our parents made that arrangement?"

Grace sighed. "Yes."

"And I was all of eleven. Neither of us were old enough to understand what marriage even is."

"My lord, I—"

"This may come as something of a shock, so please prepare yourself."

Grace fought rolling her eyes. He did have a flair for the theatrical, but this was ridiculous. "Anthony."

"That is to say, I do not believe our marriage would be much of a success. And I am afraid that my heart belongs to someone else now and I would make a dreadful husband, so my intention is to tell your father that—"

Grace held up a hand. "Your heart belongs to the Earl of Waring."

Beresford coughed and spluttered, making a good show of looking offended.

Grace did not have patience for prevarication, either. "I saw you kiss him in the cloakroom."

Beresford stopped objecting abruptly. "Why were you in the cloakroom?"

"I thought it was the ladies' necessary room."

"This house really does have too many rooms." Beresford frowned and met Grace's gaze. "I take it you are not going to use this information to bribe me into marrying you, are you?"

"Goodness no. Why would I do that?"

Beresford shrugged. "The curse of being a generally sociable gentleman who enjoys a good ball but also being a man of some means has put it into the heads of many ladies of the *ton* that I am eligible for marriage. When I told my mother a month ago that I did not intend to marry, she reminded me of my betrothal to you. You are right, it does not make logical sense for you to blackmail me into marriage, knowing what you do about where my affections lie, but… I don't know. The ladies of the *ton* are made of not much more than aspirations and subterfuge, from what I can tell."

Grace didn't know if she should laugh or feel offended. "You are safe from me. Before you rounded the corner, I was just saying to Penny that we are in an interesting situation. You and I, that is. You do not want to marry me, and I do not wish to marry at all."

"A sentiment I am familiar with."

"However, I am in a bit of a bind. I believe if you and I went to my father and told him we spoke for some time tonight and have come to the conclusion that we will not suit, he would call off the betrothal with no further questions. However, perhaps that would be hasty, because it does leave the question of what I shall do to avoid the marriage trap myself."

"You sound as though you already have an idea."

"Penny suggested I marry you anyway to get our parents off our backs and then continue to live separate lives. You must have a country estate you neglect in want of a mistress of the house."

Beresford frowned. "This is a novel idea you propose, although it is an unfair one."

"To you? I swear, if you would like to carry on with Waring, I will not stand in your way." Grace did not understand it, but she could think of no reason to stop it.

A little smile played at Beresford's lips. "Yes, very fair of you. But I meant it would be unfair to you. You are a beautiful woman in the prime of life. I would not force you into a marriage in which your only role is to play estate manager at my country house. I know we do not spend much time together these days, but when we were children, I always knew you to be friendly and kind. Do you really want to wither away in a country house? No. My conscience would not allow it."

Grace leaned against the wall. "I loathe the city. It's loud and dirty and it smells. I long for a country home where there is sunlight and fresh air, where I can walk freely without worrying a carriage will run me over. My family will not permit me to adjourn to the family estate without securing an offer of marriage from *someone*."

"And I am sympathetic to that, although the vibrancy of the city is the very thing that appeals to me. I enjoy the noise and the chaos. Alas, I will not marry you. But you may be onto something." Beresford tapped his finger against his chin. "You see, if you and I married, my mother would start to hope a future marquess was in the offing, and that is pressure I cannot bear. A man of sterner stuff than I perhaps might be willing to enter into such an arrangement, but I cannot."

"I'm afraid I don't completely follow what you are saying."

Beresford frowned. "I forget sometimes that ladies are not so conversant in the ways life is created."

"No, not that. Although…"

"You see, I would not be able to consummate a marriage to a woman. Well, I probably could, but I do not wish to. Also it would not be fair to Waring."

"You love him."

"I care for him a great deal. We have an arrangement. I do not wish to break promises I have made to him. I know that may be difficult to understand—"

"No, I believe I do understand you, Anthony."

He nodded. "We are at Christian names, then?"

"We were friends as children." She sighed. "But what are you suggesting? That I enter a *ton* marriage where we dispense with the creation of heirs quickly and then lead a life separate from my husband?"

"I mean… yes. That seems ideal, no?"

"Would I not be then occupied by the rearing of said heirs?"

"Would you? You could hire nannies and governesses, no? Assuming you found a lord on steady enough financial ground. I barely saw my mother as a child. It is partly why I resent her intrusion in my life so much now."

"Anthony." Grace found Anthony's embellished way of speaking charming but also frustrating. They were talking around the issue, at any rate. Grace understood what he was suggesting—for her to find another man willing to marry her and leave her in the country—although the real issue for Grace was that she had no idea how to do that.

Anthony was looking off at something in the distance and clearly not giving her his direct attention. "Or don't have children. It's not my business."

"In other words, the solution to all my problems is to entrap some poor gentleman into a loveless marriage."

Beresford grinned. "That's all. Shouldn't be too hard. Such marriages are prolific in the *ton*. Maybe you could find a chap who can be found frequently occupying his seat in the House of Lords so that he would be obligated to be in the city often and you can do whatever it is people do in the country."

The door of the card room down the hall opened and a couple of gentlemen tumbled out. Grace recognized them as Baron Fowler and the Earl of Caernarfon.

Fletcher Basildon, Baron Fowler, looked a little goofy these days, his hair overlong and covering his eyes, his cravats always askew. But Owen Thomas, the Earl of Caernarfon, was certainly handsome. He had dark brown hair, intelligent eyes, and a strong, athletic body. Grace didn't know him well but had always liked the look of him. He smiled at her and Beresford now.

"How are you gents?" asked Beresford. "Did Rutherford clean you out?"

Caernarfon scoffed. "Hardly."

"Rutherford has a tell," Fowler explained. "Scratches his nose when he's bluffing."

"Hello, Lady Grace," said Caernarfon jovially. He dipped his head slightly, so she offered her hand to be kissed. The brush of his lips against her knuckles was barely there, particularly through her gloves, but it was exciting all the same as he peered up at her through his dark eyelashes.

"Hello, my lord."

"Perhaps you will do me the honor of dancing with me," he said, a bit of brogue in his Welsh accent. "We promised the Duchess of Swynford we would not spend the *entire* evening at cards, so we must rejoin the crush."

"I'd be happy to oblige, my lord," said Grace.

A wry expression crossed Beresford's face and he offered Grace a crooked smile before turning to Caernarfon and saying, "I am surprised both of you are here. You have been avoiding the marriage mart, haven't you?"

Fowler sighed. "My mother has got that look in her eye. She bullied me into it. I blame Swynford."

Grace stifled a laugh. The Duke of Swynford had entered into a scandalous marriage the year before, with a woman from a family of dubious repute, and all society seemed to care about was that a duke had been taken off the market. By all accounts, it was a love match, and Grace did not begrudge them their happiness, although she supposed they did serve as an example to Swynford's friends.

Caernarfon grinned. "I shall take the lovely Lady Grace on a swift loop around the ballroom and tell my mother I tried to charm her, but she could not be charmed."

"I am standing right here," said Grace. "I am onto your scheme now."

"Indeed." Caernarfon held out his arm.

So, with one last look back at Beresford—who shrugged—
Grace let Caernarfon lead her into the ballroom.

AS A WALTZ began, Owen took Grace Midwood into his arms and
stepped into the dance. He looked around, trying to make sure
people were looking.

The only family Owen had, other than his mother, was his
married sister, and she was tucked away with her husband at their
British country estate. He felt no particular pressure to marry, but
he wanted to go through the motions to keep the ladies of the *ton*
away.

Grace was pretty. Well, more than pretty. She had a round
face with cheeks that went rosy when she smiled, which she did a
lot of the time. Her curly blond hair, currently arranged neatly
around the crown of her head, took on reddish hues in the right
lighting that reminded him of the lick of a flame. She wore an
emerald green gown now that hugged her bosom in a tremendously appealing way and skimmed down the rest of her body,
implying a tantalizingly curvy figure.

So, yes, fine, Owen found Grace very attractive.

But now was not the time for him to be entranced by a woman. Upon his father's death, Owen had taken his seat in the House
of Lords, and the country currently seemed under assault. Well,
perhaps not literally; the wars with Napoleon had ended, after all.
But now angry textile workers were protesting being replaced by
machines by destroying those same machines, and many in
Parliament worried a workers' uprising was inevitable. Whether
the uprising was containable or whether it would become a fully
armed insurrection was an open question. Owen was not entirely
sure Parliament could do much, but he felt his place was in his
seat. He preferred London to his home in Wales anyway.

"You seem to have much on your mind, my lord," said Grace.

"Please call me Owen. And yes, just a spot of bother I am thinking about. Government business, you see."

"Ah, yes, I've heard you have taken up your seat in Parliament."

"I never intended to, but then my father left us, so I decided to try it, and it turns out I am well-suited to the work."

They danced together silently for a moment, and Owen became acutely aware of the woman in his arms. She smelled vaguely of roses and citrus, her blond hair was like sunshine, and though he could feel through her gown that she wore stays that likely manufactured some of her curves, there were some things one could not fake. He had a few inches on her height, and her bosom pressed tantalizingly against him as they danced. She had a light step as well, masterfully keeping pace with the music while letting him lead her around the floor.

Owen had no interest in marrying, and thus had no interest in a young miss such as Grace Midwood. Oh, why could she not be a widow? If she'd been a more experienced woman, he would have bent his head and whispered something altogether inappropriate, she would have giggled, and then he would have escorted her to a more private location.

Lord, what was he even thinking?

The waltz ended, but Owen was, for reasons he could not quite articulate, reluctant to let Lady Grace leave his side. He held up his arm and said, "Can I find you a refreshment?"

She tilted her head as if she did not understand his meaning and said, "All right."

They traversed the ballroom slowly, the crush of people blocking much of their path. "How do you know Beresford?" he asked.

"We were betrothed as children. Our fathers were schoolmates."

That brought him up short. "You and *Beresford* are betrothed?"

"In name only. Neither of us wishes to follow through with

the betrothal, and in truth, until a few weeks ago, I thought nearly everyone had forgotten about it."

Well, that made a certain amount of sense. "I have gotten to know Beresford some in the last year and can guess at his reasons for not wanting to marry, but I am curious about yours. Beresford is handsome, no? His costume is somewhat ridiculous, if you ask me, but he is rather wealthy. I'm sure many women desire him."

"He loves another."

Owen nodded. He had long suspected that Beresford had been carrying on an affair with Lark, the Earl of Waring; they weren't very subtle, though neither had confessed aloud to Owen, who was still not entirely sure what to make of it.

"When Beresford came upon us, I was telling my friend, Lady Penelope, that I do not wish to marry because…"

It was rare to encounter a woman who did not wish to secure her own future through marriage, and Owen found he was curious about Lady Grace. "You have piqued my curiosity. Please tell me your reasoning."

Grace frowned. "Well, if you must know, I am an artist. I also hate the city. If I had unlimited means, I'd move to a home in the country where I could have an artist's studio and where the pollution and noise from the city would not bother me. Did you know that the dirt and soot in London can affect the purity of clay?"

"You are a sculptor, then?"

"Of a sort, yes."

Owen wanted to pursue that, but they'd arrived at the refreshments table, so he procured her a glass of lemonade, from which she took a dainty sip.

"I have considered marrying my betrothed anyway. Leave him to his affairs in town while I manage his home in the country, but he will not allow it. He says I deserve a true marriage."

"Aye, you do."

Grace drank the rest of her lemonade and placed the cup on a tray held by a footman walking by. She waved her hand dismissively. "Men are always presuming to know what is best for women."

"So you mean to tell me that in this hypothetical future in which you are a woman of means, you wish to deny yourself male companionship? Children?"

That seemed to give her pause, but she shrugged. "If I have my art, I do not need children."

"All right."

"Besides, this future is not so hypothetical. Beresford himself pointed out that I could marry a willing man who preferred to stay in the city while his wife retired to the country. I do not see anything wrong with this plan as long as both parties agree to the terms in advance."

Owen shook his head. He thought her naive. That was, he was sympathetic, as he was not interested in becoming ensnared in a marriage himself. His work at Parliament was far too important, and he enjoyed partaking in female companionship when it availed itself. Lady Grace, as a virginal miss, may not have realized the carnal pleasures she was choosing to forsake for her independence. Owen had always felt people should experience all life had to offer before resigning themselves to their fate.

Perhaps he should introduce Grace to the Duchess of Swynford. Her Grace was married to Owen's dear friend Hugh, and she had been resigned to a life of solitude until she and Hugh fell in love. The Duchess had thrived at Hugh's side and had recently given birth to the duke's heir, a child that, by all accounts, she doted on to an unseemly degree, insofar as women of the *ton* were generally not supposed to care for their children if they had money to throw at nannies. Wealthy aristocratic women were too delicate to care for children, according to Owen's own mother, although the Duchess of Swynford was sturdy enough.

Owen sighed. Why was his mind wandering all over?

"I find it a bit stifling in here," he said to Grace. "If I recall correctly, Rutherford has a terrace near the back of the house that offers some decent fresh air. Would you like to accompany me?"

"Not to state the obvious, but if I walk out of the room with you, people will get ideas."

"Let them. We've done nothing wrong. And I intend to do nothing wrong by you. You can trust me."

She raised an eyebrow, but said, "All right."

Owen knew he was being self-indulgent. He wasn't ready to let Grace go just yet because he was enjoying her company—particularly the wry expression on her face, as if she was in on whatever he was up to—but she made a reasonable point that people might assume they were courting.

Well, as long as neither put the other in a compromising position, it didn't matter. All he wanted was fresh air and her company.

Back in the corridor outside the ballroom, Owen paused to try to remember which doorway led to the terrace. "I think it's this way," he said, leading her down the hall.

"Would the Rutherfords approve of us wandering around their house?" she asked.

"If you invite five hundred people to your home, you must assume some of them will wander. I think this is it."

Owen opened a door that led not to a terrace but to a sitting room. He laughed. "Well, this is as good as anything. Far fewer people in here."

"What is your aim here, my lord. Do you intend for the maddening horde out there to believe you have an interest in me?"

"I *do* have an interest in you." Which was the truth. He found her so charming, he wanted to have a conversation with her in a room where he could hear her speak.

"Not in marrying me, though."

"No. But I enjoy your company and hoped to prolong our engagement this evening. You say you do not wish to marry, so can I extrapolate that this means you do not wish to mingle among the eligible bachelors with the other debutantes?"

"I came because my mother insisted, if you must know."

He could not bed her, and he would not say anything scandalous enough to offend her, but part of him wanted to use their bodies to make what he assumed would be a persuasive argument about why she should perhaps not give up on marriage.

"What are you thinking, my lord?" she asked.

"What makes you ask?"

"You have a curious expression on your face."

He stepped toward her. She was lush, beautiful, her plump lower lip begging to be kissed, her voluptuous bosom practically spilling out of her gown, those soft tendrils of hair falling around her face wanting to wrap around his fingers.

"Well, if you must know, I think it a shame for a woman to relegate herself to spinsterhood. There are so many experiences she'd be denying herself."

That seemed to get her back up. She stared at him primly. "Such as?"

He shook his head. "It is not for me to say."

She pursed her lips. "I think I know what you are implying, but in truth, I am not offended." She touched her neck, then her fingers drifted slowly across her collarbone to her bosom. Owen doubted she intended to be provocative, but his attention was...provoked. This was a woman with a great deal of sensuality. Of desire. She met his gaze and said, "I will admit to a certain amount of...curiosity."

Owen felt drawn to her as if he were pulled by a string. He stood before her and gazed into her eyes. He wanted her, even if she was completely off limits.

"I suppose if I followed Beresford's suggestion and married some nobleman who preferred London to the country," she said, her fingers tracing patterns on the lapels of his jacket, likely unconsciously, "then we could... have marital relations... a few times a year. Then the rest of our time would be our own."

"I doubt you would be satisfied with that," Owen blurted out.

"No?" Her lips parted.

No. Definitely not. There was no way a woman as beautiful and unconsciously sensual as Grace Midwood would be satisfied with a quick tumble on the rare occasions she and her husband were in the same location. Not if her husband were doing it right.

"I do not believe a woman like you, with intelligence and, I presume, some talent at her art, a woman in the prime of her life with desires of her own, would be satisfied with an absentee husband. Nor do I think you would be satisfied with a life as an idle, delicate lady of the *ton*."

She stared at him for a long moment. Their gazes met and it was like a shock to Owen's system. Lord, she was beautiful.

She stepped forward and lowered her voice. "You see my conundrum, then. You men always presume to know the right thing, but you do not know the circumstances us women often find ourselves. My options seem to be the nunnery or the glass cage of a *ton* marriage, and neither tempt me, but here we are. Perhaps I shall never be satisfied."

Something deep in Owen wanted to satisfy her. Without intentionally meaning to, he stepped forward and cupped her cheek. Her skin was just as soft as it looked.

He wanted to kiss her more than he wanted to take his next breath, but he knew he shouldn't. Instead, he stared at her pouty lips and inhaled her citrusy scent. Her lips parted and he looked up at her eyes. Their gazes met and he felt like something passed between them.

He barely knew this woman. He knew of her, moved in the same circles as she did. His late father had been friends with hers. They'd had casual conversations in the past, perhaps flirted a bit. He *liked* her, he was attracted to her, he wanted to kiss her. But he didn't want to give her the idea that *he* could be the poor sucker pulled into her marriage scheme. He had no desire to marry, and he already knew one night a year with her would not be enough.

He kissed her anyway.

It was like a thunderclap. Like something inside Owen lit up like lightning.

She melted against him and parted her lips. She put her arms around his shoulders, as if she was as caught up in this as he was, so he grasped her waist and pulled her closer. And just when he was about to dive in further, he heard a gasp somewhere to his right.

They'd been caught.

He stepped away from Grace and met her gaze again, then looked at who had discovered them. It was the Marchioness Midwood, because of course it was.

"*Grace!*" she groaned out.

Owen felt as though his fate was sealed.

Chapter Two

"YOU'VE DONE IT now," said Hugh Baxter, the Duke of Swynford, and one of Owen's closest friends.

Owen groaned and rubbed his forehead. They were in the sitting room of Hugh's home. Normally on nights like this, they gathered at their club, but Hugh's infant son had been feverish the day before. Adele, Hugh's wife, insisted that young master Edward was in perfect health now, but Hugh decided on staying nearby, just in case.

Adele now poured tea for everyone, but Owen could have really used whiskey. He cursed in Welsh, sparing the duchess.

"What has he done?" Adele asked.

Fletcher, Baron Fowler, Owen's dearest friend, said, "He kissed Lady Grace Midwood at the Rutherford Ball and her mother walked in on them. The Midwoods are insisting Owen marry their daughter."

"You *didn't*," said Adele, sounding scandalized. "What would possess you to do that?"

Owen did not know how to answer. He didn't regret it, as such, although he wasn't thrilled with his current predicament. So he just said the first thing that popped into his head. "She has very kissable lips."

Adele frowned at Owen. "Still. She's a pretty girl. Why do you look like marrying her would be a fate worse than death?"

Just then, Hodges, the Swynford butler, showed in Lark and

Anthony, who stumbled into the room as though they'd already had a few drinks. The trouble with being in a private sitting room and not at the club was that Lark and Anthony felt less like they needed to hide the relationship they still had not confessed to Owen. Owen supposed he was just supposed to accept it, although he wasn't sure he did, quite. Anthony was a bit of a ninny, in point of fact.

Anthony brandished a bottle of whiskey. "From my own store. I found this little distillery in Ireland that makes the smoothest whiskey you've ever tasted. Single-malt, aged twelve years. Shall I pour?"

"A double," said Owen.

"That bad, eh?" said Lark, sitting in a wingback chair.

"I assume you heard what happened?"

Lark offered a wry smile. "Everyone at the Rutherford Ball heard what happened. You compromised little Gracie Midwood."

Owen sighed. "All right, first of all, she is not little Gracie anymore. Lady Grace is a grown woman. Believe me. Second of all, I…" But Owen didn't want to go on because he was guilty of what he'd been accused of.

"You kissed her," Fletcher offered.

"Yes. But that was all."

"And now her parents are insisting you marry," said Adele.

"Because in reality," said Lark, waving his hands around, "she's betrothed to Beresford, but Beresford has spent the last month doing everything in his power to get out of it."

Adele stared at Lark. "Come again?"

"It was a childhood betrothal," said Anthony. "Two men wanting their children to marry and thus join their fortunes. Neither I nor Grace were of consenting age when the agreement was made, and I didn't believe anyone took it seriously, but Grace has been put through two Seasons without committing to anyone, and I think calling in this chit was a last resort on her parents' part. And it's *possible* I walked up to the Marquess of Midwood at the ball and heavily implied I was courting someone else and that Grace and I did not suit, so when his wife stumbled upon Owen making a fool of himself, they saw a new opportunity."

Owen grunted. "That's about the sum of it."

Anthony distributed glasses of whiskey and then sat on the arm of the chair Lark occupied. Lark reached up and stroked Anthony's back while sipping his whiskey and looking at Owen. It was a gesture of affection and one done unconsciously; it was the gesture of a long-time lover.

Owen knew Lark was a good person—Anthony was an open question—but this was still a difficult thing to reconcile. Owen glanced at Adele, who looked unfazed.

But it was not his main concern at the moment, so he shoved it aside. "What Midwood said was, 'I trust you will do the right thing here.'"

There was a collective groan.

"I think you should marry her," said Anthony.

Everyone turned and stared at him.

"Hear me out!" Anthony looked at Owen. "I know the lot of you are averse to marriage, the duke and duchess aside, and I count myself among your ranks in that regard, but I believe this particular marriage solves a number of problems."

"Explain," said Owen.

"I've known Grace most of my life. She really is a charming girl. And that emerald gown she had on at the Rutherford Ball really showed off her coloring, no?"

"Only Beresford would note the color of her gown and not the body beneath it," said Fletcher.

Adele cleared her throat. "Is this about to be a scandalous conversation? Shall I leave the room?"

"Fletcher will behave himself," Hugh said, glaring at Fletcher.

"Do you agree with me, Your Grace, that the emerald gown was well-suited to Lady Grace?" Anthony asked Adele.

She smiled. "I did think it was quite beautiful."

"There, you see? Appropriate conversation." Anthony smiled.

"Anyway, my point was, you could do worse."

"I barely know her, and also, she was betrothed to *you*," said Owen.

"Indeed she was, and neither of us wants to marry the other." Anthony frowned. "All right, I admit this is a little self-serving, but consider this. Your family has been nagging you to get married. And I know from the way you talk about that crumbling castle your family owns that your family's legacy is important enough to you that you would have married eventually so that you'd have someone to pass it on to." He sighed. "I cannot give her what she needs out of a marriage."

"What do you mean by that?"

Anthony crossed his arms. Lark rubbed his thigh sympathetically. "Grace is clear-eyed about me. She and I do not suit."

Lark made a noise, an odd whistle through his teeth. Anthony jerked his head toward Lark. "What? Do *you* wish me to marry Grace."

Lark crossed his arms. "No. I do not wish you to marry anyone."

"Indeed. Look, Owen, you want an heir at some point, yes? And you are also tethered to London whenever Parliament is in session. Grace loathes the city and wants to move to the country. She also has not much interest in a husband. In a lot of ways, this situation is perfect. Marry Grace, who is a lovely girl. You must have thought she was lovely enough to kiss."

Owen nodded, though he resented this whole proceeding.

"So marry her, install her at your home in Wales, and then both of you can carry on with your lives."

"Why would Lady Grace not want her husband at her side?" asked Adele.

"Grace is a potter of some skill," said Anthony. "She told me at the ball that she is only still willing to marry *me* because she wants space in the country to set up a studio where she can make…whatever it is she makes. Bowls and vases, I suppose."

"I just bought a cottage on the coast," said Owen.

Everyone turned to look at him.

Owen sighed. "Caernarfon Castle has become the project of my aunt. She wants to fix it up and open it to gawkers. I've been content to let her. And my estate functions well enough without my presence. But I just bought a cottage on the north coast of Wales that needs some fixing up. I was planning to make it my project this summer. But I could give it to Grace if she wanted to use it for a pottery. She has some skill, you said?"

Anthony nodded. "I own a few of her pieces. They are quite lovely. She's no Makepeace, but I do believe her goal when she has her own studio is to improve on her craft."

"Makepeace?" asked Fletcher.

"Gerard Makepeace. He's a master potter. Makes these vases and urns that are just breathtaking. They are hard to acquire, but I know his dealer." Anthony grinned, but then frowned at everyone's blank faces. "Philistines, all of you."

Owen sat back in his chair and downed the rest of his whiskey. He could see the wisdom of Anthony's argument. Perhaps this situation *was* a blessing. Still…

"Marriage is so…permanent," Owen said. "I don't know her very well. What if it turns out that she and I do not suit?"

"What if you do?" asked Adele. She tsked. "You gentlemen are allergic to the prospect of marriage, and I think it is ridiculous. Owen, do you even…sow many oats?"

Owen didn't understand her meaning. "What are you talking about?"

"She's asking if you've had many lovers," said Fletcher. "But politely."

"Oh. Well, no, not exactly. I've been busy with Parliament these last couple of years."

"So why not marry?"

"I don't feel ready. I don't know."

Adele shot Owen a wry smile. "Hugh, tell your friend that marriage is actually a festival of delights."

Hugh laughed. His wife stood before him, near the tray full of tea and tarts. Hugh grabbed her by the waist and pulled her onto his lap. "We've been married just over a year, have we not?" Hugh asked.

"Yes, darling."

Hugh looked intently into his wife's eyes. "I have no regrets. Do you?"

"Not one."

Hugh rested his chin on his wife's shoulder. "I don't know if 'festival of delights' is the phrasing I'd use, but marriage is certainly far more enjoyable than I ever imagined."

"Yes, but you actually love your wife," Owen pointed out.

"You and Grace may grow to love each other," Adele said. "That is quite common in *ton* marriages, is it not? If not, she is an agreeable woman and you may grow to be friends. There are a number of possibilities. Pleasing her parents by offering for her is not the worst thing that will ever happen to you."

"I've known Grace my entire life," Anthony said. "In addition to being beautiful, she is clever and practical. A good conversationalist. Kind and friendly. She has a lot of traits to recommend her."

"Why not just follow through on the betrothal?" said Lark, sounding irritated.

"Hush. Jealousy doesn't suit you, darling."

Owen looked around the room. "Fletcher, you are often the voice of reason. What do you think about all this?"

Fletcher frowned. "We are of an age in which we will look increasingly ridiculous if we do not marry. Like you, I am in no hurry, but I can't help but think that everyone here has a point. Although, of course, I will resent you for the rest of my days for leaving me as the lone unmarried man in the group."

"Lark is not married."

"Lark has Beresford."

Owen groaned. He stood and strolled over to the table where Anthony had left the whiskey and refilled his glass. "Well, I hope to see you all at my wedding, then."

LARK LIVED JUST on the other side of Grosvenor Square from Hugh, and as they left Hugh's house, Lark invited Anthony to walk home with him.

They walked silently until they were out of earshot of Lark's other friends, at which point Lark said, "So you would not marry some woman for the sake of appearance?"

"No," said Anthony. He felt strongly about this point. He felt no sexual pull toward women and knew he would struggle to consummate such a marriage. "What is the purpose of marriage if not to legitimize heirs? I have no intention of fathering an heir. I'm leaving my estate to my cousin in my will. I'm sure he'll be happy to take up my title upon my death. Likely he is already trying to engineer such an outcome."

"Hopefully that is many decades in the future," said Lark. He sighed. "You don't think marriage may have other purposes? A public commitment, perhaps? Hugh and Adele have formed a partnership, and sometimes I envy them."

"You do?"

"Marriage and love often have little to do with each other, but there is something romantic in me that appreciates a love match." They reached Lark's house and Lark paused on the front stoop. "I think you must too, which is why you refuse to marry Lady Grace."

"I do like her. Thus I want her to have a real marriage. Owen likes her enough to have kissed her, so there is some potential there. He can do things for her that I cannot."

Lark nodded and walked up the steps of the front stoop. Anthony followed him. When Lark opened the door, his butler was waiting there and took both of their coats. Anthony nodded at him in acknowledgement. Lark paid his staff handsomely for their discretion, and Anthony had long stopped caring what anyone in the house thought of his presence there. Lark proceeded up the stairs, presumably headed for his bedchamber, so Anthony followed.

Once they were in the room, Lark said, "Part of me wishes I could marry you."

Anthony paused, surprised by the sentiment. "What makes you say that?"

"I love you. We've been together for nearly eighteen months now and I do not see myself ever tiring of your company. I wish that we could walk arm-in-arm in the park the way married couples do, because I often want to touch you in public but of course cannot do so. And, well…"

Lark's valet appeared at the doorway. Lark dismissed him with a hand gesture.

So, they were now quite alone. Anthony sat on the bed and began to wrestle off his boots.

"Couples who marry do often give a part of their heart to each other," Lark went on. "Even if they are not a great love story, they have some affection for each other, usually. And, well, you have not just part of my heart, Anthony. You have my whole heart."

Anthony stopped what he was doing and looked up at Lark, who stared back at him with the kind of earnestness that could break him. "Lark."

"I'm serious. But of course, we cannot marry each other, so it does not matter."

"It does matter," said Anthony. He succeeded in pulling off his boots, and then he stood. "I love you. You have my whole heart as well."

Anthony took Lark into his arms. Lark sometimes seemed to love Anthony a bit resentfully, as if this relationship was not what he wanted in life. And yet now, Lark put his arms around Anthony's shoulders and held him tightly. Somewhere in the back of his mind, Anthony still worried he'd lose Lark to a marriage to a woman—and that would be a true threat because Lark was attracted to men and women equally, and also was not the sort of man to commit infidelity—but for now, they had each other.

"We have a marriage of sorts," Anthony said now. "I realize we live in separate homes and manage our lives separately, but at night, we have a partnership."

Lark nodded against Anthony's shoulder. "I agree."

Anthony slid his fingers below Lark's chin and lifted it. Then he kissed Lark soundly.

"Let us go to bed," Lark said, rather breathlessly. "I need you tonight."

And Anthony went, because he needed Lark, too.

Chapter Three

"CAERNARFON IS WELSH, isn't he?" asked Penny.

"Yes," said Grace. "And it's Ca-nar-von. That's how he says it."

"Do you think he will offer for you?"

Grace flopped down on the settee. They were in the Midwood family sitting room, awaiting what promised to be a parade of female callers wanting the gossip on what had happened between Grace and the earl. Penny had come over early to confer with Grace before the horde descended. Grace stared at the ceiling now. "I do not know if he will offer."

"I guess the more important question is, do you want him to?"

Grace had been thinking about this nearly nonstop for the three days since she'd been caught with Owen. He was a handsome man, there was no doubt of it. His dark hair was trimmed into the latest fashion, brushed forward toward his face, and he had unusual eyes. She hadn't been able to tell their color from the lighting in the Rutherford ballroom, but she supposed they were hazel or green. He was quite tall, with broad shoulders and an athletic body. He didn't seem to care much about the latest fashion, and his dress, whenever she'd seen him, had been appropriate but simple. Only white cravats, no garish colors.

How would he be as a husband? What she knew of him indicated he'd be courteous and kind. But was that enough to build a marriage on?

"We hardly know each other," said Grace.

"Do you think him handsome?"

Grace sighed and sat up. "Yes. Incredibly."

"A fine start. Do you think he is a good man?"

"I do, but I only know that from his reputation." And she only knew that much because she'd asked every person she came into contact with in the last three days what they thought of him.

Penny nodded. "Perhaps that is all you need."

Grace disagreed. Marriage seemed like an altogether unwieldy institution. Her own parents barely tolerated each other; they rarely spoke and were never affectionate. It seemed to Grace that marrying a man who was practically a stranger to her would yield something similarly cold, which Grace had no interest in. On the other hand, the kiss she'd shared with Owen had been anything but cold. It had made her feel hot all over, in fact. But how could she reconcile those two things?

Saunders, the Midwood butler, knocked on the doorframe. "Misses Elizabeth and Helena Hastings would like to know if you are in to callers."

Grace stood. She glanced in the mirror above the fireplace to make sure her hair didn't look too wild. "Yes, Saunders. Please show them in."

The two sisters arrived in a cacophony of female giggles and tittering. Grace was already exhausted.

"We've heard the news."

"Has he offered?"

"Is he handsome?"

"When is the wedding?"

"Ladies!" said Penny. "Calm yourselves. The earl has not offered yet."

Elizabeth cleared her throat. "Apologies, but goodness! You must tell us what happened."

"Nothing."

"Come, Grace, that is nonsense," said Helena. "*Something happened.*"

"I was chatting with the Marquess of Beresford, and then the earl walked over. He asked me to dance, and we waltzed, which was lovely. He is a sprightly dancer. Then he got me a lemonade and we continued to talk. We were looking for the terrace for some fresh air, but walked into the empty sitting room accidentally. Then he kissed me…and my mother walked in."

"No," said Elizabeth. "You have to tell us more than that. What was the kiss *like?*"

Grace sat back down on the settee. "It was a dream," she said with a sigh. Grace didn't have a wealth of experience with kisses. She'd only kissed one other man, in fact; he'd been a baron who had courted her the previous Season. But that kiss had been naught but a peck on the lips. But Owen's kiss had made the Earth move. Owen had kissed Grace like he was a starving man and she was a roast beef. But in the best way. Owen had passion and strength and he'd made Grace *feel* things—tingles, warmth, *desire*—she'd never felt before. Which made Grace circle back around to her current internal debate: she didn't want her parents' dead marriage, but she *was* curious.

All the ladies in the room said, "Aw" simultaneously.

Would he offer? That was the question. Grace hadn't had the opportunity to speak to Owen since the ball, nor had he called on her. She'd written a short note the previous day just to say she'd enjoyed her evening with him, and he'd sent back a brief response:

The pleasure was all mine. I would like to call on you soon. –O

It was all so frustratingly vague.

"Are dreamy kisses enough to base a marriage on?" she asked her friends.

"I thought you didn't want to marry," said Penny.

"I don't, but… Maybe it won't be all bad."

"Caernarfon has several properties in Wales, I heard," said

Elizabeth. "And his family owns a castle. A *castle*, Grace."

Grace sighed. She hoped one of those homes had space for a pottery studio. A castle might serve as inspiration for some of her sculpture; likely the castle itself had some old gargoyles or statues of dead kings or something along those lines. On the other hand…

"Wales is so far from London." And Grace had never been to Wales before.

"I'm sure it's less than a week's travel," said Helena. "What do you say, ladies? If Grace marries the Earl of Caernarfon and moves to Wales, we could make a bit of a holiday of it and go visit her."

"Yes, of course we will visit," said Penny.

"I am grateful," said Grace. "But do you really think marrying Caernarfon is the right thing to do?"

"You may not have much choice," said Elizabeth. "But I think this is an opportunity for you. Caernarfon is a handsome, wealthy man. He's not that old, less than five and thirty. You wanted to live at a house in the country, and he has more than one. This may be your best option."

Grace remained unconvinced.

"What happened to the Marquess of Beresford?" asked Helena. "I thought you were betrothed."

"He's in love with someone else," said Grace. "I saw them kissing at the Rutherford ball. That was actually what started this whole thing. I could never be his wife. I would hate to compete with that."

"Will he marry her?" asked Elizabeth.

Unwilling to explain the truth about Beresford, Grace just said, "There are circumstances that make me doubt it, but I do not know."

"Who is this lady?" asked Helena.

"I do not know and did not ask," said Grace. "But I spotted them in a coat closet."

Helena laughed as if this were the most delightful thing she'd ever heard. "Beresford has a secret lover! What a delight! I shall ask Patricia. She knows everything." Patricia was the Hastings girls' older, married sister.

"We should let it lie. Beresford is no longer my concern." Grace hadn't intended to set the gossip brigade on Beresford. She doubted even Patricia would know about Beresford and Lord Waring, but she didn't want anyone digging too hard.

"So let us review," said Penny. "Your engagement to Beresford is off."

"Apparently he told Father that he and I do not suit shortly before Mother discovered me with Caernarfon."

"And you kissed Caernarfon and it was dreamy. And it could be the solution to your problems. Your parents would leave you alone if you married him. You could make all the pottery your heart desires." Penny looked off into the distance. "Surely a castle is big enough to have a room you could use for that."

"I suppose."

"I think you should marry him," said Penny. "Caernarfon is also a politician and is often in town to attend to…whatever Members of Parliament attend to. So you'd have your privacy, at least most of the time. And if your family is going to force you into a marriage anyway, I daresay Caernarfon is a far better option than many alternatives."

"He is quite handsome," said Grace. "I just worry we won't have anything to talk about."

"But will that matter if he's in London and you're in Wales?"

A good point. "I suppose not." Grace shook her head. "I hear what you ladies are telling me, I just… Well, I can't think of any reason to say no to him if he asks."

"So is that your answer decided?" asked Elizabeth. "If Caernarfon offers, will you say yes?"

"I…yes. Yes, I will agree to be his countess."

OWEN APPROACHED THE Midwood residence with trepidation.

He'd never done anything like this before. He knew the Midwoods because his parents traveled in their social circle, but he did not know the marquess well and was worried how he would react to Owen's presence.

It wasn't that Owen *never* wanted to marry, it was just that he'd wanted it to happen at a time in his life when he felt more sure of himself. In the three years since his father's death, Owen had been struggling to adjust to simultaneously managing his family's holdings and keeping his work in Parliament. He'd thought about marriage, but had saved it for a perhaps mythical time when he'd feel less overwhelmed, at which time he'd feel prepared to settle down. Instead, he found himself in front of the Midwood house.

He steeled himself and climbed the stoop.

The butler immediately showed Owen to the Marquess of Midwood's study on the house's second floor.

The marquess was a thin, delicate man with graying hair and a kind face. He had a reputation for getting on well with everyone.

"Ah, Caernarfon," he said, standing and butchering the pronunciation of Owen's title.

"Hello, my lord." Owen doffed his hat. "I suppose you know why I am here."

"Come in, come in. Please, have a seat." Midwood smiled.

Perhaps this would be all right. Owen swallowed. "I admit to being a bit nervous."

"Ask me the question."

Might as well just get this over with. "I've come to ask for your daughter's hand."

Midwood nodded. "Yes, I expected you would. She's a beautiful girl, Grace is. I'm enormously proud of her, and I want her to have a good husband. I want her to be provided for. Tell me, my lord, can you do that?"

"Yes, sir." Owen paused to formulate a way to express his

wealth without bragging. "I own an estate in northwest Wales that is quite profitable. Sheep farming is our main industry, and we've been selling wool to textile factories and the like. I also own a house here in town and recently purchased a cottage on the north coast of Wales. Oh, and there's drafty old Caernarfon Castle. Technically I own that, too, although my aunt is currently overseeing its upkeep. But my point is, yes, I can provide Grace with a comfortable home and whatever she needs. She will never want for anything."

"What of your obligations to Parliament?"

"I come to town when Parliament is in session. I often stay in London, in fact. But I do travel out to my estate to handle the business there with some regularity."

Midwood nodded. "Would Grace travel with you?"

"If she desires. I intend to let her choose where she feels most comfortable living." Owen decided to omit that her predilection for the country and his for the city meant they'd likely be spending time in separate residences. Before he made any vows, he intended to discuss that with Grace, to find out if she meant what she'd said when she expressed a desire to live in the country, apart from any hypothetical husband. Since his stomach was still in knots over the prospect of going through with a marriage, that arrangement suited his purposes.

Midwood gave Owen a long look, and then said, "I have been asking around about you, and everyone has only the best words. I feel satisfied that you will make a good husband for my daughter. I can offer a modest dowry."

Midwood stated the figure, which was more than Owen expected. He didn't much care about the dowry; he had no need of Midwood's money. Perhaps he would set the money aside for Grace's use, however she decided to use it.

They shook on the deal, which bothered Owen a bit. It was like a financial transaction, not like a major, life-changing event.

Midwood stood and said, "I have a connection to St. Paul's. I believe I could reserve the church for the wedding in a month's time, unless there's a reason the ceremony needs to happen sooner." He shot Owen a pointed look. "Is there?"

"No, sir. A month will be fine. Or however long you need to arrange it."

Owen stood. Midwood grasped his hand and shook it again. "Welcome to the family, son."

Thus emboldened, Owen asked about Grace's whereabouts, feeling like she should be a part of this decision. Midwood escorted Owen to a sitting room down the hall from his study. Lady Midwood appeared as if from nowhere as well.

Owen's heart pounded. Everyone's eyes were upon him. He'd hoped to have a conversation with Grace without everyone watching.

"Do you think I might have the opportunity to have a word with Grace?" Owen asked. The "without her family staring at us" was left implied.

"No need," said Midwood.

Perhaps they could speak once the betrothal was official. "All right."

Grace stood, looking at him expectantly.

He stepped forward. "Lady Grace, I…" Well, here went nothing. "I've come to ask for your hand in marriage."

She hesitated. Owen imagined he could see the same conflict in her eyes that he felt in his own heart. But she took a deep breath, smiled, and said, "Yes. I will marry you."

Chapter Four

T HE NEXT MONTH was a whirlwind. Grace's mother dragged her to the modiste, the perfume shop, the jeweler, and a half dozen other places in London. Grace had to stow all her worldly possessions into trunks. She wasn't finding time to work on her pottery, so she packed up her wheel and her other supplies one afternoon. Everything was to be sent via coach to Wales, so when Owen's men came to take all but her essentials, Grace sacrificed some her dignity to emphasize to the men that the large crates contained her most prized possessions, including several ceramics, and they were to be treated with utmost care. Still, she feared the crates would arrive in Wales with her finished works smashed to pieces.

Grace's mother took charge of the errands and the wedding planning, but there was something oddly rote about it. Sometimes Grace stopped and thought, *This is a* wedding. *When it's over, I'll be living somewhere else entirely.* Mother was treating this like any other series of errands. Whenever Grace opened her mouth to talk about how all of this made her feel, Mother shut her down. So Grace found herself overwhelmed, and the only person she could talk with about it was Penny, who had no experience with marriage and couldn't entirely relate to her. Grace had hoped the advent of her wedding would be a way to become closer with her mother, but Mother remained as distant as ever, which was frustrating. Was Mother not upset Grace would soon be leaving the house? If she was, she showed no sign of it.

Owen was apparently also busy, because he rarely stopped by. But he did call on her a few days before the wedding wearing a very stylish black coat. The fabric looked so fine that Grace wanted to run her hands over it.

"I apologize for being scarce, my lady," he said, eyeing the open door. They were alone, but Grace's mother was just across the hall in the other sitting room.

"We have both been busy."

"I wanted to tell you of my plan for after the wedding. Your father has offered to host the wedding breakfast here. After that, we shall begin the journey to my property in Wales. Unless something unusual happens, the journey takes five days."

"Five days!"

Owen nodded, looking chagrined. "I know it's a distance, but I know the route well. There are a series of inns I usually stay at. The sooner we get on the road after the wedding, the better so that we can travel the first leg before it gets too dark."

Grace was alarmed by how perfunctory all this sounded. "As romantic as five days in a carriage sounds, can we slow down for a moment?"

He frowned. "What do you mean?"

She led him over to a sofa and gestured for him to sit beside her. He complied, his expression blank, likely evidence of confusion.

"We're going to be *married*, my lord, and yet I can count the number of conversations we have had on one hand."

Understanding dawned on his face. "All right. What would you like to know about me?"

She had no idea where to begin. "Well, all I know about you so far is that you are an earl, you are Welsh, you have two or three homes depending on whom you ask, and you intend to whisk me off to Wales the moment our wedding is over."

"You said you wanted to spend time in the country."

"I did, that is true. And I had prepared myself for this eventuality. Would it be all right if my friends came to visit me after I am settled?"

"Of course. You may invite anyone you wish. You will be the lady of the house."

"Do you have more than one home?"

He smiled. "I have a townhouse here in London. It is modest but suits my purposes. The estate in Caernarfon will, I think, be to your liking. My ancestors built the place, but I've made some modern embellishments."

"Is it true you own a castle?"

He laughed. "I do, yes. Well, the family does." He leaned back on the sofa. "Do you want the whole history?"

"Perhaps the abridged version."

"Caernarfon Castle was built by Edward I when he was going about hammering Welshmen and Scots. Edward II was born there. One of my ancestors acquired the property and the title through circumstances too complicated to bother with. Some good deed the Crown wanted to reward during the time of Queen Anne, is how I recall it. So we Thomases have been responsible for the castle's upkeep ever since. Currently, my aunt oversees it."

"So you don't live in the castle?"

"No, I live in the estate. The castle is not really habitable. Too drafty, no modern conveniences. We can visit it when we arrive, though. I haven't seen it in quite some time. Oh, and I just purchased a cottage on the coast. It's in a little seaside town. There's not much of a beach there, as the coast is quite rocky, but there is a lovely view of the Irish Sea. The cottage is just a short ride from the estate."

"Do you speak Welsh? I've heard it spoken. It sounds nothing like English."

"I do. My mother thought it was important to teach us the language, since it is beginning to die out."

Grace took a moment to absorb everything she'd just learned.

She hadn't meant to administer an exam to Owen, but she'd wanted to clarify some of what she'd heard through her friends. In truth, she wasn't certain how spouses were meant to speak with each other. Her own parents were closed off and formal at nearly all times. Grace loathed that level of formality, found it stuffy and old-fashioned, and she wanted her own marriage to be less stiff, but she had no idea where to begin to make that happen. Even now, things with Owen felt awkward, something Grace wanted to fix. She wanted to feel comfortable with him, like she would with a friend. They weren't quite there yet, but perhaps they would be.

It occurred to her that a little cottage on the coast might make an ideal location for her pottery studio. She decided to keep that in mind.

"Is your intention to deposit me in the country and then turn around and come back to London?" she asked.

"No. I do actually have some business to attend to in Wales, and I want to check on the cottage. I hired a fellow to oversee some repairs and want to see how well they were done. But I do not intend to stay overlong. A month at most. Parliament is currently in recess, but I will have to return soon enough." He paused. "Is that…is it dastardly of me to whisk you off to parts unknown and leave you there?"

She smiled, because it was in fact what she most desired. "I've told you I loathe London. It will be difficult to be so far from my family, but I will adjust."

"Are you certain?"

"Yes." She was not, in fact, especially broken up about leaving her parents. "All I want is a place to make my pottery."

"Well, that you shall certainly have. We can find a room in the house somewhere, if that suits you."

"I'd love to build an outdoor kiln."

Owen tilted his head. "I am not certain what that would entail, but I imagine we could make that happen."

Grace studied him for a moment. He really was quite striking;

pale skin, dark hair, a strong body. She liked the timbre of his voice, the slight burr in his accent. She knew something of relations between men and women and could see herself kissing this man, and…more. Even now, he was close enough to touch and her fingers itched to do so.

She felt a brief pang as she considered that she would only have this man a few weeks out of the year. But this was exactly what she wanted, wasn't it? She'd have room and privacy in the country to develop her craft. She'd already spoken to her dealer, and he had an office in Anglesey, not far from Caernarfon, and he was willing to dispatch an agent to pick up her pieces to ship back to London for distribution.

Her future husband, of course, had no idea that pottery was anything more than a casual hobby for her, and she wasn't ready to enlighten him just yet.

This was her plan. This was everything she'd been wanting for years.

"What about me?" she asked. "What do you want to know about me?"

"The crates you packed. Pottery…equipment?"

"Yes. A wheel. Some clay, although I'll have to acquire more in Wales. I know the shop I use in London gets supplies from Staffordshire. That's not far from Wales is it?"

"No. Closer than London." He tilted his head. "Beresford says you're pretty good. You take this seriously."

"I suppose he did buy a few pieces from me. But yes, I love it. When I was a girl, I had a governess whose family made pottery, and she taught me how. I find the process of making pottery soothing to my nerves. Until recently, I had a potter's wheel set up in the kitchen here, which is not ideal. I always felt like I was in the way. And I fire my pieces at a studio a few blocks away. But having my own kiln would allow me to experiment with how heat affects the clay, to try different glazing techniques, to really explore the craft."

"I don't know what any of that means, but I can promise I

have plenty of space. But surely your life is not just pottery. What else do you like to do?"

She smiled. He didn't even know her, and he was ready to give her everything she ever wanted. "I have a few close friends I socialize with. I'm useless at needlepoint. I like to read."

"Any good books lately?"

"There's a lady writer who publishes anonymously who writes the most delightful comedies. I just read one called *Emma* about a woman who acts as a matchmaker for all her friends but becomes too arrogant and gets her comeuppance. In the end, she finds her perfect match with a childhood friend. Charming, no?"

"It sounds it."

She looked him over. He seemed earnest. Her greatest fear was that they'd have nothing to talk about with each other, but she imagined she could see the depths of Owen's intelligence in his eyes. He seemed passionate about his home and curious about her life. So she said, "I do believe we will find things to speak about on our long journey to Wales."

He let out a breath and took one of her hands. "I just hope you do not feel trapped in this situation."

"Trapped? No. Do you?"

"No, not at all." He looked up and met her gaze. "You are one of the most beautiful women I have ever seen. In our time together, you have always been friendly and witty. I cannot imagine being married to you would be in any way a hardship."

"Good. I know this is not exactly what either of us wanted, but I think we…can make the most of it."

Owen smiled. "My friend Fletcher—Baron Fowler—called this an opportunity."

"And perhaps it is that."

He leaned over and kissed her forehead. "I would like to talk more, but I have business to attend to this afternoon. I suppose we will have plenty of time on our journey out to Caernarfon."

"I look forward to it," she said.

OWEN ARRIVED AT the church on the morning of his wedding still not quite believing this was happening.

He was frankly baffled by how traditional this was. He knew so many gentlemen of the *ton* who had been caught in similar situations to his but had procured special licenses and rushed into weddings. Owen had in the past wondered if he would fall for someone scandalous, an opera singer or a servant, someone he bedded in advance of his wedding and simply could not keep away from. His sister had been reading those sentimental novels about dukes falling in love with their governesses and other such fiddle faddle, and maybe that had sunk into Owen's brain. And there was Hugh, who had fallen in love with his bride and practically dragged her to the altar.

Owen liked Grace, but did not know her well enough to love her, and, well, here he was, marrying a virginal lady, the daughter of a marquess, exactly the sort of woman his family wanted for him.

His mother was over the moon.

He peeked into the sanctuary and saw his mother sitting in the front row, already crying. His sister and brother-in-law were seated beside her. Hugh, Adele, Lark, and Anthony sat just behind them. The rest of his side of the aisle was occupied by his various friends from Parliament, from Eton and Oxford, and the few of his Welsh cousins who could make the journey in time.

"You're really doing this," said Fletcher, who stood at his side.

"Yes. It will…it will be all right."

"Are you trying to convince me or yourself?"

"Remains to be seen."

"I am the lone person in our circle without a mate, you know." Fletcher leaned against the wall.

Owen was trying to talk himself into entering the sanctuary and taking his spot at the altar. He didn't have time for whatever crisis Fletcher was having. "Lark isn't married."

"He has Beresford, as I continue to remind you. Even if they can't marry, they have each other for…companionship."

Owen grunted. His stomach kept flopping over. He could not explain why he was so nervous.

The priest walked over and told Owen it was time.

And so, a few minutes later, Owen waited at the altar for his bride, worried his heart would pound right out of his chest. And then suddenly, she was there.

Grace wore a pale blue gown and a crown of flowers around her head; her hair was braided and coiled into an elaborate twist. Her skin was creamy, her cheeks rosy, the expression in her eyes earnest. The gown itself was made of some gauzy fabric that seemed to float about her body, giving Owen a mere tantalizing hint of what might lay underneath. She smiled. Then she walked toward him.

The ceremony itself was over quickly, and Owen would not long remember what he said there, but he would always remember what Grace looked like as she stood before him. She was radiant, her big blue eyes sparkling as she gazed back at him. He wanted to touch her, to hold her, to kiss her. The longer the ceremony went on, the more his mind wandered, mostly toward what they would do once he got her alone. And then the priest pronounced them husband and wife, so Owen dipped his head and gave her a chaste kiss.

And then they were married.

There was an elaborate breakfast planned at the Midwood house, so Owen opted not to linger at the church and instead bundled his new bride into the waiting carriage and let out a breath as they slowly made their way to his new in-laws.

He looked at his wife now. His *wife*. This woman would be tethered to him one way or another for the rest of his life. He didn't resent that at all, but he was struggling to truly compre-hend it.

"You're beautiful," he said, because it was true.

She met his gaze. "I don't know what makes a good marriage, but my friends assure me that the fact that I find you handsome and kind is enough."

Owen chuckled. "Well, some of that remains to be seen."

"Are you saying you are not handsome or kind?"

"I can't speak for my relative handsomeness, but I am not always kind. I try to be, but I am not perfect. Besides, I thought this was a marriage mostly in name."

"Yes, but we will need to spend some time together. This multi-day journey to Wales, if nothing else. And someday you may want an heir."

Owen had the sense that Grace might not know entirely how heirs were conceived, and he did not relish showing her. Well, he did, because he wanted to bed her more than he wanted to partake in the feast awaiting him at the Midwood home, but he'd always enjoyed sex more when both participants were enthusiastic. Would a blushing virgin like Grace be the sensual partner he hoped she'd be, or would she grimly bear him, viewing the conception of heirs as a duty more than an opportunity for pleasure?

"What are you thinking?" she asked him.

He reached over and played with an errant lock of her hair. "My thoughts are…inappropriate."

"That is all right. I want you to be honest with me. What is on your mind?"

"That you are a gorgeous woman and I am curious about what your body is like under these prim wedding clothes."

She blushed furiously, which he found rewarding.

"My lord, I—"

"Owen. We are married now. Call me Owen."

She seemed flustered, blowing out a breath and looking toward the front of the carriage. "My mother has explained about relations between men and women…."

Oh, his poor sweet virginal bride. Owen slipped an arm around her and pulled her to him. She stiffened.

"Relax," he said. "I can promise you this. I would never hurt a woman, least of all my wife. I will not force you to do anything you don't want to do. I want you to feel safe with me." And he found that was true. Grace was his *wife*. He was responsible for her. Something primal in him wanted to protect her.

She tentatively put a hand on his chest. She wore pristine white gloves that went past her elbows, and he had on his finest dress coat, a pale-yellow waistcoat, and two shirts, and yet he could feel the heat from her body passing right through all those layers of fabric. She flattened her hand just below his shoulder. Owen pressed his hand against hers gently. Surely she could feel how his heart pounded now.

She looked up and met his gaze.

He kissed her.

He didn't even think about it. One moment he was examining the deep blue of her eyes, the color of the Irish Sea on a sunny day. He cupped her cheek in his hand. Then his lips were upon hers. He had to taste her. This last month, he'd kept his distance because he didn't think he'd be able to keep his hands off this beautiful woman, but now she was his, at least legally. He'd been truthful when he said he'd never hurt her, but given the way she melted against him now, she wanted to kiss him as much as he wanted to kiss her.

He licked against the seam of her lips, and she opened for him. She let out a startled gasp when his tongue curled into her mouth, but she also put her arms around his neck and pulled him close. He put his hands on her back and held her there. Warmth and arousal spread through his body.

Oh, yes. She was a blushing virgin, but there was something wild in her, an untapped sensuality that he couldn't wait to unleash.

The carriage slowed. Owen pulled away with great reluctance and lifted the curtain on the window. They had stopped in front of the Midwood house. So he would not be exploring this with her now.

Tonight, though. They would have tonight.

Chapter Five

OWEN REGARDED GRACE skeptically as the last of her trunks were loaded into his traveling coach. "There are just so many," he murmured.

"I am moving houses," she explained. "I need all my things."

She smoothed a hand down the front of her dress. She'd changed out of her gauzy wedding gown and into a more sturdy traveling costume, although she missed the gown. She'd felt beautiful in it. The expression on Owen's face when their eyes had first met from opposite ends of the church sanctuary was not one she'd forget anytime soon.

Her parents and her sister emerged from the house then. She'd told Owen she'd miss her family, but she wasn't entirely sure that was true. Her sister was only ten years old; they had never been close. Her father was kind but distant, preferring to spend his time on business matters rather than with his family. Her mother spent most of her time on her rigorous social calendar. The person Grace had been closest to as a child had been her nanny, an older woman named Anne, who had died four years ago.

Perhaps that was why it didn't seem like such a hardship to travel across the country to take up residence in her new husband's estate. She could build her own family there. The only thing keeping her in London were these people who barely knew her. Her father petted her head and her mother made a big show of hugging her while her sister looked on indifferently, likely anxious to get back to whatever adventure her dolls had been on when she'd been interrupted to come outside to see her off.

She looked at Owen, who smiled and rocked on his heels.

It was not the way of aristocratic parents to give their children much love and affection, not when they could hire nannies and governesses to show off their wealth and status. But if Grace ever had children, she'd make sure they knew they were loved by their parents.

And now she was anxious to be off. She walked over to the carriage.

Owen shook hands with Grace's father before he followed her over. Then he grasped her waist and lifted her inside. She settled into her seat, and once he'd climbed in, he rapped on the roof. The carriage slowly rumbled down the street.

Owen had changed as well, into simpler clothes. Sleek brown trousers, a brown jacket, a fine lawn shirt, heavy Hessian boots.

"A little later than I wanted to leave," Owen said, sliding his watch back into his pocket, "but we should still make it to the first posting inn by dinner time."

"You make this journey often?" Grace asked.

"A half dozen times a year, yes. Well, perhaps less frequently since I took up my father's seat in Parliament. My sister's husband owns a house in London and in Surrey, so I do not have to travel far to see her and her family. But the estate in Wales does beg my attention sometimes."

"I was asking if your drivers know the way and where to stop," said Grace. "My mother took us to Bath last year, but the driver had no knowledge of the way, and we kept getting dreadfully lost. The inn we stopped at to rest seemed...disreputable."

Owen chuckled. "Yes, my staff knows the way, and more importantly, I only stop at reputable inns on my journeys west." He winked.

Grace realized that they'd be spending their wedding night in one of those inns.

"This first inn," Grace said, "the one we're to stay in tonight. Is it nice?"

Owen nodded. "Yes. We're getting a late start, but I anticipated that, so we're only going as far as Oxford tonight. I attended school there and know the town quite well. The inn I've chosen is lovely. I've stayed there before. And they are expecting us, so we will have the best room they have available."

"Wonderful." She was nervous about the night, though. She'd never spent time in an intimate space with a man. She supposed she was allowed now that they were married—that this was expected of her—but it was different and quite intimidating.

"You're nervous."

"As I said earlier, I have a sense of what is expected of me, but, yes, I am nervous."

"No need to hide that. I want you to be honest with me. I hope not to frighten or intimidate you, but rather that we grow close."

The streets of London were...bumpy. The carriage rumbled and shook down the street. After one especially extreme bump, Grace felt herself fly off her seat. Owen caught her and held her close to his side.

"The streets of London are a travesty," Owen said. "Parliament should spend the money to fix them, but Prinny needs a new pavilion or something, so we must take our own lives in our hands just to leave the city limits."

Grace smiled and smoothed down her skirts. "I do not know much about politics, I will admit. Is that the sort of thing you vote for? To pay to fix the roads?"

"Among many other things, yes. The Crown, of course, has some say, but Parliament determines where the country's money is spent. That is, we gather money when people pay taxes and then determine how to spend it. We *should* spend it on the people of England, but Prince George has other ideas."

"What does he want to spend money on?"

"Mostly himself." Owen sounded resentful.

"Have you met him?"

"Yes, once, and my impression is that he is just as ridiculous as the cartoons in the illustrated newspapers would have you believe. He is…well, he is a very large man. He likes to parade around in what look like military uniforms, although he has never served in any military capacity that I am aware of. And he is constantly asking Parliament for money to build new houses or buy art or whatever his whims dictate, as if he does not have enough."

"I've never met anyone royal. Well, I saw Princess Charlotte from a distance at my debutante ball. She was…well, lovely is the wrong word."

Owen chuckled. "Indeed."

"I hate to say such things. You think of princesses as they are in fairy tales. Beautiful, graceful. Charlotte is…she is short. Her nose is too big for her face. Her clothes were beautiful, and she has a lovely smile, but…"

"I know."

"My mother gave me this book, translated from the German. *Grimm's Fairy Tales*. Do you know it?"

"I know of it. I have not read it."

"They collected these folktales and published an anthology of them, and my favorites were about the princesses. In those stories, terrible things often happen to them, but they are always the most beautiful women, and the princes in those stories fall irrevocably in love with them. Often it is up to the prince to save them, in fact."

"I would not have taken you as being fond of a damsel in distress narrative."

"I am not, as such. That is, women should be able to make their own way in the world, although I am not so naive as to think that is possible with our current laws and customs, which is how I came to be in a carriage with my brand-new husband. But I am fond of the love stories. That is, in a story like 'Cinderella,' this girl has basically been forced to act as a maid for her evil stepmother, and she toils with little complaint, and then some magic occurs and she meets a prince. He is handsome, too, that is the key to these stories. Always the most beautiful people. A number of things happen in the story, but in the end, the prince takes Cinderella away from her wicked stepmother and they live happily ever after. That is what I like about that story." Grace sighed, thinking of the first time she'd read the tale, and how satisfying the ending was. "However, my point was just that, in these stories, the royalty are often the kindest, most beautiful people, but our royalty is…not that."

"It certainly is not. Then again, they aren't all bad. I have heard that King George is even rather kind and thoughtful when he is of sound mind. But they are not royals because they possess any innate qualities. They are royals because they were born into the royal family."

"Yes, of course."

The carriage hit another rut in the road. Grace did not fly as far this time. She reached out for balance, and her hand landed on Owen's knee. She looked up and met his gaze. He gave her a soft smile, and then put his hand over hers. They both wore gloves, but Grace appreciated the gesture. He was trying to make her feel comfortable.

She said, "I will say, talking with you feels easy. It is the rest of it that makes me nervous."

Owen looked like he wanted to say something but thought better of it.

Eventually, he said, "For now, we just need to speak. It is a few hours ride to Oxford, and we are, unfortunately, still in London."

Grace settled into her seat. "I feel so foolish."

"Why?"

"Because married couples who know each other even less well than we do have managed to get married and…have relations…since the beginning of time. I feel like nothing anyone has told me has prepared me for this. And I like you! And yet…"

Owen nodded. "I think I understand. Well, try not to worry too much. Most of…relations, as you put it, is instinctual. You more or less do what feels right in the moment."

"Do you have much experience with women?"

Owen hesitated. "Some, yes. I don't know if 'much' is accurate."

"I suppose all men do. I am not jealous, to be clear. I was just hoping one of us would know what to do."

Owen barked out a surprised laugh. "Yes, I suppose that would be helpful."

"Because if I knew nothing and you knew nothing, we'd just be two people who knew nothing, fumbling around in the dark."

Owen started genuinely laughing then. Grace laughed with him, a bit caught up in the mental image of two naked people flailing, not knowing what to do.

"I can assure you, I know exactly what to do," Owen said.

He surged toward Grace and claimed her lips, kissing her deeply and cupping her cheek in his hand.

Grace felt overwhelmed. Her body went hot everywhere. She imagined there was a red flush spreading across her skin.

Tentatively, she reached over and touched his shoulder. The simple wool coat was soft and expensive, and she ran her hand over the fabric. Which meant she was touching his shoulder, his chest, the top of his back, the back of his neck.

"Is this all right?" she asked when he broke the kiss to move to her neck.

"Touch me wherever you like," he murmured.

It felt good to touch him, to learn the contours of his body as well as she could through all his layers of clothing. The fabrics were fine, though, and well fitted to his body. He smelled good, too, like pine, maybe, or mint, it was hard to say exactly what it was. What he did to her felt wonderful, too, the way he licked at her skin as if it were covered in sugar, the way his fingers splayed on her hip, the way he grasped her possessively. She was *his*, technically, because they were married, but she found she wanted to be.

When her fingers went to the buttons of his coat because she had to know what his skin felt like underneath, he jerked way.

"Did I do something wrong?"

"No. No, not at all." Owen sat up and tugged at the edge of his coat. "I loved what you were doing, but I'll not have your first time be in a carriage."

"Oh."

"You are beautiful and very desirable, I must say. And I am eager to relieve you of your lovely gown when we finally arrive at the inn tonight, but for now, I believe we must behave ourselves."

"Yes, of course." Grace paused, feeling flustered. "Why?"

Owen shot her a sidelong glance. "I am rapidly forgetting, but it just seems… I mean, you are my wife, I like you a great deal, it feels…sordid. Cheap. To be with each other in that way in a moving carriage just isn't right. Not to mention, the ride is quite bumpy. We may be more prone to injury."

Grace couldn't help but giggle. "Injury. All right."

"Just trust me, my dear. We will both have a great deal more fun in a bed and not in the tight confines of this carriage rolling through the potholes of London."

Grace reached over and took his hand. She held it in both of her own. "I trust you," she said.

"Good. Now I suppose we must find a way to pass the time."

Grace nearly laughed again at how ridiculous this all seemed. "Well, you said we could just talk. Maybe one of us could tell a story or something. Could you tell me about your childhood or your schooling? Or Wales? I know so little about Wales."

Owen smiled. "Well, despite the amount of time I spend in London, I am rather fond of Wales…"

OWEN LED GRACE into the Hound & Deer and knew he was in a lot of trouble.

She wore a cloak around her travel costume now, and most of her hair was covered, but sprightly curls still peeked out, and her face was striking. Every part of her was beautiful. This was perhaps the main reason Owen had not yet found regret for any of his choices. And he was about to see all of her.

He was also starving, though, so they went straight to the dining room, in search of the inn's proprietor.

Mr. Madden was indeed in the dining room, speaking happily with a customer. Madden was a round man and always had a smile on his face. He saw Owen approach and his grin grew wider.

"My lord, it is wonderful to see you!" Madden said after parting company with the customer he was talking with. "I received your letter and have our best room set up for you. This must be your lovely bride."

Owen shook Madden's hand. "Yes, if I may introduce the Countess of Caernarfon."

Madden took Grace's gloved hand and kissed her knuckles, and Owen was surprised by the spike of jealousy. Madden, of course, had a wife of his own and was just being charming to customers.

"If your carriage is outside, I will see to your luggage," Madden said.

"Yes it is. I spoke with a porter outside."

"I will check on them in just a moment. Can I interest you in dinner before you go up?"

"Yes," Owen said. "That is, we broke fast after the wedding this morning, but there were so many well-wishers, we were barely able to eat a thing."

"That is the way," said Madden. "At my own wedding, I think I had but a single grape. Here, come over here and sit at the table by the fireplace. I'll send Mrs. Madden over to take care of you while I see to your luggage. We have roast chicken tonight that my customers seem to be enjoying."

As Grace sat, she lowered the hood on her cloak to reveal her shining blond hair. "This is a nice place. I've stayed at a few coaching inns, and many of them are far less nice than this."

"I'm afraid this is the most luxurious of the inns on the route to Caernarfon. But I thought it would be good to stay here on our first night."

Grace blushed, which was endearing. She had an easy blush, it seemed, her pale skin going pink whenever Owen made even the vaguest of innuendos.

Mrs. Madden came over and her small fleet of helpers soon provided Owen and Grace with roast chicken and beautiful roasted vegetables and potatoes and bread and cheese and ale. Grace ate daintily, but with the enthusiasm of someone who wanted to act more ravenously.

"I will say, my lord, that it surprised me somewhat to be referred to as the Countess of Caernarfon. And I know that this is my title now, but I am not yet used to it."

"I confess I am still getting used to the fact that I have a wife."

"I appreciate that this whole situation seems to bewilder you as much as it does me."

Owen had to smile at that. "Perhaps we should just embrace how odd this feels."

"What do you mean?"

"Why bother to pretend this is normal when it does not feel normal?"

Grace laughed. "Fair enough." She ate a bite of chicken. "Everything on this table is delicious."

"Well, eat up. You may need your energy."

Grace blushed again.

Once they ate their fill, Mr. Madden appeared again and escorted them to their room. It was on the third floor, which provided them with a view of the Thames. They were just a few minutes' walk from the university, which had Owen feeling a bit nostalgic for his time there, but right now, he had more immediate concerns.

"That will be all for tonight," Owen told Madden.

Madden winked. "Of course, my lord."

Their trunks had been brought up and were situated along one wall. Owen spared a thought for his driver and the footman who were tagging along on the journey; they'd be sleeping at the inn tonight, too, but in a less well-appointed room than this. Owen had allowed his valet to stay behind in London, leaving him to take care of his pregnant wife, so Owen felt a bit like he was traveling with minimal staff. But he was also capable of dressing and undressing himself, and he could hire someone in Caernarfon if he felt it necessary.

He was on his own now, for certain. He looked at his bride, who was taking in the room.

The four-poster bed had fresh linens, there were plush chairs for sitting, an adjacent room with a large bathtub should they decide to bathe in the morning, a table in the corner, a large painting of the university over the table. There was also a privacy screen near where the trunks had been set.

"This is nice," Grace said.

"Our home for the night."

She hung her cloak on a hook on the wall. "Well…"

Owen gestured toward the privacy screen. "I suppose this is the awkward bit."

"Honestly, I would be glad to be no longer wearing these stays. Now I must determine which of the trunks contains my night rail."

"Yes. I have night clothes somewhere as well, but I do not believe they will be much necessary. Only if you feel more comfortable."

"What did you have in mind?"

Owen liked that a little edge had crept into her voice. "I could help you out of those stays."

She raised an eyebrow, which might have been the sexiest thing Owen had ever seen.

GRACE STOOD IN just her shift, which she was pretty sure was transparent as she stood in front of the room's fireplace. Owen, it turned out, was delightfully fussy, though, so he was carefully folding each item of his clothing as he took it off. He was down to just his breeches now.

"Owen, look at me."

Owen stood up and turned around. He had a wide, muscular chest covered in dark hair. Grace hadn't seen a nude man…ever, but she had seen stableboys without shirts on occasionally. That had not prepared her for the jolt of arousal her husband's body sent through her.

She closed the space between them and put her hands on his shoulders.

"Are you stalling because you are nervous?" she asked. "Or because you find me repulsive."

"I assure you, I do not find you repulsive."

"But you are stalling."

"I suppose. I feel some amount of pressure to make this feel good for you, but I can't say I have some legendary reputation as a lover, so I am a bit at a loss."

"Yes, but I have no reputation at all, so how would I know if you were a skilled lover or not?"

Owen raised an eyebrow. "You'd know. I'll make sure you know." Then he let out a little growl and kissed her.

It was hard not to feel vulnerable, standing as she was before him wearing nearly nothing. When Owen put his hands on her waist, his skin felt hot against hers. But she found, oddly, that she trusted him. She barely knew this man, but he'd only ever been kind to her, and he was handsome and strong and something about the way he kissed her made her skin tingle.

"May I touch you?" he asked.

"Yes," she said breathlessly. "Everywhere."

Owen's kisses grew hungrier. He licked into her mouth and nibbled at her lip. She put her arms around him and played with the hair at the back of his neck as they kissed and was surprised by how soft it was.

Then Owen scooped her up and carried her over to the bed.

He lay her there and then he undid the buttons on his breeches.

"I don't want to terrify you," he said, pausing.

"You won't."

"I'm going to muck this up."

"You *won't*."

Grace's gaze traveled down to the buttons on Owen's breeches. She wanted desperately to know what he was hiding. She felt arousal flooding her body, nearly painful between her legs, and although the sensation was not new to her, it had never felt like *this*. This was almost tangible.

So she grew bold, hoping to spur Owen along. She sat up and wriggled her shift up to her waist and then pulled it off over her head, revealing her entire body to Owen.

He groaned. "You are breathtaking," he said.

She felt self-conscious but tried to hide it. That wasn't too hard, given that Owen clearly liked what he saw. He let go of the buttons holding up his breeches, letting them slide down his hips. Then he worked to take them off, obscuring what hung between his legs somewhat. When he stood back up again, Grace had to admit she was a bit startled. How was *that* supposed to fit—

"Relax," Owen said, climbing onto the bed. "Lay back."

She didn't relax—her heart was beating too fast—but she did lay back, her head sinking into the pillow. Owen lay down beside her and put a hand on her hip. It did not escape her notice that they were still naked, that the lamps near the bed shone bright enough that she could see every inch of Owen's skin, and that Owen now lay close enough to touch and smell and taste. Tentatively, Grace kissed Owen's cheek, his jaw, his neck. His skin was salty and warm, but she liked it.

He shifted his weight on the bed so that he was closer to her, so that their bodies touched from their shoulders to their knees. She could feel him hard between them, and it should have scared her, but instead it excited her, as if her body knew instinctively what needed to happen here and was urging her forward.

Owen gently pushed one of her shoulders so that she was on her back. He nudged her knees apart with one hand. He placed his fingers on her collarbone and then slowly ran them down her chest, over the rise of her breast.

"Tell me if anything does not feel good or if you want me to stop," he said. "And please touch me wherever you like."

The angle was awkward, but truth be told, Grace was most curious about Owen's cock. Men and women were far more different than even Grace had imagined. Owen had dark hair across his chest, on his forearms, on his shins, but his shoulders and buttocks were bare.

Owen cupped her breast and tweaked her nipple, which pulled a moan out of her. It was like she had strings in her body that he was pulling, that everything in her body was connected somehow, that she could feel his touch on her breasts between her legs. She reached over and ran a hand over his buttocks and was surprised by how smooth his skin was.

"Yes," he murmured, shuffling closer to her.

He kissed her, licking into her mouth. He ran his hand from her breast to her belly button to right between her legs.

"Tell me if this is too much," he said.

She responded by shifting her hips so that his fingers would be closer to her core. He groaned in response.

He moved with painstaking slowness, so much so that she wanted to tell him to hurry up and get there. Instead, he teased her, circling the tips of her fingers at the spot between her legs she'd found on her own, late nights when she was alone and curious. He pressed against it, with exactly the amount of pressure to make her feel tingles everywhere.

Then he slid his fingers down. He slipped one inside her.

It felt good, but also strange.

"You're wet for me," Owen murmured. He sounded grateful for that.

She felt like she was on the verge of something, that something big was about to happen. And perhaps it was, because then Owen shifted his body again so that he was above her, his hips between her legs. He dipped his head to nip at her lips and then asked, "Are you ready for me?"

She didn't know, but she said, "Yes."

She kept her eyes wide open, watching everything he did. He took himself in-hand and steered his cock toward her center. She felt the blunt head of it between her legs. There was a searing pain at first. She gasped and bit her lip.

Owen hesitated. "Are you all right?"

Somehow she knew that this would pass and said, "Keep going."

Owen pressed forward slowly, giving her body time to adjust. But her body did open up to accommodate him as he slid forward. He groaned as he pressed all the way in.

"Does that feel good?" she asked him.

"Amazing." He kissed her again. "You feel amazing."

She wanted to ask him to describe it, but she wasn't sure she could put into words what she was feeling right now, let alone expect him to answer. The pain eased once he started moving, thrusting his hips forward and pulling back, waking up every feeling in her core. It was incredible. He began to pick up speed and it felt even better. She grasped his shoulders and let her head fall back, moaning at how good it felt to have him moving inside her.

That feeling that something was coming returned. Owen snuck his hand between them and pressed his thumb against that spot between her legs. He rubbed for a moment and then everything exploded.

She threw her head back, the greatest pleasure she'd ever experienced ripping through her. She gasped and moaned and probably made all manner of unladylike sounds, but she had no control over her body anymore. She jerked and shook and rode that feeling. Then she looked up at Owen, whose facial expression looked lost.

He grabbed her face and kissed her hard as he continued to pump his hips. Then he pulled back slightly and moaned. He stopped moving and his whole body went slack suddenly.

Everything seemed to come to a natural conclusion. Owen slid out of her and rolled onto his back, his breathing still hard. Then he put an arm around her and pulled her close. She rolled and rested her head on his chest.

"Was that all right?" she asked.

"Yes. That was…" He was still panting. "I have no words. But it was great. Was that good for you?"

"It felt amazing. I had no idea it would feel like that. Good. Great. My mother explained it like something I'd have to endure, but I already want to do it again."

Owen laughed. "We will, my dear, we will in good time. I need a while to recover. Men cannot simply go at it without ceasing."

"Why is that?"

"I have no idea. You'd have to take it up with the Almighty."

Grace laughed at that. She did feel good. She felt like her trust in Owen had not been misplaced. He'd just shown her something amazing, he kept asking for permission to make sure she was still all right, and now he held her like he didn't want to be separated from her again. She felt closer to him now.

But also sleepy.

"On second thought, I may close my eyes and dream instead," she said with a yawn.

Owen reached for a blanket that had fallen off the bed during all their activity and draped it over their bodies. "All right. Let us sleep," he said.

Chapter Six

THE NEXT THREE days and nights played out similarly. They spent their days in the carriage, although Owen insisted on stopping midday for luncheon. They found a safe place to pause, usually a field or wooded area where they could lay out a blanket, and they'd walk around, stretch their legs, and eat whatever he'd procured from the inn they'd left that morning.

Sometimes they napped, but Grace found it hard to sleep in a moving carriage. Often they talked. They talked about unimportant things, like the plots of novels Grace had read or some bit of gossip one of Owen's friends had spotted in a scandal sheet. They talked about their childhoods, telling stories about trouble they'd gotten into or moments of triumph. Owen had struggled in school, until suddenly he didn't; he'd had a teacher at Eton who finally made mathematics make sense, and another who helped him understand history. Grace wished she could have gone to school, but she'd taken to reading like a fish to water and had grown up reading whatever books she could get her hands on.

"This is what you do every time you travel west?" she asked on the second afternoon as the carriage rumbled over a difficult dirt road. It was almost bumpier than the ragged streets of London.

"Normally," Owen said, throwing out a hand to brace himself against the carriage as it hit another bump. "I try to get there as soon as possible and only stop if I absolutely cannot stand to be in the coach a minute longer. You are unused to the trip, so I thought it might do us some good to have a more leisurely luncheon. And I am actually enjoying making this trip with you, so I find I am not in a hurry."

Grace smiled at that. And she appreciated the long breaks, because all the sitting in the carriage was making her backside hurt.

They spent their nights in a series of coaching inns, making love in a progression of ricketier beds. Grace hadn't slept much, but she didn't regret anything, because being with Owen was maybe the greatest thing that had happened in her entire life.

Well, that was exaggerating a little.

Except no, it wasn't. This whole trip had shown her more of the country than she'd ever seen before. And Owen seemed eager to show her all of it.

The journey had taken them not just through Oxford, but also through Stratford-on-Avon on their way to an inn in Birmingham. Owen explained that Stratford was where Shakespeare was born. They didn't have time to take in a play, but they did stop at the church where Shakespeare was buried.

"His grave seems so modest for a man we have grown to revere," said Grace.

"Yes, well, I suppose he had his preferences. No need to build a marble effigy if one is not a royal or absurdly wealthy."

"Quite. But this is something. It says, 'Blest be the man that leaves these stones, cursed be he that moves my bones.' Astonishing."

"He just wanted to be left alone. I have some sympathy for that."

"Me, too."

The stop in Birmingham was not so bad, because it was a small city, at least, and the inn was well appointed. It was hard for Grace not to admire the sorts of places Owen liked to spend the night. Grace didn't know much about money or finances, but she could tell Owen had much more money than her parents, or at least, he was more willing to spend it.

Late that night, they lay in bed together, Owen absently stroking Grace's arm. "I feel terrible for taking you from your family," he said.

"Don't."

"Are you certain? My mother spends most of her time with my sister these days and I only see her a few times a year. I miss her sometimes."

"You and your mother are close?"

"I suppose we are. She doted on me when I was a child."

"My family and I are not close. My father is friendly enough, but rarely home. My mother is cold and standoffish. My sister is only now coming into her personality. I was often left alone as a child, so I had to learn to entertain myself. My family…they were not harsh or cruel or anything like that. I've heard of families who are. But I don't feel like I'm leaving behind people who have much affection for me. I imagine I will see my family when I return to town and I will write them letters from Wales, but…"

"I am sorry to hear that you had so little affection in your home. But dare I ask, how did you entertain yourself?"

"Reading and art. It's part of why I took up pottery. I can work for hours and not notice time is passing."

"Oh," said Owen. "I suppose I have some sympathy for that. I like to keep busy. And I've been living alone in London more or less since my father passed, so I have some familiarity with finding things to occupy my time."

Grace nodded, feeling like he understood her.

After Birmingham, the scenery became much more rustic, but it was hard to deny how beautiful the countryside was. Most of it was flat, but there were farms and fields and little houses and inns.

They crossed the border into Wales, but it didn't feel like much of a change. The terrain, even the accents of the people they encountered, were the same.

"You did not bring a valet with you," Grace said as they rode one afternoon.

"No. My valet's wife is about to have a baby, I could not ask him to be away from her. I can forego his services for a month. And as you've seen, I do seem to be able to dress myself."

"But does he not help you into your clothes and take care of your grooming?"

"Indeed, he gives me a closer shave than I am capable of myself." Owen rubbed his jaw, which was shadowed with dark stubble. "And I will admit, it is harder to get into my more stylish clothes without some help. Especially my boots. But there will be no need for formal evening wear in Wales that I anticipate."

"What, no balls? No house parties?"

Owen smiled, perhaps understanding her sarcasm. "No, my dear, I intend to show you my home, get you acquainted with the staff at my house, show you my favorite places. At night, we shall have intimate dinners without being bothered by the need for social niceties. Will you miss it terribly?"

"I will not miss it at all. That is, I do like my more beautiful gowns, but I do not believe I shall miss the sorts of balls my mother was forever dragging me to in the hopes I'd choose some wealthy lordling to marry."

"You landed me."

"And may I never go to one of those balls again."

Owen chuckled. "That is good, though. I've worried constantly that I'm taking you from a life you loved."

"You aren't. I suppose many women love the balls and the clothes and the socializing, but not me. I like quiet and I like my art." She raised an eyebrow at him. "And if you like, I can help you with your boots."

Owen winked, perhaps appreciating the innuendo. "And I can introduce you to my family, so if you do find yourself at loose ends and in need of conversation, they are available. My aunt handles the castle maintenance, and she's a real character. Her name is Morvith."

"Morvith?"

"Yes. Spelled M-o-r-f-u-d-d. Here is your first Welsh lesson. Two Ds in a word make a *t-h* sound."

"Will I need to learn Welsh?"

"No. My staff all speak English, as does Morfudd, even though she resents it a little. She is a widow and never had any children, although she helped raise a local girl named Gwen, one of her late husband's nieces. Like you, Gwen has recently come of age but seems to largely loathe courtship rituals, at least according to Morfudd's letters."

"It's not that I disdain courtship—"

"No, I know. You were betrothed to Beresford as a backup in case you met no one else. I can understand what a trial that would be."

"You do not like Beresford."

Owen sighed. "It's not that I dislike him. He is not my favorite person, though, it's true. He's arrogant and ridiculous and now that he and Waring are—" He stopped himself abruptly.

"It's all right. The night we… Well, at the Rutherford Ball, I had caught Beresford kissing Waring. I know they are in some sort of relationship. I don't understand it, but it is not my place to get involved."

"I agree. I try not to ask much about it. I suppose if they care for each other, they aren't hurting anyone." He sighed. "At any rate, Beresford has been a feature of my life in London for the better part of a year, so I have learned to…tolerate him." Owen shook his head. "And we shall eventually reach my estate. I'd like to introduce you to my family. I believe you and Morfudd will be fast friends."

"Then I shall like to meet her."

"I just worry about you all alone out here when I go back to London. I do not want you to be lonely or bored."

"I can't imagine I would be. This is what I wanted, after all. And like I said, I am good at entertaining myself." And it was what she wanted. They'd had plenty of time to chat about

Owen's home and what he liked about it, and it sounded splendid, if remote. A five-day journey meant that Owen couldn't be going back and forth too often, so she would not see much of him, but maybe that was for the best. Despite all the lovemaking, they still barely knew each other. This way, they would both have their freedom.

"I will be fine," Grace said, taking Owen's hand. "The only thing I ask in return is that you stay faithful to me."

"Of course."

"I know I may seem naive, but I know how men are." She knew how her father was, at any rate. She didn't know for certain, but she suspected that he was not spending all of his nights at his club or on business matters. "Many have mistresses, and it would not be hard for you to keep one with your wife all the way out in Wales. But I cannot stand the thought of you with another woman. On this point, I feel quite strongly."

"You have nothing to fear from me, my lady. If it is fidelity you want, I can manage it."

"Good. I trust you. Do not betray that." She tried to make her voice as threatening as possible.

"I won't."

He looked serious. Grace believed him. She did not believe they had a marriage in name only. She'd been at the ceremony, and she'd been with him the last several nights, and it was clear that even if this were not a love match, there was affection and attraction between them. And after the nights they'd spent together, the idea of Owen with another woman made her want to pluck out her own eyes.

Instead, she sealed his promise with a kiss.

"WELCOME TO CAER Newydd," Owen said as the carriage pulled up to a grand house. "The *newydd* implies the house is new, but that only means it is two-hundred years old instead of five hundred some odd. Although apparently some mate of William the Conqueror built the *original* castle, or so the rumor goes, but the pile of stonework up the road was built by Edward I, and we Welsh have resented the British ever since. Edward hammered the Welsh before he hammered the Scots, you know."

"I did not know."

"My aunt will happily lecture you on notable moments in Welsh history. I warn you, there are loads of Llewellyns."

"Does your aunt live here?"

"Morfudd keeps a house in town, but once she hears we are here, I imagine she will invite herself over."

"So who is here now?"

A groom ran up and helped them out of the carriage. Owen led the way up the stairs to the front door.

"Just the staff, I should think," said Owen.

The front doors suddenly flew open and a very tall man in livery stood at the door.

"Lord Caernarfon. Welcome home."

"This is Driscoll," said Owen. "Driscoll, this is my lovely bride, Grace."

"Welcome, my lady. My lord, I will have tea service in the grand parlor if you'd like to adjourn there while we take care of your luggage."

"That sounds nice, thank you." Owen turned to Grace. "Would you like the tour first or would you rather have something to eat?"

"Definitely something to eat. I'm famished."

Owen imagined a house of this size would make Grace feel overwhelmed. Owen felt overwhelmed sometimes; Caer Newydd was much larger than his home in London.

He led the way to the grand parlor. But first, they had to cross the main entrance, and what the staff referred to as the vestibule. It wasn't really a vestibule. The vaulted ceiling, the columns, the wide-open space was all a bit cold for Owen's taste, although he was used to it. The rooms inside were much cozier.

He held out his arm for Grace, and she cupped her hand around his elbow. As they walked across the vestibule, Grace said, "This is...grand."

"It's ostentatious, I know."

"Did I know you owned a house like this?" Grace sounded awed. "I suppose I did, but this is..."

Owen grinned. "I suppose I do have a few spare pounds to spend on nice living quarters. There's actually a whole wing of the house I don't really use. It's too much for a single man without a family. But now that you're here, if you want to spend some of my money to redecorate, I am open to it."

"Did you decorate this house already?"

"Some of it. A lot of it was my mother. But I made some modernizations a few years ago. I'll show you when we go up to our rooms later."

"Rooms? Will we not share?"

Owen smiled. "That is not customary. Surely your parents kept separate bedrooms."

Grace frowned. "Yes, but you and I shared a room and a bed on the road, and I thought that—"

"The lord and lady of the house have adjacent chambers upstairs, but you may sleep in my bed if you like. Anytime you want."

They arrived at the grand parlor, which was just a few steps down a hallway from the vestibule. The parlor was luxuriously appointed; Owen had seen to its decoration himself, and now that he looked again, he felt how dark and masculine it was. But there were two high-backed chairs that faced each other across a small table, situated in front of a fireplace, where a small fire was already burning. Owen pulled out one of the chairs for Grace, then he sat across from her.

The cook came in a moment later with a cart for tea. Owen was delighted to see that in addition to a teapot and cups, there was a tower of cakes, biscuits, and small sandwiches.

"Grace, this is Mrs. Jones, our cook. She bakes the best biscuits in Wales."

"My lady, it is wonderful to meet you," said Mrs. Jones. "I have soup cooking downstairs if you'd like that, too."

"This will be fine," said Grace. "Save the soup for dinner."

"Yes, my lady." Mrs. Jones bowed and left them.

Owen poured tea. He gestured at the milk, honey, and lemon that also sat on the cart.

"A little milk," said Grace.

So they had tea together, and Owen enjoyed watching Grace taste one of Mrs. Jones's biscuits, which really were light and crisp and very good.

After tea, Owen said, "Our luggage has probably been moved upstairs by now. Would you like to see our rooms?"

"I would."

A grand staircase off the vestibule led them upstairs. There were five bedrooms on this floor, which felt like more than anyone should need, but Owen supposed if he had more family, they'd take up more space. When he'd written ahead to say he was coming, he'd asked that the master bedroom, which was where he'd been sleeping the last few times he'd stayed here, and the adjacent lady's rooms be cleaned and decorated.

The staff had done a good job. Owen took Grace to his room first. A four-poster bed dominated the room, and it was covered in dark blue bedding. After his father died, he'd swapped out the furniture, finding that sleeping near so many of the late earl's things was too maudlin, so some of the furniture in his room here had come from London. He'd also changed the art on the walls to be more his taste: a watercolor of the northern coast of Wales, a painting of what was left of Caernarfon Castle, and a painting he'd bought in London of the Thames near Westminster at dawn.

"This is lovely," said Grace.

"Come with me," Owen said. He led her into another chamber. "I did not know the last time I was here that I would be bringing home a bride, but I can have some of these old clothes moved if you need more space for yours. This is my dressing room, and if you come through here…" Owen led her through a doorway, "this is the bathing room."

Grace looked around. Owen was quite proud of the room. He'd had tiles installed so that when he got in and out of the tub, water splashing about wouldn't ruin the floor. "And watch this!" He turned a knob on the tub and water flowed out.

"Impressive," said Grace. "I didn't realize water ran like that outside of London."

"One of my modernizations. I had iron pipes installed in this part of the house. It was very expensive, but at least the staff don't have to lug buckets of water upstairs just so I can bathe myself. Now come through here."

He led her into a mostly empty dressing room. "This is your dressing room. I'm afraid we share the bathing chamber, but you can use this space here however you like."

"It's lovely," said Grace, sounding genuine.

"And here is your bedchamber."

A door in the dressing room opened into a bedroom. Owen wasn't entirely sure what to expect, but this room had also been cleared of his parents' things. This had once been his mother's room, but there was no longer any trace of her, and Owen was grateful. The bed was covered in cream-colored bedding. A pale armoire stood across from the bed. Someone had hung a watercolor of flowers and a framed embroidery Owen recognized as something his sister had done when she was a girl, of a red dragon.

"You may, of course, redecorate however you see fit," Owen said.

"You keep saying that."

"I don't have much of an eye for decoration, and I imagine in the coming years, you will spend more time here than I will. I want you to feel at home." Owen frowned at the watercolor. "This is quite dull, for example, but we have other art available to hang here if you'd like to see it."

"Perhaps not today. I am quite tired."

"Yes. Of course." Owen looked around. "I see the trunks have been brought up but not unpacked."

"I should like to oversee the unpacking myself," Grace said. "This, for example, is my potter's wheel." She put her hand on a large crate. "And I am still not quite sure where it should go. We should keep it boxed up until we decide."

"Of course. Whatever you think is best."

"You are allowed to disagree with me, you know."

Owen smiled. "Like I said, I am merely trying to make you feel at home here."

She walked over and put her hands on his shoulders. He enjoyed that she'd gotten bolder after the nights they'd spent together. He wanted her to be as aggressive as she wanted, to initiate intimacy between them on her terms. Frankly, he was happy to accommodate her in all things.

This beautiful, clever woman was his bride. He could scarcely believe it.

He kissed her.

"What was that for?" Grace asked as she pulled away.

"You're the most beautiful woman I've ever seen. I can't believe you're mine."

"And you're mine," she said. She kissed him back.

Someone nearby cleared his throat. Driscoll stood in the doorway. "Dinner will be served in the dining room in one hour," he said.

"Driscoll, could you send a footman or two upstairs to help us unpack?"

"Of course, my lord." He bowed and left.

"Well," Owen said. "I suppose we should get to it."

Chapter Seven

Back in London, Anthony strolled into his club one evening and was immediately confronted by Matthew Clairborne, an earl and politician who was working on some sort of education reform bill in Parliament. Beresford only knew that because Clairborne had been quite vocal about said bill and there'd been much ink spilled about it in the newspapers Lark insisted on reading every morning. A bothersome habit, to be sure, although sometimes Beresford got bored and read those papers himself.

"Where is Caernarfon?" Clairborne asked.

"On his honeymoon. Surely you occasionally deign to read society columns. Caernarfon married Midwood's daughter. Wedding of the year! Quite a spectacular feast afterward, too, in fact."

"Is this your way of rubbing it in that you were invited?"

"I do try to place myself in the most high-profile social situations so that all may bask in my power and beauty."

Clairborne frowned. "Right."

"Why are you asking after Caernarfon—and asking me of all people? Despite securing an invitation to his wedding, I am not on his list of favorite people."

"When you bother to show up for votes in Parliament, you often vote with him, and I've seen you conversing with him in this very club, so I assumed you were friends. I do not, in fact, read society columns. That is women's business."

Beresford saw right through what Clairborne was saying there and decided to ignore it. "Well, all I can say is that Caernarfon is in Wales for at least another fortnight, likely ensconced in a love nest with his new bride…who, as it happens, was betrothed to me until six weeks ago, if you should like to take me down a peg. She's beautiful and came with a large dowry, so Caernarfon won the day, I suppose." Beresford crossed his arms. "But of course, society columns and scandal sheets are beneath you, so you will tell me none of this signifies."

"You speak too prolifically, Beresford."

"So I'm told. What do you want with Caernarfon?"

"His vote on my education reform bill. But it will come up for debate and voting before he returns, I'm afraid."

"I suppose that gives you a week to invent a faster conveyance."

"Indeed. Well, thank you for the information, Beresford. I will count on your vote should you bother to show up."

"Of course."

Clairborne sighed. "My sister has long been fond of Caernarfon. She will be sad to hear he's been taken off the market."

"Is she looking for a husband?"

"She is indeed on the marriage mart this year. My aunt has been escorting her to balls. Surely you've seen them."

Anthony tried to remember what Clairborne's sister looked like. "She's tall, yes? Your sister, I mean. Auburn hair, freckles?"

"That's her."

"And her name is…Margaret?"

Clairborne rolled his eyes. "Matilda."

"Yes, right."

"I take it by your lack of attention to detail that you will not be asking her to dance at the next ball."

"I daresay I feel obligated *now*. I am not in the market for a wife myself, though."

"Nor am I advocating for you to offer for her. I am just saying, she is on the market now. I'm making conversation."

"Ah, I see. Well, tell *Matilda* to save a dance for me at her next appearance, eh?"

Clairborne assented and loped off.

Anthony was aware of the fact that Owen didn't like him, likely because Owen harbored a familiar prejudice against men who dallied with other men, but at least Lark's other friends were more accommodating. Anthony set out to find them when he was accosted by another MP, this one Jacob Tipton, the elderly Duke of Foxborough.

"I say, Beresford," he said, placing his cane in Beresford's footpath.

Anthony fought not to roll his eyes.

"Can I count on your attendance at Parliament next Thursday?"

"I will consider it. What is the occasion?"

Foxborough let out a husky chuckle of a laugh. "Right to the chase you go! I feel we must rein in the spending of the Prince Regent. He has asked for more funds to decorate one of his palaces, but do you not think the money brought in from British taxpayers should go toward improvements?"

"Certainly the roads in London would be top of my list," said Anthony, willing to indulge the old duke. "I nearly lost a wheel on my favorite barouche the other day because of a large divot in Haymarket Street."

"Capital! I agree wholeheartedly. So I can count on your vote?"

"I will give the issue the attention it deserves." That was Anthony's stock answer for most issues in Parliament. His attendance was sporadic and mostly depended on how bored he was any given day, but he did have a seat in Lords and had once been the deciding vote on a very important bill regarding the safety of factory workers in Yorkshire. That is, fewer factory workers would lose limbs to the machinery now that safety precautions were in place; Anthony felt good about that.

He found Lark next, standing near a fireplace, staring at the fire as if it held the answers to life's questions.

What Anthony wanted to do was pull Lark into his arms from behind and hold him there until he spoke about whatever was bothering him. Alas, they were in public, and Beresford knew they'd gotten careless and were doing a poor job of hiding their affair, so he really should behave himself. Instead of touching Lark, he walked up beside him and said, "Schilling for your thoughts?"

Lark looked at him and raised an eyebrow. "Not a pence?"

"Inflation, you know. Cost of goods these days. I am just trying to keep up."

"You spend too much time in Parliament."

"There are a lot of men here who feel the opposite. It seems everyone has a bill and would appreciate my vote on it."

Lark frowned.

"What is it?" Anthony asked.

"I heard a terrible rumor that someone in Parliament wants to advance an anti-buggery bill. It would mean anyone caught could be hanged."

"Is that not already a law?" Anthony tried to sound casual.

"Likely it is, but it's one of those laws nobody sees a need to enforce. In *this* case, some MP in Commons wants to make an issue of it. He has a notion that this is a way to attract votes from the general public, since he has to run for his seat instead of being born into it."

"How many buggerers do you think there are in London? A few hundred?"

"Are you keeping count? Did you write down their names as they paraded through your bedroom?"

"Hush. Jealousy is unbecoming. And anyway, what I mean is that this is a bill that would apply to a very small portion of the population—and it is a population that means no harm to others. This MP in Commons, how do buggerers affect his life? They don't! Why bother to kick up dust about something that is already illegal?"

"My concern is that he means to enforce the law. And I don't know if you knew this, *Beresford*, but you are guilty of the crime."

Anthony waved his hand dismissively, although he wondered what Lark meant to say by using his title instead of his given name. "Any law would have to get by Lords as well, and I can assure you, the preoccupation of the peerage is mostly lining their own pockets or doing good deeds so that they can impress people and thus line their own pockets. Not to mention you have many other friends in Parliament, so why ask me?"

"Everyone else will know the issue bothers me and will wonder why."

Anthony put his hand on the fireplace mantel and leaned in a way he thought would be sexily casual. "And you don't want them to know because you so enjoy my hard—"

"Hush." Lark put up a hand. "You idiot. We cannot discuss—"

"Relax, Lark. I am jesting."

"Well, refrain from jesting before both of us end up at the wrong end of a noose, you jackass."

Lark's tone was *not* jesting. "Are you cross with me?"

"A little, yes. You have no sense of self-preservation. Being wealthy and powerful does insulate people from scandal to an extent, but if this bill passes, it's over for us."

Beresford paused to understand what Lark was saying, but couldn't parse it. "What do you mean by that? It's over for us in that we'll both be hanged? It's over for us in that we'll have to go underground? Or it's over for us in that our relationship with each other will be over."

"I don't know. Maybe all of those. I just know this is bad news."

"You can't mean you would end our relationship over a piece of legislation."

"If it meant keeping you alive? I would."

Anthony wasn't sure what to do with that. He was touched. He was frustrated.

"The bill may not pass. Lords won't see this as a priority. But if it does, I'll be careful. I'll stop spending time with you in public if that's what it takes. But you can't just throw this aside because of fear."

"I can, in fact, do that if it means not watching you *hang*." Lark was whispering and practically spit that part out.

"May we postpone further discussion on this until or if the bill actually passes? Because I intend to vote against it, and I have friends I can talk into voting against it."

"Yes, but what will they think of you if you do?"

"I can make an argument that has nothing to do with me. The bill is a waste of time, it's solving a problem that doesn't exist, innocent people could get caught up in the witch hunt, that sort of thing."

"And you're pushing it because *you* don't want to get caught in the witch hunt."

Anthony crossed his arms. "Let us not make more of this than it needs to be."

Lark threw up his hands. "Fine. You asked what I was upset about and that's what it is. And while I adore you for your optimistic outlook on life and the way it never appears that anything bothers you, sometimes you are too cavalier and take too many risks. And, as I've said repeatedly, I point all this out because I don't want to see harm come to you."

"And what about you?"

"*I* don't matter."

"I think you do."

Lark frowned. "Whatever. I can weather a storm. You have a title, you actually do show up for your seat in Parliament, you have a reputation you need to protect. I'm…"

"*You* have a title."

"But I don't care about my reputation."

"I don't, either. I'd give the title to my cousin tomorrow if it meant we could stop fearing doom lurking around every corner." Anthony grunted. "This isn't a problem yet. Can we push off fretting about it?"

"For now. Fine."

"Good."

Hugh and Fletcher were approaching from the other side of the room.

"May I point out," Anthony said, "that Hugh's father-in-law is repeatedly rumored to flounce around in women's clothing and visit molly houses, and though I know that's not true, and the press has gone easier on him since his daughter married a duke, the rumors still pop up periodically. And yet, he carries on in Parliament. And he's so far up Prinny's backside, he—"

"I take your point." Lark walked away from the fireplace, a sign the argument was over.

"Trouble, lads?" Fletcher asked.

"No," said Anthony. "At least none that Lark isn't looking for."

"You think I *want* this?" Lark said. "You think I want *any* of this?"

"I think you're overreacting."

"Bloody hell." Lark stalked out of the room.

Anthony considered going after him, but he figured Lark needed time to cool off. Instead, Anthony dropped into a chair near the fireplace.

"What was that row about?" Fletcher asked, sitting across from Anthony.

"Politics," said Anthony.

"Silly thing, politics," Fletcher said.

Anthony gave Fletcher a once over. Fletcher also stood to inherit a title—his father was a marquess—so he would eventually have a seat in Parliament as well. However, he'd long been disinterested in both politics and idle gossip, which made it difficult for Anthony to come up with things to speak with him about. Anthony tossed about for some topic of conversation and recalled that Fletcher was a patron of the arts.

"I say, Fletcher, have you yet had time to see the new opera at the Royal Opera House? I heard it is a take on *Pygmalion*."

"No, but I am taking Lady Louisa Petty to see it at the end of this week. Do you plan to see it as well? It's a new composer, Donizetti. He is quite young. I'm curious to see if the new opera is good."

Anthony smiled. Fletcher's Italian pronunciation of the young composer's name indicated he was, in fact, a fan of Italian operas. "You will have to tell me your thoughts. Although I often go to the opera to be seen, and rarely to, you know, see the opera."

"Lady Louisa loves opera, and so I must hold my tongue as she listens."

Ah, yes. One mustn't let it be known that one liked art too much. It was not what men did. Anthony did like opera, or he liked the spectacle of a good production, but he liked socializing with his peers more. "I did like that production of *The Magic Flute* they put on last Season. The costumes were beautiful."

"Lady Louisa and I saw that three times. She thought it was wonderful."

Anthony took this to mean Fletcher also enjoyed it but did not want to say as much.

Hugh looked on, not saying anything. Hugh had rarely been seen at the Royal Opera House, and so might have thought Anthony and Fletcher were speaking gibberish.

It was probably time for Anthony to take his leave anyway. Find Lark and smooth down his ruffled feathers.

"I should be off. But Swynford, before I go," Anthony said, standing back up. "May I have a word?"

"It's fine," Fletcher said. "I can entertain myself. Deal myself a game of whist. Work on my skills."

Anthony pulled Hugh into a quiet corner and relayed what Lark had told him and a brief summary of their argument. Then he said, "You must have some influence with your father-in-law. Can you make sure this bill never makes it to the floor?"

"I can't make sure of anything, but I can come up with a cover story and convey that it's…unnecessary. Isn't buggery already illegal?"

"Technically, but it's one of those cyclical things. Every, oh, thirty years or so, someone decides the *sin that shall not be named* needs more attention, and that men who seek their pleasure with other men should be burned at the stake. The MPs in Parliament need an issue to throw attention off something they plan to do that they think will be unpopular, is my guess."

"I can't do anything about Commons."

"No, but if Lords doesn't take up the bill, it won't become a law."

Hugh nodded. "All right. I'll try. But please, for the love of all that is holy, do not get caught. I'd prefer it if neither of you hanged."

"If Lark ever speaks to me again, I promise, I will be the soul of discretion."

Chapter Eight

OWEN'S AUNT MORFUDD turned out to be a complete delight. She was preoccupied by the maintenance work at Caernarfon Castle, but she was happy to speak about anything Welsh. The first night they all dined together, Morfudd taught Grace a few Welsh words. "I always start with *draig*," she'd explained. "Say it with me."

Grace repeated the word. "What does it mean?"

"Dragon," said Morfudd with a wink.

The next day, Morfudd escorted Owen and Grace on a tour of the castle, which was far less charming than Grace had hoped. One heard the word *castle* and pictured something grand, but Caernarfon was mostly a broad brick facade with few windows. Inside, there wasn't much to see. There were many empty rooms, and parts of the castle that were inaccessible because walls had caved in and the rooms were too damaged.

"What I'd like," Morfudd explained, "would be to turn this into a museum of Welsh history. But for now, I'd settle for using some of the empty rooms to show exhibits about the history of the castle. The first English Prince of Wales was born here, you know, and we have never forgiven Edward I for the dishonor."

"The English Prince of Wales feels like a contradiction," said Grace.

"The Welsh people could not abide by a Prince of Wales who spoke English. *Cymru rydd!* But Edward I insisted his son be dubbed Prince of Wales, and since he was a baby, he did not speak English, because he did not speak anything, and we let him get away with it. And so Llewellyn the Last was the last Welsh Prince of Wales. Unless you count Owain Glyndwr."

"I do," said Owen. "*Cymru rydd!*" He turned to Grace. "That means 'Free Wales.'"

"Although, to be clear to your English bride, we are not so revolutionary as to advocate for Welsh independence," said Morfudd. "At least not out loud."

"I see," said Grace, appreciating Morfudd's attitude.

"We do still speak Welsh to keep the language alive, and we have a few of our own old habits and traditions, although we are of course also part of England as well. A bit of a duality, especially now that Owen here has taken his father's seat in Parliament. In the *English* Parliament."

"Yes, well. King Charles I bestowed the title upon our family, so I suppose we do owe the government something," said Owen. "I am, in fact, the tenth Earl of Caernarfon."

"That is remarkable," said Grace.

"I suppose it is."

"Come," said Morfudd, bustling along. "Let me show you the rest of this pile of bricks."

Two days later, Owen brought Grace to the cottage he'd bought on the coast, although "cottage" felt too humble a word for it. The house was small compared to Car Newydd, but it still had several rooms.

"I have not had time to furnish it much," Owen explained as he showed her around the property. "I'm not even entirely sure why I thought I should buy it. But it's lovely, isn't it?"

And it was. Large windows on the northern exposure of the house looked out at the Irish Sea, which was the house's main feature. Inside, Owen hadn't done much except put a bed in one of the bedrooms and a table and chairs in one of the sitting rooms.

"I think in the summer, this will be a wonderful place to be,"

Owen said.

"I agree," Grace said, already imagining what she could do with the space. She even walked into the garden behind the house, which was overgrown but quite large. She could put a kiln here. She could put her potter's wheel in the room at the back of the house, and add shelves to accommodate her supplies, and…

Yes. She wanted to make art right here, so close to the water she could smell it.

She didn't say anything to Owen, but she figured he'd tell her what he said whenever she asked a question about changing something, which was to give her his full permission.

It was a little bit annoying, how nice he was being. She almost wished he would stop her.

Because the truth was, she was enjoying his company immensely, and she knew that he wanted her to have her way because he wouldn't be here much. And the thought of that made her sad.

"I do love the water," Owen said as they stepped outside to look at the sea. "I find it calms me."

Grace understood that. Owen put an arm around her shoulders and she closed her eyes, hearing the gentle sound of the waves rolling against the rocky coast. There was little else around, save for some other cottages in the distance. It was a peaceful spot. Grace hated to leave it.

"Must we rush back to your estate?" Grace asked.

"We have some time, although I'd like to get started back home before it gets dark."

She looked up at her husband's face. One surprising revelation of their nights together was that Grace felt insatiable, constantly wanting more of her husband. How could that be? They'd made love every night since their marriage, but Grace still wanted more. They'd barely been able to keep their hands off each other when they were alone. Sometimes she wondered if this was normal or inappropriate, but certainly the feeling was mutual, so she decided not to wonder too hard.

Grace put her hands on Owen's shoulders and raised an eyebrow. He looked a little startled at first, but he smiled. "Oh. Er, have I showed you the bedroom?"

"Is there furniture in it?"

"I slept here once shortly after I purchased the cottage because I wanted to see what it would be like to sleep so near the sea at night." He took her hand and led her down a short hallway. He opened a door. "There's not much more than an old mattress."

"Mattress" was a generous description. It was a pallet on a simple wooden bed frame with several blankets draped on top of it. There was a trunk off to the side and a simple armoire in the corner. Grace stepped into the room and walked over to the armoire, which she opened. It held a couple of changes of clothes for Owen—two shirts, a jacket and pair of breeches made of simple broadcloth that looked old enough to be ten years out of fashion—but little else. This wouldn't do as a place to sleep for Grace, but she didn't plan to sleep here tonight.

"You are generous with your funds," Grace said. "If I were to set up a proper bedroom here, would I bankrupt you?"

"No. That is, my funds are not unlimited, but I intended to furnish the cottage and had set aside money for it. A proper bed is not too much, so long as it is not made of gold."

"You may have to tell me to stop spending your money at some point."

"My man of business has an assistant. I can dispatch him to help you manage the money. Or to tell you which expenditures are too great."

"A proper bed, some chairs, maybe a table to put in that main room. Nothing extravagant."

Owen put an arm around her shoulders. "I trust you not to bankrupt me."

There was something magical about this cottage. It was not large, but it was enough. Space for Grace's pottery supplies, space for her to sleep and keep some clothes. She probably couldn't stay here for many days at a time—she did not know her way around a kitchen, and the one here was small—but the ride wasn't too long. An overnight now and then would be workable.

"I see the ideas flitting about your head," Owen said. "Are you mentally decorating?"

"Yes," said Grace. "How sturdy is that bed?"

"Why do you ask?" Something sly crept into Owen's voice.

Grace grinned. "Oh. I did not mean to imply anything. Just whether one could sleep on it without it collapsing."

"Yes. Like I said, I did it once. It's not very comfortable, alas. But it might serve a more immediate purpose."

Grace turned to look at Owen. He winked at her. Grace felt wanton and inappropriate, but she had not expected to enjoy herself with Owen so much. She could not get enough of him. Currently, Owen was dressed in a functional brown jacket and trousers, hardly his most dashing kit, and yet Grace still felt drawn to him. He was breathtakingly handsome, and Grace found that, rather than frighten her as her mother implied he would, seeing Owen out of his clothing was exciting. His broad chest, his strong arms, his sturdy thighs, all of these things made Grace ache when she beheld them.

She hadn't known she could feel this way. Sometimes, when she looked at him, she felt like her skin was on fire.

But more than that, the way Owen held her made her feel safe and cared for. The previous night, they'd shuddered to climax together, and after, Owen had held Grace to his chest, like he was unwilling to let her go, and Grace didn't want him to anyway.

And this was her *husband*. Her married friends had told stories implying they barely tolerated their husbands, but Grace wanted to spend nearly every minute with hers. She supposed this feeling would wear off eventually, that once the heady days of their early marriage matured into something steadier, they'd irritate each other the way Grace's parents did, but for now, it was wonderful.

But he was leaving in a few weeks.

"Perhaps," she said, "we should make the most of your re-maining time in Wales."

"What did you have in mind?" asked Owen.

Grace stepped away from him and tugged at a ribbon on the bodice of her gown. She wore simple muslin today at Owen's urging—no expensive fabric that might be damaged in salt air—and loosening the bodice meant the dress could be slipped off easily.

Owen's expression darkened. "You are incorrigible, my dear. But on the other hand, it would be a crime not to christen this space."

Grace giggled. She reached over to Owen and slid his jacket off his shoulders. "I am getting my fill before you depart."

"I will have nothing left when I go. I will be a hollowed-out husk of a man. And I will regret none of it."

He bent down and kissed her. Yes. This was perfect. This was what Grace wanted. A memory made in this room in her new cottage.

Owen slipped her gown off. She had yet to hire a lady's maid and Owen had urged her not to dress to the nines, so she hadn't bothered with stays today, not thinking they were needed under her loose muslin dress. Owen groaned as his fingers clutched the fabric of her shift.

"I don't want to leave you here," Owen said.

"It's truly all right."

He nuzzled the space where her neck met her shoulder. "I could bring you back with me."

"I want to stay here. I already told you it's what I want."

"I feel guilty leaving you alone."

"Owen."

He lifted his head and looked at her.

"I am allowed to have visitors, no?"

He nodded. "Of course. So long as they are not bachelors." He looked at her sternly.

She laughed. "Never. I thought to invite my friend Penelope."

"Penelope… Thistledown?"

"Yes. She is my dearest friend. I mean to write to her the next time I am near paper and a pen and invite her to stay at her convenience. She and Morfudd and your various employees can keep me company in your absence."

"So practical." Owen held Grace close to his chest. "I admit, I did not expect to like you as much as I do. I feel drunk whenever I am around you. You are so beautiful and clever and I cannot believe you are my wife."

"It's true."

He smiled and kissed her. "Perhaps you have bewitched me."

"I know of no witchcraft."

"I suppose not."

"Owen?"

"Mmm."

"The time for speaking is over. Let us…how did you say it? Let us christen this house."

"Indeed."

IN BED THAT night, Owen held Grace as she slept against his chest and wondered again if all of this was a terrible mistake.

He did like Grace. He'd never been with a woman like her, always curious and excited in bed. His past lovers had always seemed to have ulterior motives or made him feel like he was one in a long line, but Grace always put her entire focus on him. She was inexperienced but had good instincts, and Owen thought that if he could spend the rest of his life in her arms, inside her, he'd die happy.

But he had to leave soon. He'd gotten a letter that morning that Parliament was being called back into session in ten days.

He wanted to bring her back to London with him, but every time he brought it up, she insisted she wanted to stay back. That had always been the arrangement, after all.

She stirred now. Owen stroked her back, marveling in how soft and smooth her skin felt under his fingers. She propped herself up on his chest and looked down at him. "You are stubbornly awake."

"Apologies."

"What keeps you awake?"

Owen sighed. "Swirling thoughts, I suppose. I am trying to invent a faster conveyance than a carriage so that I might make the journey between here and London in a matter of hours instead of days."

"Not looking forward to the long trip?"

"Wishing I could pass between here and my home in London faster or at a whim."

"The trip is arduous."

That wasn't what he meant. What he wished was that he could go to London, take care of his business in town, and be back in Grace's arms that same night. But perhaps that was just his lust talking.

"I know we've discussed this at length," he said, "but I'll take you back to London if you wish. Unfortunately, I must go because I have business in town."

"I am certain." She paused and looked to the side. Her long hair cascaded around her shoulders, and Owen's fingers itched to comb through it. Then she said, "Imagine spending your whole life confined to one house, only leaving under intense supervision, having your every move watched like a hawk. Did you know, I always behaved myself? Kissing you at the Rutherford ball was the most scandalous thing I have ever done. One reason I wanted to marry you was freedom. And I recognize that I am tethered to you, and that I am now in Wales instead of closer to my home in London. But I am no longer under my father's thumb. I am no longer subject to my mother's scrutinizing gaze. And that is liberating. I do not relish the two of us being separated, but I—"

Her answer surprised Owen. "When we first agreed to this, that was essentially what you said. You wanted to live in the country."

"I dislike London, to be honest. I dislike how loud it is, how smoky, how crowded. And spending time at your cottage on the sea today—it's so beautiful, Owen. The sea air is lovely. I want to stay here. It's better even than what I pictured."

"And you want freedom."

"Yes."

"And to make sculptures."

"Yes. I intend to convert part of the cottage into my studio. Just so you're aware."

"Of course."

"And I feel like I made the right choice in husbands because you are allowing me to do that." She smiled. "Owen, hear me when I say that our arrangement is what I wanted and that you need not feel guilty for bringing me here and giving me a lovely home. Our arrangement... It has far surpassed my dreams. I will miss you, of course, and I hope you do not stay away too long, but this is what I want. I promise."

Owen nodded and tried to internalize that. Perhaps he was imposing his own sadness about their parting on her, something she did not seem to feel. She wanted to be here. She was satisfied with their arrangement. Why was he fighting this? He'd wanted a marriage with minimal interruption to his life, and that was exactly what he was getting.

"Just promise me," Owen said, "that no other man but me will warm your bed."

"I promise," she said, not even pausing to think. "You are my husband."

"All right." He leaned up and kissed her forehead. "I did not anticipate us being together in bed like this, though, even when I agreed to this marriage. It is a happy bonus. You are so beautiful." Owen cupped her cheek. She leaned into his touch. "Perhaps I am a little sad to leave."

She laughed softly. "You want me to go back with you to London so that we can keep doing this. You want to use my body."

"Well...yes."

She lay down beside him. "Perhaps this will serve as an incentive for you not to leave me alone too long. I do enjoy your company. I shall not be sad if you choose to visit more frequently than you originally proposed."

"Good to know."

"And we can write letters when we are apart. My friends have said I am a good writer. I had the best governess money could buy."

"Oh." He supposed he should not have been surprised by that, given how much she read. She spoke and had the quick-thinking skills of someone who had gone to school, even though she hadn't. "I am not the strongest writer, but I will happily respond to letters from you, especially if you wish to keep me up to date on your plans for my estate."

"I promise not to change too much."

Owen found he was astonished by the talents of his new bride, not just in bed, but the fact that she wrote letters—there were some aristocratic women who were barely educated because of old-fashioned notions of women being docile servants to their husbands—and she made art. What couldn't she do?

"Change whatever you like," Owen said, "except my study. I decorated that myself and would like for it to stay as-is."

"I don't see much in this house that needs changing, but the cottage is like a blank canvas."

"Then paint away on that canvas, my dear."

She smiled again and snuggled up to his side. "Thank you, Owen."

"For what?"

"For giving me exactly what I wanted. I am grateful. You will never know how much."

"Well. This has all been unexpected. But you're welcome."

TOWARD THE END of Owen's time in Wales, he took Grace on an extended tour of the grounds around Caer Newydd.

"One thing you'll note about Wales," Owen said as they walked arm-in-arm, "is that the Welsh have a tendence to cover any open bit of land with sheep."

"I had spotted quite a lot of sheep." There were indeed several milling about on the grounds around them as they walked.

"My family has been selling wool to textile mills for generations. The work is handled these days mostly by Arthur Williams and his family."

"Your employees?"

"Yes. Although I believe Arthur and I are distantly related as well. His house is just over the way here."

Grace hadn't known what to expect. Whenever she'd read about tenant farms on these large estates, mostly in novels, there were always tales of rotting roofs on crumbling cottages, a sure sign that the landlord was neglecting his tenants. However, Arthur Williams lived in a sturdy-looking cottage on the estate with a thriving garden beside it.

"I sent a note yesterday that we were coming so Arthur would know to expect us." Owen knocked on the door.

A man with graying hair answered the door. His face lit up when he saw Owen.

"Ah, Owen, my boy. I am glad you are home." He pulled Owen into a bear hug.

"Just for a few more days, but I wanted to introduce you to my wife. Grace, this is Arthur Williams. Arthur, this is the new Countess of Caernarfon."

"How do you do?" she asked.

"Well, you're a pretty one!" said Arthur. "Please come in. The whole clan is here."

Grace quickly found herself overwhelmed with the sights and

sounds of Arthur's large family. "Arthur's sons and nephews do most of the labor on the sheep farm these days. They're responsible both for the maintenance of the farm in terms of things like the shelters we use in bad weather and the fences and those sorts of things, and they tend to the sheep and shear them on regular schedules. Then the wool is bundled up and shipped off, thanks to Arthur."

Grace nodded, eyeing the people filling the room. In quick succession, she was introduced to two of Arthur's sons, their wives, and several of Arthur's nephews. Arthur's wife, Bryn, offered Grace refreshments, and although Grace and Owen had eaten lunch before walking here, she did help herself to a biscuit.

Everyone in the room seemed eager to meet Grace. She shook many hands, endured many hugs, and was mollified somewhat by Owen continuing to beam at her while he introduced her to all of the people in the house. A few children ran by, too, but Grace had no idea to whom they belonged. The group was perhaps more of a collective, all of them assisting each other and helping raise the children.

"It's a lot, isn't it?" said one of the women as everyone spoke over each other.

"It is," said Grace. She'd never been to a family gathering like this. On the rare occasions her parents hosted dinner parties or social gatherings, they tended to be formal affairs with a particular stodgy rhythm, where everyone went through the motions and no one ever spoke over anyone else. They also rarely had family over. Grace's mother had no siblings, and Grace's father had only a brother that he did not often speak with. "My family doesn't gather like this. I've never seen anything like it."

"I know precisely what you mean," said the woman. "I'm Gwen. I'm Alex's wife."

"Which one is Alex?"

Rather than be offended, the woman laughed. "Arthur's son. The taller one with darker hair, standing over there next to the table."

"Ah, yes. Of course. I apologize, but it was a lot of names to learn all at once."

"No worries. I was an only child, so I understand where you're coming from. I found my first few gatherings with the Williams family to be overwhelming, but it's got its charms."

"I imagine it does."

"This group of people loves each other more than anything, and they love the earl as well." Gwen gestured across the room, where Owen and Arthur were laughing together. "The Williams' have been tending sheep on Caernarfon land for generations, so we all treat each other like family. My husband and the earl played together as children. And the earl makes sure our homes are well tended to and that we always have everything we need."

"That's lovely."

Gwen nodded. "You'll get used to the noise in time, I'm sure."

Grace laughed. She didn't think that was true. "Owen—the earl—has been showing me how to manage some of the affairs of the estate, and while I think I'm taking to the work, I've never done anything like this before. I had never been to Wales before moving here a few weeks ago. Everything has been wonderful so far, but you're right, I'm completely overwhelmed."

"Well, my lady, perhaps some of us can be of service. My husband and his brother and cousins do a lot of the physical work, but we women are keepers of the knowledge." Gwen tapped her temple. "My sister-in-law Carys and I do some of the management work. If you ever have any questions, you are free to call on one of us. Send a note or just stop by. My house is just a few steps that way." She gestured to her right.

"Thank you. That is kind. I will likely take you up on that."

"We ladies must help each other out."

Grace smiled. "I agree. And if I can do anything for you, please let me know."

"I will, my lady." Gwen winked. "I've forgiven you for being an Englishwoman, by the way."

Grace chuckled. "Thank you for that."

As they walked back to the house a while later, Owen said, "Convenient of Arthur to gather everyone to the house."

"Yes."

"You were a bit inundated back there."

"It's just that I am not used to any of this. That is not a criticism to be clear. I love how quiet the house is. I love that I can sit outside and hear only birdsong or the breeze through the trees. And I do like that most of the people I've met are friendly and far less formal than my own family. But it will take a bit to get used to it."

Owen nodded. "I probably should have warned you."

"There was no need. Perhaps my stoic British upbringing is the unusual one."

"When I was a child, I was made to understand that certain occasions called for formality. I learned all the protocol, I learned how to address my peers and ask a lady to dance and defer to my social betters and all that. But when we were here in Wales, my family generally let all of that fall away. My father, God rest his soul, had his employees call him by his Christian name, and he'd get out there and shear a sheep or two himself. He and Arthur were great friends, and all those men you just met? We terrorized the adults when we were boys. My mother, too, has little need for much formality unless it's called for. So what you just saw was a big part of my childhood."

"My mother would faint," Grace said.

Owen laughed. "I do hope that is not the case."

"Father would adjust, but he can be a bit awkward. But my mother was the daughter of a very old earldom, and she is distantly related to the king. Unfortunately, she insists on living up to that at all times. I admit, I did often wish she was more affectionate when I was growing up. On the other hand, it was all I really knew."

"Do you find me overwhelming?" Owen asked softly.

"No. How can you ask that?"

"I fear that I like the sorts of physical affection your parents would surely find scandalous."

"Yes, likely true, but *I* like that physical affection, and my family is many miles away."

Owen paused and turned to Grace. He smiled. "I do hope you enjoy your time here."

"I believe I shall."

Owen looked around. They were approaching the house. He gazed up at it. "I shall miss both you and this place when I return to London, but I'm afraid Parliament has been called back into session and I do not have much choice."

"Write me letters," said Grace. "Tell me everything."

"You must do the same. Especially since you have some competence at letter writing. Tell me all about everything happening here and with you. I shall endeavor to return as soon as I can."

Grace smiled, although she felt sad now that Owen's departure was imminent. She had enjoyed her time with him far more than she expected to. But this was what they'd agreed to, and anyway, Grace was anxious to get to work on her pottery.

She hadn't felt right taking time away from Owen while he was here, but as soon as he was gone, she planned to set up her studio at the cottage. Her fingers itched to get back into the clay.

"I shall keep busy," she told Owen. "Hopefully the time without you shall fly by."

He leaned over and kissed her cheek. "I shall return before you know I'm gone."

Chapter Nine

A DINNER PARTY at his mother's home was the last event Anthony wanted to attend. He'd considered inviting Lark just to have an ally, but his mother insisted the guest list stay small for some specific reason.

He learned what that reason was as soon as he was seated for dinner, next to a Lady Eugenia Trestle, the daughter of the Earl of Rainsford.

He'd walked into a trap.

No one at the dinner table said what Anthony's presence at this dinner implied. The Earl and Countess of Rainsford were perfectly pleasant. The countess kept up a steady stream of conversation with Mother, mostly society gossip. Anthony's Uncle George, his mother's untitled younger brother, kept the earl entertained, bouncing around various parliamentary business. This left Anthony to speak with Lady Eugenia, likely by design.

She was pretty, albeit very young, barely nineteen. Her hair was pinned atop her head in an elaborate nest of curls that must have taken her lady's maid an hour to assemble. She had porcelain skin and flushed cheeks and impeccable table manners.

And she was dull as dirt.

Anthony fished for topics. Had she read any good books recently? No, she didn't really read. What did she think of the weather? Oh, it was pleasant, she said amiably, even though

London had been a rainy, muddy mess for three days. How did she like to occupy her time? Needlepoint and promenades in the park.

"Have you read Shakespeare?" he asked at one point. "Or seen any of his plays performed?"

"Oh, no. Papa thinks the theater is vulgar."

"Even Shakespeare? The greatest British writer who has ever lived?"

"Indeed. Why do you ask?"

"I was just thinking of idioms Shakespeare invented. 'Dead as a doornail,' for example. That was Shakespeare." And that was how this whole dinner was making Anthony feel.

As the men began to retire toward the lounge for whisky and cigars, Anthony's mother hooked a hand around his arm and pulled him into the hallway.

"We must discuss your betrothal."

Here it came. "What betrothal? As you may recall, *my* betrothal became null as soon as my would-be bride was caught *in flagrante* with the Earl of Caernarfon. And now my betrothed is married to him."

"You must get married."

"I must do no such thing."

"The Rainsford girl is lovely, isn't she?"

"She has all the brainpower of a lamprey. We'd have nothing to talk about."

"Your job is not to talk, Anthony. Your job is to carry on the Beresford legacy."

"Right. And I cannot bestow the title on a cousin because…"

"Because it is your duty to carry on the title. I like Lady Genovia."

"Eugenia."

"Regardless, she is pretty and biddable."

Anthony lowered his voice. "She is boring and vapid."

"The society papers are saying things about you."

"I'm sure they do. It's probably all true."

Mother looked positively steamed at that point. "Anthony. Sowing a few oats when you are young is one thing, but you are four and thirty and you have an important title. Perhaps Lady Eustace is not what you want—"

"Lady Eugenia. You don't even know your prospective daughter-in-law's name."

"Perhaps she is not to your taste, but you must choose someone, and soon."

"Why the rush?"

"The things I hear about you, Anthony. They are too horrific to repeat."

"Then don't repeat them. I am finished with this conversation." He walked into the lounge to get a cigar.

Uncle George and the earl were friendly enough company that Anthony lingered at the house after the Rainsfords departed to have another snifter of whiskey. He regretted it as soon as Mother brought up the subject of prospective wives again. As soon as her mouth opened, Uncle George made himself scarce.

"I agree, Eugenia is a bit of an empty vessel," Mother conceded. "Perhaps we can find someone with more than clouds between her ears."

"Mother…"

"I know you do not wish to marry, but I wish you would, because you could very well tarnish the family name otherwise."

"And so what if I do? What if, for example, I do not wish to marry because I am, in fact, in love with someone completely inappropriate."

"Surely she cannot be so inappropriate as to not be your marchioness. You do not socialize with the other classes."

"It was a hypothetical. I was curious about how you would react. Swynford's mother did not approve of his bride, you know. The daughter of an earl! But because she'd been on the shelf so long and there had been rumors about her father, the dowager did not approve. And yet Swynford married her anyway."

"Are you telling me you are having an *affaire* with a woman of ill repute."

"No… I'm not having an *affaire*. There's no woman. I'm trying to make a point."

"If she comes from a good family, I don't care if she comes from a lower rank."

"Of course." Anthony sighed and spared a thought for Lark. "I wish you would not meddle."

"I wish *you* would recognize that you have duties, Anthony. You inherited your father's title, God rest his soul. That comes with certain obligations."

"Obligations I did not want and never asked for!"

"And yet you live on the money you inherited from the title."

Hard to argue with that. "Still, the title is mine, should I not be the one who decides what to do with it?"

"Your one job as Marquess of Beresford is to produce a future Marquess of Beresford."

And that was when Anthony ran out of patience. "Well, thank you for that, Mother. I believe I shall be heading home now."

"I know you are disinterested in acting like an adult, but you are a fully grown man, and you have responsibilities. You need to select a bride. The Season is nearly over, so I will give you a year. Find a bride by the end of next Season."

"Mother."

"I'm serious, Anthony. You cannot squander your prime. Do you know what they say about you? There is too much speculation about why you have not yet married."

"And if I don't choose a bride by the end of next Season?"

"That's not an option." Mother stared at him for a long moment. "If you do not choose a bride, I will choose one for you."

As Anthony walked to Lark's house, just a short distance from his mother's, he reflected on the empty threat. His mother couldn't force him to marry. He'd already inherited the title. She didn't have any leverage over him. He was the one in power here. And if he decided his cousin should become the next marquess, that was his decision, was it not?

He'd worked up a good, frothing anger by the time Lark let him in. Anthony stormed past Lark and into Lark's parlor, a tastefully decorated room where he kept a good supply of brandy.

"And how was the dinner party?" Lark asked, closing the door behind him.

"Mother insists I marry by the end of next Season, but… she cannot force it, can she?"

Lark pressed his lips together for a long moment. Then he said, "You knew this was a possibility."

"And I knew that as long as Grace Midwood remained unattached, I could postpone the decision."

Lark sighed. He walked over to the cabinet and got out two glasses. "And you kept stringing that woman along, even though she's beautiful and could have found someone she actually cared about instead of Owen."

"Neither she nor Owen seemed too sad about it at the wedding."

"Look, I support your project of postponing marriage as long as possible, but you must know that each of your actions has consequences and not just on yourself. Things had a…positive resolution where Grace Midwood is concerned, but if you choose to postpone marriage and the rumors that you and I both know are circulating get louder, the title you refuse to pass on becomes worthless anyway. If you *don't* marry, you'll be a pariah, and I know that is not what you want."

Anthony grunted. "What I want is to be with you."

Lark poured two glasses of brandy. "I know. But…we knew this wasn't…that is, we can never go public because we'll both be hanged and… I never expected…"

"We thought it was a quick affair," Anthony said. Instead, they fell in love, but Anthony knew better than to voice something so flowery. "We didn't intend to grow so fond of each other."

"Yes. Quite. And we both knew that at some point we'd have

to marry."

"And end our affair."

"Yes, of course."

"But can you tell me," Anthony said, walking over to Lark to accept a glass of brandy, "that if I found some biddable debutante next Season and married her, you'd be willing to let me go?"

"It would…involve some hardship. But what choice do I have? I could not…that is, you'd have to father children, and I can't… Just picturing you with…"

"You'd die of jealousy."

Lark let out a breath and his shoulders dropped. "I do not like this situation any more than you do, but I am also realistic. If we both are seen around town together and we both postpone marriage until our hair begins to go gray, people will talk."

"Let them talk."

"I do not think you fully appreciate how much a tarnished reputation will put you out with the rest of society. As it is, people think you're…"

"A lovable scamp?"

Lark rolled his eyes. "People find you bothersome. Never serious. Carefree."

"Is this why society does not like me or why you do not like me?"

"Anthony, this thing between us, it cannot be forever. We both have obligations."

"And now you sound like my mother."

Lark let out a frustrated grunt. "I wish it were different. I'd marry you tomorrow if I could. I certainly like you better than any woman I've ever courted. But this is not the world we live in. Two men cannot…."

"Lark."

"We cannot be in love," Lark said.

Anthony set his glass aside. "And yet we are." He cupped Lark's face and pressed their lips together. He felt Lark surrender.

Something had changed in their relationship. What had started as a bit of fun had turned into something far deeper, and Anthony thought that, if Lark would let him, he would spend the rest of his life ensuring that Lark was happy.

"To the devil with obligations," said Anthony. "To the devil with *duties* and *responsibilities*. I never wanted to be a father. My father had four brothers, each of whom had several sons, and thus I see no reason why the oldest of my cousins should not inherit the title. I did not ask for these obligations. I was merely born into a titled family."

"You're not being realistic."

"Perhaps. But Mother also gave me until the end of next Season. A lot can happen in thirteen months."

"I do not expect the whole of society to change in that time," Lark said, putting his hands on Anthony's waist, "but I suppose if we have a clear last day of our affair, we might as well make the most of our time together."

"Do you intend to leave me for some debutante next Season?"

"No, but—"

"Do you not also have the same so-called obligation? You shall be a duke someday, shall you not?"

"Yes, but—"

"Hush then, with this talk of obligation. We are free-thinking men who can make our own decisions, and this is a new century. It's not like when our parents were having their marriages arranged. Society is changing."

Lark shook his head. "That may be, but it is not changing *enough*. Not for what you and I are to each other to be socially acceptable."

"I am content to keep it a secret. Men like us have had secret affairs since man first walked on Earth, I am certain of that. I do to want our affair to end."

"You live in a fantasy world."

Anthony smiled. "Perhaps I do. You should come live in it with me."

"If only."

"Come, let us drink this fine brandy and talk of less serious things."

Lark looked like he wanted to protest, but he nodded. He picked up his glass and walked over to sit by the fire.

As Anthony sat in the chair beside him, Lark said, "We're not finished with this discussion, you know."

"I know. But we are for tonight."

Chapter Ten

Dear Owen,

I hope you're well. I have two important items for you.

First, Morfudd wanted to pass on the attached inventory from the east wing of Caernarfon Castle. She says the windows are beyond repair and must be replaced. Apologies for being the bearer of bad news.

Second, the sheep farm has yielded the following profits this quarter...

The first few letters were simply about business.

Once Owen had arrived back in London, he and Grace started trading regular missives. The first few were rather formal, accounts of what Grace was spending money on and various news about the estate. Apparently she'd been meeting with Gwen and Carys Williams, the wives of two of Arthur's sons, and they were sharing with her the ins-and-outs of the wool operation. Owen felt pretty good about that; at least Grace was not alone.

Owen received the letters and passed most of the information on to Jonathan Truitt, his man of business. He cared some about how Grace and Morfudd were spending his money, but he didn't feel that the particulars of windows or the fabric used for curtains needed much of his attention.

Owen had to admit to a certain amount of disappointment. He and Grace had not known each other long, but their weeks together had been...pleasant. Shouldn't that have merited a more interesting letter than an inventory of purchases and profits?

No, their time together had been more than pleasant. He spent his entire walk to Parliament one morning trying to land on a better adjective. Exciting? Perhaps in a way. Warm? Too mild. Thrilling? Too much. Lovely. Pleasurable. Delightful.

He was so lost in thought, he didn't see Rockingham approach him as he reached Westminster.

"Doing sums in your head?" Rockingham asked, pulling Owen out of his reverie.

The Duke of Rockingham was a maybe ten years older than Owen and regularly haunted his seat at Parliament. He was loud and pushy, but he had a dry wit Owen found amusing most of the time. Owen was hoping to win Rockingham over to a bill he was working on to fix a number of London's busiest roads, inspired by his rocky trip out of town the previous month. He was swimming upstream, though; the Prince Regent wanted to redo the whole map of London to make it easier for him to get between his various residences, and Owen did not think he should earn that right at the expense of the people who lived where Prinny wanted to put roads. Owen thought fixing the existing roads, making them smoother and better for traveling on, was a good compromise.

Thus Owen didn't want to alienate Rockingham by saying something untoward. "Woolgathering," Owen mumbled. "How are you, Your Grace?"

"Fine, fine. I heard you hitched yourself to a pretty young lady and that is why you were late returning to the new session."

Owen hadn't been late. He'd arrived the night before Parliament opened. All he had missed were a few social gatherings. But he said, "Yes. We honeymooned at my estate in Wales."

"The Midwood girl, right? I always liked Midwood. I suppose anyone that plain would come with a nice dowry."

Owen bristled at that. "Have you met Lady Caernarfon before?"

"No, I don't believe so. My wife says she's perfectly pleasant to look at. She must be getting up in the years, though."

"She's beautiful," Owen blurted. He sighed. "Apologies, Your Grace. She was betrothed to Beresford since childhood. That is why she did not marry previously. They broke their engagement—"

"Of course they did." Rockingham raised a sardonic eyebrow.

"Indeed. I just mean to say, I find her beautiful and we had a lovely honeymoon, and I am happy with this turn of events." Although *happy* also seemed insufficient.

"Good, good. These things are…that is, my own marriage was arranged. And my duchess is quite dear to me after our many years of living together and raising our children. I didn't mean to imply your wife wouldn't be. It just seemed rather sudden. My wife loves to gossip, as you know, and I'd heard nothing about you even courting until I saw the announcement of your wedding in the paper."

"We did not make a big show of it, it's true. But it wasn't hasty or improper in any way, if that's what you're implying."

"No, no. It's all to the best. Young people these days have elaborate weddings, and they make such a big show of being in public and flaunting their love, and it's all rather tawdry, if you ask me. A more modest affair such as yours is much more to my taste. I am glad you are happy."

"Thank you, Your Grace. And if I might have a moment of your time, perhaps we can discuss a more serious matter."

"I'd be delighted."

Owen was still smarting from Rockingham calling Grace *plain* that evening when he wrapped up his business at Parliament and opted to walk to his club. Grace was anything but plain. She was the most beautiful woman Owen had ever been with, by a long distance. He'd found his bed felt rather lonely without her in it, a sentiment he had not anticipated. But he hadn't pushed his point because he hadn't wanted to look like a lovestruck idiot to Rockingham, who had agreed to sign on to Owen's bill about the roads, mostly because he agreed that Prinny's plan was a fool's errand.

So Owen felt somewhat accomplished as he walked into the club. He found his friends in their usual spot near the fireplace and took the fourth chair. Almost immediately, a staff member handed him a snifter of whiskey.

"You look tired," Fletcher observed.

"Long day, but I'm fine. Parliament business."

"The thing about the roads," said Lark. "I read about it this morning."

"Yes. Bad enough we have that new Regent Street, but Prinny wants to travel between his various houses without such burdens as needing to make turns. So if he has his way, he's going to level half of London to build a series of roads connecting his palaces, with Carlton House at its nexus."

"What an eyesore," said Lark.

"I am merely proposing a compromise, that we make the roads more passable by investing some money in cleaning them up, rather than building new roads."

"This is why I won't take up my seat in Parliament," said Fletcher. "If you spend your days talking about roads, I would certainly fall asleep."

"This is a small thing I can do to make a difference, and if I make the right allies, I can then do bigger things that make bigger differences for the people of London," said Owen. "I find that gratifying."

"I should appear at Parliament as well," said Hugh, "but now that construction is underway for my mother's new house, I'm afraid that is stealing most of my attention."

Owen smiled to himself. Hugh's mother, the Dowager Duchess of Swynford, was an imposing woman. She and Adele got along reasonably well, sometimes, but Owen could understand Swynford wanting her out of their home so that he and his wife might have more privacy.

He was less fond of his friends' lackadaisical feelings about Parliament. Owen felt he had a certain obligation to the work, and that if he was smart about it, he could make the country better. His father had always been involved in Parliament. And while it was true that attendance at the House of Lords was often just over half of its membership, so Hugh and Fletcher were hardly the only men who rarely bothered, part of him wished his friends would take it more seriously.

But conversation had already moved on.

Owen found his thoughts straying back to Grace as the men discussed the plans Hugh had for the new house. Presumably his mother would not live forever, so Hugh saw the house as an investment for the future of his family, perhaps a home he and Adele could retire to once their children were grown.

"Is Beresford joining us?" Fletcher asked, pulling Owen's attention.

Lark shook his head. "I asked him to stay away tonight. He has been…too free with his affection of late. I am trying to remain inconspicuous."

That didn't surprise Owen. He didn't think much of it until Fletcher said, "To what end?"

Lark let out a heavy sigh. "Wealth and power only provide so much cover. Anthony's family is pressuring him to marry."

"Why should that affect anything?" asked Fletcher.

Lark looked at Fletcher, appalled. "I know it may seem I have little regard for institutions, but I do in fact care for other people. And although Lady Caernarfon was spared the indignity of a farcical marriage with Beresford, whichever young miss his mother picks out will not be. And, well, I do not want to be the reason for her misery."

"You know," said Owen, "marriage seems like a formality until you are in it."

Everyone turned to look at Owen. Hugh shot him a wry smile.

Owen tried to think of how to explain. "I barely knew Grace when I committed to honor her for the rest of my days. I expected to keep her in Wales while I continued to live my life as I always had in London."

"You meant to pick up where you left off with that actress you were seeing last summer," Fletcher said knowingly.

"Oh, no, that was disastrous and does not signify, but I meant… I don't know. I can't explain it now, but even though my wife is in Wales and has no way of knowing what I am doing in London, I find that my impulse is to stay faithful to her. That is, before we married and she was more of an abstract concept, it didn't feel important to do more than the minimum to honor my commitments, but—"

"You needed to perform your marital duties, you mean," said Lark. "Father children and the like."

Owen hadn't given much thought to children, but he nodded. "That sort of thing, yes. But I just spent a month with her, speaking with her every day, sharing my meals with her, and some other things of course, and I found that I quite like her. And so I do not want to betray her while I am here in London. I made a commitment to my wife and I intend to honor it."

"Noble of you," said Fletcher. He sounded a little sarcastic.

"Hugh understands me," Owen said, gesturing across the table at his friend.

Hugh smiled. "I do, although my wife is actually here in London."

The implication being that it was easier to stay faithful when one's wife was in proximity. Owen shrugged it off. "My point is," Owen said, "I did not expect to feel so beholden to my marriage when I agreed to it, but now I do, and I believe what Lark is worried about is that if Beresford—or if Lark himself—should get hooked into a marriage, they might feel similarly beholden, in which case they will no longer be with each other. Am I near the target?" He looked at Lark.

"Bullseye," said Lark. "Should Anthony marry a young woman, I would need to respect that relationship. There will be pressure on Anthony to ensure his title is passed to a direct descendant. I would be the thing preventing that from happening."

That puzzled Owen a little. "Forgive me if this is too intimate a question, but is Beresford the sort of man who is not attracted to women at all?"

Lark grimaced. "I fear he is. I have not been burdened with quite the same affliction, but…" He stared at the ceiling. "No, that is wrong, it is not an affliction. It is just how some men *are*. How we were created by God. I believe that. I believe that some men, and presumably some women, are attracted to only their own sex, or they are attracted to many kinds of people, or they are attracted only to the opposite sex. Anthony has this friend who never gave other men a single thought until he became a widower, and now he lives in Shropshire with another man, and they're raising his children together. It sounds very quaint, but they lie that his lover is his butler so that no one expects, because they'd be hanged otherwise, so there is that." Lark leaned his head back on the chair and placed a hand over his eyes. He groaned.

"I'm sorry," Hugh said softly.

"I know. I apologize for sermonizing. I have just found myself struggling lately with this particular lot in life. I have fallen in love with someone I have no future with, and part of me thinks I should end the affair so that he can go off and get married and carry on with his life. But another part of me cannot bear to stay away from him, and it is a terrible place to be." He sat up and looked at Owen. "I am glad you and Lady Caernarfon have made something together, that from the sounds of it, you get on well. I am happy for you. I hope that one of these days we will all get to spend more time with her and get to know her better. I do not mean to visit my own misery on this group, but Fletcher asked, and…"

"I do miss her," Owen said. "I had not expected to. And then she sent me this letter." He pulled it from his pocket. When Lark held out his hand, Owen handed it over.

Lark took a moment to look over the letter. "Oh, this is dreary."

"What is it?" asked Hugh.

"It's basically just an inventory. So many pounds for glass for windows at…your castle." Lark glared at Owen for a brief moment. "Should we all have such burdens as a castle. But then it goes on to list things Lady Caernarfon bought. Curtains. A settee. Some…clay?"

"She likes to make pottery."

"All right. And she can pay for all of that because, according to this letter, Owen is making quite a bit of money from a sheep farm?"

"I've been selling wool to a textile mill. But you see what I mean, right?"

"Does she even like you?" Lark asked, handing back the letter.

"I thought so."

"Maybe she just feels awkward conveying emotion in a letter," said Hugh. "You could write her a letter telling her what you just said to us. That you miss her."

"I suppose."

"It might at least get you a less dry letter. I've gotten more exciting letters from my solicitor," said Lark.

Owen slipped the letter back into his pocket. "So what you're saying is, I should send the sort of letter I'd like to receive."

"Yes," said Hugh.

"And please, for the love of God, do not talk to her about roads," said Fletcher.

IT TOOK NEARLY every one of Owen's footmen to carry the crate of Grace's pottery equipment into the cottage. She got their help setting up her pottery wheel and carrying her recently purchased clay into a dark cupboard where she could wrap it up and keep it cool so it wouldn't dry out.

She stood in front of the house as the men finished, when another woman came by.

"Helô, sut mae?" said the woman.

"Pardon?"

"Hello. Are you English?"

"I'm afraid I am. I hope you do not mind my presence here."

"Oh, not at all, not at all." The woman had a thicker accent than Owen and Morfudd, whose accents were a bit watered down by spending time in England. It was more like that of the Williams family, who were locals. "Were you the one who purchased this cottage? I'd heard the previous owners were selling it. Well, it was just Old Man Owens and his daughter and son-in-law, who decided to move to Liverpool. What can you do?"

"My husband purchased the cottage. He is from this region."

"Oh, indeed? Well, if you teach your children a few Welsh phrases, you should have no quarrel with me. But I thought I knew everyone in this town. Who is your husband?"

Grace hesitated. This woman—she was perhaps a decade older than Grace—seemed friendly, and Grace did not want to intimidate her. "The Earl of Caernarfon."

"Oh, my lady, I did not know!"

"Please do not worry about that. I do not need special treatment. I was hoping to blend in here a bit."

The woman winked. "Well, Lady Caernarfon, my name is Catrin Davies. I live just down the street. I was out for my afternoon constitutional when I spotted your men carrying those great crates inside and I became curious. New furniture I presume."

"Yes, but also a potter's wheel."

"Oh, aye, do you make pottery?"

"I do. I intend to use this house as a pottery studio, not as my primary residence."

"Oh, how nice. And certainly you have that big estate up the road."

A wagon pulled up then. When the driver hopped off his perch, he said, "Lady Caernarfon?"

"'Tis me. Is this the brick?"

"Yes. Where should I put it?"

Grace told a footman to help the brick man carry the bricks to the back garden.

"I intend to build a kiln," Grace said to Mrs. Davies, who was staring at her strangely.

"Oh, I wondered. It looks like only enough brick for a fireplace."

"It will be a bit like an outdoor oven made of brick, where I might bake the clay after I finish molding it."

"I would love to learn how to make pots," said Mrs. Davies said a bit wistfully. "I had an artistic inclination as a girl, but then I married my husband and had children. But now that my children are a bit older, I'm interested in pursuing that again."

"Once I have everything set up, I will invite you over for a lesson. I haven't had many students, but I believe I could teach you how to do it."

"Yes? I would adore that." Mrs. Davies smiled. "You must be newly married. I hadn't even heard the earl had found a wife."

"Yes, the wedding was about six weeks ago."

"I've just mentioned, I am married as well. Local boy, of course, not nearly someone so fancy as the earl. But the earl's family… They've been a part of this town for generations. My husband is his cousin, technically, if you follow a few circuitous branches on the family tree."

"Is he? So we are distantly related by marriage, then."

"Family, yes." Mrs. Davies smiled. "Mostly I keep house and help my husband with our sheep. But my husband is also a blacksmith and I have always envied a bit that he has time to pursue a craft. I can barely sew, not able to do much more than mend my children's clothing. But I like to paint, and pots might be fun."

"I make all sorts of things, but we can start with something practical. I'll teach you to use the wheel to make bowls or plates."

"I would like that. Just send word to number twenty-seven on this road. Maybe a half mile that way." Mrs. Davies pointed. "I must say, it was lovely to meet you, my lady."

"The feeling is mutual. My husband has gone back to London for business, and I should very much like to have friends here while he is absent."

"Then let me give you your first language lesson. Here in North Wales, *sut mae* is a standard greeting. It basically means *How goes it?* So when you meet a Welshman on the street, that is what you say. Some of my neighbors are a bit precious about the language, so it helps to know a few phrases."

"Thank you for the tip. You've been extremely kind."

"Oh, no bother at all. If you show me how to make a dish, I'll consider it a good deal."

Grace smiled. "Agreed."

Chapter Eleven

Dear Grace,

Thank you for your last letter. You asked what I am working on. My friends inform me my bill to improve the roads in London's too dull to bother writing to you about, so I will tell you that I am also currently working on a bill that will allow for the forward march of industry without depriving workers of their livelihoods. I believe it may come to pass that soon machines will do the work of many people, but until that happens, perhaps we can help the workers. There is resistance to this idea in Parliament, but the case in favor is that if we allow men to make an honest living, they are less likely to riot. You may have read in the newspapers that there has been armed resistance to the proliferation of these machines to make textiles and other products, but one thing I believe some of my fellow Lords have yet to fully appreciate is that the reason these men are resisting is that the machines are taking their jobs from them. I do not wish to stand in the way of industrial progress, as these machines can make fabric much faster than a weaver can, but at the same time, I pity the workers who have been replaced…

Owen's latest letter, while not overtly emotional or intimate, did reveal the inner workings of his brain in a way he might not have even realized he'd shared. Grace particularly liked this letter and tucked it away in the trunk where she'd been storing all of his correspondence. There was an inherent kindness in his work in Parliament, like he genuinely wanted to make British society better, betraying that he wanted to help people rather than—as Grace was certain was true for most members of the House of Lords—lining his own pockets.

Usually, his letters were just as to-the-point as hers had been, but often he finished his letter with a bit of sentimentality. In this letter, he said:

Although I am keeping busy, I find that I am missing you.

Not exactly a love confession, but Grace treasured it. He missed her! Hopefully that meant he was not pursuing affairs across London—Grace's heart would shatter if that turned out to be the case—and that he was being honest. It was hard to know. Grace felt like she knew her husband, but they'd barely spent a month together before he left for London again.

But perhaps she should set a model. Rather than simply telling him what work she had completed in his absence, she should tell him more about how she felt. That she was *thriving*. She found herself well-suited to the work of running an estate. She was good enough at sums to do some simple bookkeeping, and she like having several large projects to oversee. In addition to the Williams family, Owen had staff that saw to his other business ventures. Those businesses mostly ran themselves, but every now and then they needed someone to make a quick decision. There was no time to write to Owen in London and wait for a reply. Owen's advisers were good men who gave solid advice, so she found that if she listened to them and applied her own logic, she was able to answer those questions.

She'd had no idea she could manage any of it. That she seemed to be good at the work came at something of a surprise. That Owen's staff was so competent gave her time to pursue her own interests as well, so she was getting the pottery studio up and running, and taking the liberty of redecorating the parts of Owen's house she didn't care for, making it more her home.

In short, she had everything she'd wanted when she left her parents' home. Except she did not have her husband, and it often took as long as a week for her letters to reach him and for him to write back. She was surprised by how much she missed him, although the reminders of him everywhere in the house certainly contributed to that.

She couldn't dwell on it, though, because Penelope was due at any moment.

Indeed, she arrived within the hour, with her old friends Elizabeth and Helena Hastings and a small staff in tow. Naturally, unmarried ladies couldn't travel great distances unchaperoned, so the Hastings matriarch—Lady Lenora Hastings—and a small cadre of footmen had come along as well. They pulled into the drive, in front of Caer Newydd in a caravan of three carriages.

Goodness.

The rest of the day was a whirlwind of getting the guests settled and issuing instructions to the staff, and by the time they settled down to dinner, Grace was feeling overwhelmed and a little nauseous.

"The staff here has such charming accents," Elizabeth said over their second course.

"It is the native accent," Grace said. "Most of the folk I've met here sound like that. A few don't even speak much English."

"Is it true your husband owns a castle?" asked Helena.

"He does. We can visit it this week, if you like. It's not really habitable, but the family is repairing it. The earl's aunt can take us on a tour of the grounds, perhaps."

"I had no idea the earl was so wealthy," said Lady Lenora.

"Oh." Grace had no idea how to respond to that. "Well, I—"

"Let us not be so frank with Grace." Penny rolled her eyes. "Discussing the earl's finances without his presence here is gauche, don't you think?"

Lady Lenora bristled. "I suppose."

When the time to retire finally arrived, Grace was exhausted. When Penny inquired about how she was feeling, she said, "I am fine, but I had become accustomed to my solitude here, I suppose. I'm finding all the company a bit overwhelming. Not that you aren't welcome. I am enormously happy that you—and everyone—are here. I am truly happy to see you, Penny. I just need a little time to adjust to hosting."

They were seated in the drawing room, just the two of them after the Hastings ladies went to bed.

"Do not worry about anything," Penny said. "You're a fine hostess. Maybe we can find something to occupy Lady Lenora's time so she is not so…blunt. Honestly, though, she has been like this for the entire week it took to get here, and I am quite ready to throw her into the sea. Just give the word if she bothers you."

"Oh, she's fine. No worse than my mother."

"True."

"Penny, I am grateful to see you. Although I am happy to say that I am not as lonely here as I expected. Owen's aunt, who runs the castle, comes for dinner once a week and is delightful company. I've befriended a few of the women in the family that runs the wool operation. And Owen has a cottage a couple hours ride from here where I've set up my pottery studio, and I've made a few friends in the town there. The people here are kind and friendly, and the sea air is refreshing."

"So you are happy here, is what you are saying."

"I missed you! I would not have invited you to visit if I didn't. But yes, I am actually happy here. I love it here in a way I do not love London. And there's so much to do that I am rarely bored."

"I am glad to hear it. I worried about you being so far from home."

"I've missed you, my friend, but I feel content here."

"And how was your husband while he was here?"

"Nothing but pleasant. He's given me permission to style the cottage however I like and to make a few changes here. Most of the furnishings are things he chose and I haven't really felt inclined to change them, but I think he believed that he was stranding me here, and thus gave me permission to do whatever I needed to feel at home here, cost being no object. I just bought those blue chairs. Do you like them?"

"I do. A handsome addition to the room."

"It's everything I always wanted. I just wish my husband were here, too. I find some days that I miss him."

"He's been busy at Parliament, I hear," said Penny. "Peter keeps mentioning seeing the earl there." Peter was Penny's older brother.

"Tell me about what's going on in London. Have you any suitors yet?"

"I've done a bit of promenading," Penny said with a wink. "Actually, Baron Beckwith has shown some interest."

"He is a handsome fellow." It was largely agreed by the young women of London that Baron Theodore Beckwith was the best-looking eligible bachelor in London. "How do you feel about him?"

"I certainly would not turn away his affections. I just hope he does not meet someone new before I return to London."

"You are beautiful and charming, Penny. How dare he look at anyone else."

Penny smiled at that.

"Anyway, perhaps it is for the best that my husband is in London. He spent a month with me here before returning to the city, and it was lovely, but sometimes I worry our relationship may sour."

"In what way?"

"Well, I can't help thinking of my parents. After many years of marriage, they loathe each other."

Penny nodded knowingly. "But then, I have doubts they ever liked each other. There's no reason to think you and the earl will end up like that. My parents are quite fond of each other, even after all these years. Why, just before I left London, they celebrated their anniversary, and it was quite a fete. Father could hardly keep his hands off Mother, and she giggled the whole time. Embarrassing, if you ask me, but nice in its way. It's honestly given me some hope that if I find the right man, I can be happy well into my old age, just as they are."

Grace supposed that was something. She still felt she'd made the right decision, that it could be that once the initial euphoria of the wedding wore off, she might grow tired and annoyed with Owen—she had always assumed this was what would happen in a marriage. But she hadn't anticipated the pleasure Owen had shown her, nor had she expected to like his company so much. She supposed Penny was right that not all couples succumbed to the fate that her parents had.

"Well," said Grace. "What else is going on in town?"

Grace wanted to hear more about the goings on back in London, but as Penny told a long story about a bit of gossip pertaining to one of their mutual friends, Grace found her energy waning. Penny paused as if she anticipated a laugh, but Grace said, "I'm sorry. I'm exhausted."

"Go to sleep. We can resume our talk tomorrow."

A solid night's sleep did Grace a lot of good, although she woke up the next morning with her stomach still unsettled. Indeed, it proved a bit of a challenge to keep the Hastings girls occupied. They took a walk around the estate. They admired Owen's sheep and horses. They ran into one of the Williams brothers—Alex or Artie, Grace still had trouble telling them all apart—who indulged the ladies with some jokes about sheep. The day after that—once Grace sent word to warn Morfudd—they went to Caernarfon Castle.

Grace did everything she could to keep her guests entertained, and she did have a good time. She'd always liked Elizabeth and Helena, though they were not as close as Grace was to Penny. And it was nice to be around other women, to indulge in gossip, to hear about what she was missing in London. Truly, it was gratifying that she wasn't truly missing anything except for the exact things she'd been looking to escape.

But after a full week of playing hostess, Grace felt as though she'd been drained. Penny and Morfudd both noticed, and Morfudd agreed to take the Hastings to town that day to give them a taste of Welsh culture. Penny stayed behind to keep Grace company.

"Are you sure you're all right?" Penny said. "You've seemed not yourself the last day or two."

"I'm fine, truly. I might be coming down with something, though. I'm sure it's nothing serious. But you're right, I have not felt quite myself the last few days."

"What is wrong, precisely?"

"Mostly I'm just tired, which I attribute to having to entertain. And...I'm nervous, I suppose. Unsettled. I've never hosted on my own before and I want to make sure all of you are having a good time, so I've been putting some extra pressure on myself, perhaps more than necessary."

"As long as you aren't seriously ill," said Penny warily.

"I do not believe I am. A bit overwhelmed, is really all it is. A good night's sleep and I'll be fine."

"All right. We shall be out of your hair soon enough."

"Please stay as long as you like. I will try to be less fussy about everything."

Penny smiled. "I love you like a sister." She gave Grace a quick hug. "I would do anything for you. If you need us to leave, we will."

"No, no. Stay. I like having you here. I think Lady Lenora just unsettles me."

"She is quite intimidating."

Grace giggled at that.

"And perhaps next time I come visit," Penny said, "I will leave the Hastings behind."

"Oh, I would never presume to—"

"Grace. It is just the two of us here."

"All right. The Hastings are...a lot to manage," Grace conceded.

Penny laughed. "I do adore you, my friend. I am glad we made this journey."

"I am, as well. Truly, come visit anytime you like. The one thing I regret is that I am so far now from my friends." Although, to be honest, Grace had mostly only missed Penny. She didn't have many other close friends. Grace intuited that the Hastingses mostly tagged along with Penny so that Penny would not have to make the five-day journey alone.

"Maybe Baron Beckwith has some use of a country home near the Welsh border."

Grace laughed. "If only."

It was odd to reflect on that, though. Grace had spent so much time alone when she was in London, and now here, in Wales, it felt decidedly different. She dropped in on Gwen sometimes just to have tea together. She had regular dinners with Morfudd. She'd been teaching Catrin Davies how to do some basics with clay. And now she had a house full of guests. She was more social now than she'd ever been before, despite being so far from London. And she liked it. But it was different than the life she'd known back in London.

"I'm having fun," Grace assured Penny. "But I will sleep for three days after you all leave."

Penny laughed. "And it will be much deserved."

ALL YEAR, THERE had been a series of rebellions in which textile workers, worried about being replaced by machines, had destroyed the machines. They called themselves Luddites, after the legendary figure of Ned Ludd, someone Owen didn't think had actually existed but who had allegedly broken a loom in protest or something. Owen could never remember the details.

The problem, of course, was that the machines could weave fabric much faster than humans could, so textile manufacturers—some of whom Owen had worked with—did in fact want to replace their workers with machines. Owen understood that. Why wouldn't you want to make fabric faster and cheaper?

He felt bad for the workers who were losing their jobs, too.

But he didn't think destroying expensive machines was the answer.

The other problem Owen was having now was that Parliament was still in session deciding what to do about the rebellions, and all Owen wanted to do was go home to his wife.

It was a very odd position to be in, especially since Grace was several days' journey away, and he hadn't expected to miss her so much. But every time she sent him a letter, he felt like he could hear her voice again.

They'd talked about this. It was what they wanted. Owen couldn't let himself get distracted.

"It's quaint that you think you can compromise," said a voice standing near where Owen sat in the sitting room outside Lords.

Owen looked up. Lord Edgerton and the Earl of Canbury stood over him. Canbury nervously worried a piece of paper in his hand.

Owen tried to remember which bit of legislation Edgerton had most favored. He tended to side with the Prince Regent, so he was likely discussing the roads. Owen's secretary had been circulating a proposal to fix the existing roads rather than create new ones, and this was likely the thing Edgerton was most likely upset about.

"You'll have to be more specific," Owen said. "I'm currently working on several important pieces of legislation."

"You think you can fill in a few holes in London's major thoroughfares and call it an accomplishment?"

It was the roads, then. "It's cruel to remove people from their homes just because Prinny wants a more direct route to the very expensive waste of money he calls a house."

Canbury seemed to fret at this. He'd always been a bootlicker, constantly seeking favor from the Crown.

Owen felt bad for his opinion of Canbury, especially now that the man's daughter was married to Hugh. Then again, he supposed having one's daughter find a good marriage was not enough to change one's temperament. Canbury was powerful because he had the ear of the Prince Regent, but he had a lot of enemies, too. Owen had never taken him too seriously. But Edgerton usually had more sense. Owen couldn't comprehend why he was being so blunt now.

"Your bill is dead," Edgerton said. "We're approving the new road in exchange for the Crown foregoing asking us for more money for his home in Bath."

"Do we not have more pressing matters than whether Prinny gets his road?" asked Owen. He held up the sheaf of paper he'd been reading. "These are letters from several textile manufacturers imploring me to do something about the protests."

"What are we to do about angry men?" asked Edgerton.

"Seems like a job for Commons," said Canbury.

Owen stood, not enjoying having other men stand over him. "I do not understand why you bother to attend if you think you have no role in the government."

"Of course we have a role," said Canbury.

"But Edgerton would just as soon we hand over all of our funds to the Prince Regent so that he can spend them as he pleases."

"Not as he pleases. I made a more viable compromise than fixing the roads. What do you intend to do?"

"It would have cost less money to hire some street cleaners. Now a hundred people will need to find new homes, for no clear reason, and we have to build a new road from scratch. All so one man has a more direct route from one grand palace to another."

"You are far too compassionate, Caernarfon. And besides, don't you own several grand estates? You are hardly in a position to judge."

"Perhaps not, but I am also not arguing that we should tear down houses, where people *live* in order to build a road over them! This new road is intended to help one man. Why can't we do something that helps more than the man who is spending our treasury's money on *nonsense*."

"He defeated Napoleon," said Canbury.

"No, he didn't. Did Prinny put on a uniform and march into France? He did not. Wellington won at Waterloo. Prinny wears costumes and pretends he's a soldier."

Canbury bristled. Edgerton just smiled.

Owen sighed and folded the letters he'd been reading. He slipped them into the leather portfolio he'd been carrying them in. "I intend to vote against the new road," Owen said. "And I intend to do something about the Luddite rebellion. But if you'd like to sniff Prinny's shoes in your spare time, far be it from me to stop you."

Owen didn't wait for a reply and instead left the room. But as he left, he realized he'd be stuck in London sorting all this out for the foreseeable future.

With his friends at the club that night, he said, "How did *I* become the member of Parliament most interested in the rights of regular people? I'm a bloody earl."

"Something in your blood gets riled up when the English government begins to assert its authority," said Fletcher.

"Joke's on the Crown," Owen replied. "I own the castle their ancestor built to threaten the Welsh."

"Yes," said Lark, "but despite several generations of your family worming their way into the British aristocracy, part of you still takes pity on anyone the Crown wants to oppress."

"What has you so upset, precisely?" asked Hugh.

Owen knew exactly what the issue was, but voicing it to his friends felt…embarrassing. "Do you want my honest answer?"

"We won't judge," said Fletcher.

Owen rolled his eyes. "Yes, you will, but honestly, the situation is that I suspect most of my fellow members of Parliament, even those in Commons, would just as soon side with the business owners and not bother about what is causing the rebellions."

"The Luddite situation," said Lark.

"Yes. To me, the obvious answer is to find other jobs for the rebels, because truly, all they want is to be able to earn enough to feed their families. And I think they have the foresight to know that now it's textile mills, but soon machines could take over the way we make everything. Imagine if you no longer need a man to work a printing press, but instead newspapers are printed by mechanical means. Or what if machines made, I don't know, clothing or food. Thousands of artisans would lose their jobs. I applaud these technological advances, but what do you do about all the people whose skills become obsolete?"

"It's nice that you care," said Hugh.

Owen grunted. "The problem is that I feel a moral and ethical obligation to see this through, at least as long as Parliament remains in session, because I worry that without a voice like mine, the Tories will let the rich and powerful level London to build more palaces." Owen paused and rubbed his forehead. "I am pontificating."

"It's fine," said Lark. "You let me blabber on last week. 'Tis now your turn."

Owen nodded. "Well, I suppose part of me might prefer I were more heartless, because more than anything, I want to leave for Wales right now so that I can lie with my wife again." That was the crux of it. He felt an ethical obligation to stay in London, but what he wanted more than anything was to be with Grace.

"Ah," said Lark. "I see the issue here. You installed your lovely wife, who you like, contrary to all conventional knowledge, at your distant home and miss the touch of a beautiful woman."

"I suppose I could write and ask her to come here, but that is not our arrangement."

"Can't hurt to ask," said Hugh.

"She has her own obligations in Wales. According to her last letter, she now has two pottery students she is teaching, plus she is managing my estate and helping my aunt oversee the castle renovation work. There was also mention in one of her letters of her feeling a bit under the weather and not being able to travel much, even locally, although I suppose that was a month or two ago." Owen shook his head. "It is uncouth to discuss such things."

Fletcher frowned. "It sounds like you miss her."

"I do."

"And not just physically."

Owen nodded. "I suppose that's true. We exchange letters regularly, but it is not the same as speaking with her, and I find that, the more intimate our letters become, the more I want to see her. Is that mad?"

"It makes sense to me," said Hugh.

Beresford walked in then, looking more morose than he usually did. Owen watched him speak to someone across the room before strolling toward the fireplace where Owen and his friends sat.

Beresford stopped by Lark's chair and asked, "Women are still banned from this club, correct?"

"Yes," said Lark.

"So my mother cannot foist any unwitting unmarried young ladies on me here? I am safe?"

"For now."

"Anyone want to vouch for me that I can find my own wife without my mother's intervention?"

"No," said Lark without hesitation.

Owen must have been glaring, because Fletcher said, "You'll have to excuse Caernarfon. Marrying your fiancée seems to have worked out for him and he's acting like a lovesick fool because she's in Wales."

Beresford smiled ruefully. "Is it bizarre that I think it's good that she has someone who wants her like that?" He sat on the arm of Lark's chair. "I've always been fond of Grace, albeit not in a romantic way. She has a good heart."

"Yes," Owen muttered miserably.

"What I mean is, I like her and have long hoped she could find what I could not give her. It's unfortunate she's in Wales and you are here, Caernarfon, but she deserves to have a husband who genuinely cares for her."

Owen nodded. "I appreciate that, but it does not solve any of my present predicaments."

"He feels obligated to see through his various endeavors in Parliament," Lark said to Beresford.

"I'll happily vote against that road bill," Beresford said. "Most of the House of Lords is trying to stay in Prinny's good graces, but the road plan is foolish and pointless. Why no one is interested in your compromise bill, which would make the roads more passable for *everyone*, I do not know, unless the point is to ensure that the poor suffer as if they caused their own misfortune, and horrible roads are just the sacrifice we make as the aristocracy to make sure no one enjoys them."

Owen nodded. "I agree, obviously. It just feels like an uphill battle. Whenever you show the smallest bit of compassion for the less fortunate in Parliament, the other members begin to look at you as if you are threatening to walk into their vaults and steal their money yourself."

"The thing with money is that it is never possible to have enough," said Beresford. "It's like gambling. Or cake. Once you have a taste of it, all you want is more."

"Making money is like cake?" said Lark, deadpan.

"I know you understand me. I am making an observation."

"Do you want more money?" Lark asked.

"I don't think about it much because I've hired people to worry about my money for me. But honestly, who doesn't?"

Fletcher cleared his throat. "If we're done with the politics lesson, I believe we were discussing Owen's problems."

One by one, the men of Owen's close social circle started to leave, until Owen was left with just Fletcher and a snifter of whiskey.

"You do seem sad," Fletcher observed.

Owen wanted to laugh with how obvious an observation it was. He knew Fletcher meant well, though.

Owen and Fletcher had been close since they'd roomed together at Eton. Fletcher had things he was passionate about—art, his family—but he loathed politics. He cared deeply about his friends, but he often acted like he hadn't a care in the world. Owen felt privileged to know his friend's true character underneath his nonchalant surface. And now Fletcher was looking at Owen like he was actually concerned.

Owen took a deep breath. "When I agreed to marry Grace, I didn't think it would be this difficult. Maybe I should go back to Wales."

"It would take you a fortnight just to get there and back. Can you spare that much time?"

"Not if I'm the only one in Parliament who cares about what happens to anyone who doesn't have a mound of coin and an entailed estate."

Fletcher frowned. "I won't pretend to know much about women or love, but maybe if you plan to return home as soon as this vote occurs, it might help alleviate some of what you are feeling."

"That is a possibility."

"That way, you won't feel like you are abandoning your work, but you can see the light at the end of the tunnel, as it were."

That made some sense. Seeing Grace as soon as he could would be something to look forward to. "Thanks, Fletcher."

"And if that doesn't work, I have a good store of whiskey at my house."

Chapter Twelve

Dear Owen,

I hope you do not mind, but I've commandeered the room at the back of the coastal house for a studio. There is a small pottery operation in the town, in fact, and they have allowed me to use their kiln until I am able to construct my own. I have enclosed a cost estimate for the studio expenses this quarter.

I could not wait for it to be running properly to get my hands on the clay! I made you the vase in this box. I do not know if you have need of a vase, but I do recall that the Duke of Swynford's house has a lovely garden out back. Perhaps the Duchess of Swynford can help you find some nice flowers for it. I chose the glaze colors based on things that remind me of you, so I hope it is to your taste or goes well with your decor in London. The blue matches almost precisely the color of the walls in the main parlor at Caer Newydd, although, to be honest, the color reminds me of your eyes.

I have met a delightful woman called Catrin who lives just a short distance up the road. She has taken a keen interest in pottery, so I have been teaching her how to work the wheel. She has such a talent for it that we may soon have our own pottery company right here at the house…

The box had been a curiosity, but as soon as Owen had seen the letter, he nearly ripped it in his eagerness. It was foolish of him to get so excited about Grace's letters, but somehow, he still got a thrill whenever the post arrived and a letter in her hand was among the contents.

She'd *made* him something. And she'd put some thought into it.

The box itself had been carefully packed. He had one of the footmen fetch him a hammer so that he could use the claw to pry the nails out. Inside, wrapped in blanket surrounded by crumpled up newspaper was indeed a vase. He pulled it out and looked at it.

It was exquisite. It was about eight inches wide at its widest and eighteen inches tall with a rounded belly and then a twist through the middle that opened up to a top that reminded him of the bloom of a lily. The piece was gleaming white, though she'd painted a blue lily and some leaves on the belly of it. He'd never seen anything like it, and the piece struck him as quite beautiful. She'd carved a swirly *GT* on the base—for Grace Thomas, he assumed.

He put the vase in a place of honor in his dining room, far from frequent foot traffic, but in a safe spot where it could be admired.

Thus he invited commentary on it when he hosted a dinner party a week later.

He had not originally intended to host a large party. Originally, he had just wanted to have Rockingham round for dinner to talk Parliament business, but then Beresford overheard him mention Rockingham's name and had chimed in that Rockingham had a niece on the short list of potential brides and insisted on inviting himself. And then Lark, in a jealous pique, had invited himself as well, and suddenly Owen was hosting a dozen people for dinner.

Beresford was the first to arrive at the dinner party, and as Owen poured him a glass of sherry, he said, "I thought you did not want to marry."

"I don't." Beresford's tone was hard.

"Then why insist I invite Rockingham's niece to this party?"

"So that I can verify that she is just as dull as the rest of them, and then report back to my mother that she will not do."

"Right." Owen handed him the glass.

Dinner was fine, if a little awkward at times. Owen had put Rockingham at his left so that they might discuss the Luddite rebellions. Rockingham seemed to not have any particular conviction but was interested in stopping the rebellions—*"Those machines are so expensive, it won't do to have angry workers destroy them"*—but in the end, Owen secured his vote.

His niece, a lovely girl named Charlotte, seemed intelligent and charming. She wasn't the prettiest girl Owen had ever seen—like Rockingham, she had a nose that was too big for her face and she paled in comparison to Grace—but he found nothing objectionable about her. Beresford seemed unmoved, though, as though meeting her was just another item to strike from his list. Lark watched every interaction between them like a hawk.

Hugh had brought his wife, who was always delightful company. And Fletcher had brought his friend Lady Louisa, reasoning that there should be a few women at the party so that Charlotte did not feel too singled out. And then Owen had invited two other MPs and their wives to round out the table, but they all seemed disinterested in discussing government business.

After dinner, Owen urged his guests to their respective gender's rooms. Wine and conversation for the women in the front sitting room, brandy and cigars for the gentlemen. Lark and Beresford lingered after Owen saw everyone out of the dining room, and Beresford said, "I've been staring at that vase all night. It's quite striking."

Curious about where Beresford was going with this, Owen said, "Oh?"

"Is it a Makepeace?"

"A what?"

"The artist, Gerard Makepeace. He's a pottery designer. He makes the most beautiful vases. I have several of his pieces in my home. Rutherford has a few, too. Didn't I mention it at the ball? Makepeace is extraordinary talented, although also reclusive. I keep telling the proprietor at the shop that sells his work that I'd love to meet him, but apparently he is not interested in interacting with the adoring public." Beresford took a step closer to the vase and leaned down to look at it. "I suppose you are the sort of philistine who just spotted it and thought it would look nice in your dining room."

"I will admit to knowing little about pottery," Owen said, feeling amused now.

"He's like this," Lark said to Owen. "One learns to grow patient with it."

"Do you mind if I pick this up?" Beresford asked.

"As long as you're careful."

"Of course!" Beresford picked up the vase and turned it over. "Hmm. This looks similar to Makepeace's mark, but it says GT instead of GM. Now I'm curious. Do you know who the artist is or did you just pick it up because you like lilies?"

Owen laughed. "Actually, Grace made it."

"Grace? Your wife, Grace? My former fiancée, Grace?"

"Yes, that Grace. She turned my seaside cottage into a pottery studio and she made and sent me that. It arrived a few days ago."

"Oh." Beresford put the vase back on its end table. "Gracie made this? Little Gracie Midwood."

"Grace Thomas, the Countess of Caernarfon, but yes."

"Hmm. Interesting that Gerard Makepeace and Grace Midwood have the same initials." Beresford waved his hand. "A coincidence, I'm sure. This really is a beautiful piece, though. Grace is far more talented than I knew."

Owen nodded. "I know little about pottery, but I did like the vase. I suppose I should put flowers in it or something, but I like it sitting there empty. It feels more like it is worth displaying on its own, and not just used as a functional item."

"Indeed," said Beresford, giving the painted lilies another look. "It's a beautiful piece. It should be displayed."

Lark turned to leave the room. "If we're done here, I could do well with a glass or five of whiskey."

LARK HAD SEEMED angry all evening, so when they finally retired to the bedroom in his house, Anthony said, "All right, let me have it."

"Pardon?"

"You're clearly upset with me. So I'm telling you that there's no need to keep it bottled up. Yell at me. Tell me to go to the devil. Let me have it."

Lark had dismissed his valet a few minutes before and was presently fiddling with the cufflinks on his shirt. Anthony had already rid himself of his coat and breeches and sat on the bed in his shirt and drawers, waiting for Lark to come to bed.

But first, they needed to resolve whatever fit Lark was silently throwing.

"I'm not—" Lark started, but he shook his head. "I'm not angry at *you*. Well, I am a bit, because you made me think you intended to consider Lady Charlotte a viable option for a wife and then ignored her through most of dinner. But that's not my main issue."

"Then what is your main issue?"

"How long can we carry on, Anthony? Realistically. You're making light of this situation, which is what you always do, but you agreed you'd find a wife by the end of next Season. Where does that leave us?"

"Lark."

"My family feels less invested in my securing a wife. And now that Laurence is courting the Everleigh girl, I suspect soon enough there will be a baby to whom I can bequeath my title." Laurence was Lark's younger brother. "Laurence was always the more responsible one anyway. Or, I don't know, perhaps my father will outlive us all."

Beresford nodded at that. Lark's father, the Marquess of Beaufort, seemed impervious to the ravages of time. He'd just turned sixty but had the energy of a much younger man and kept up a lively social schedule. Beresford sometimes joked that, at the end of time, after society crumbled, all that would remain would be cockroaches and Beaufort.

"But you could marry," Beresford said. "That is, you are not cursed to only find men sexually appealing. You are fond of women, too. You've lain with your fair share of them."

"Yes."

"But you don't want to."

"Not tomorrow. Who knows what the future holds, but I do not feel I *have* to, and certainly not while I am still carrying on with you. Which brings us back around to my larger point, which is that you will not be mine for much longer. And I find myself torn between ending things now to spare myself the heartbreak later, and holding on to you for as long as you're still mine."

"Heartbreak?"

"You know as well as I do that the main reason we are still together is that we are… emotionally attached."

"Emotionally attached."

Lark finally succeeded in pulling out his cufflinks and placed them on his bureau. "We love each other. That's not news."

"No. I just wanted to hear you say it."

"You don't want to get married."

Anthony rubbed his face. "No. I truly do not."

"Charlotte Rockingham is a perfectly nice girl. That story she told at dinner about the fox that got loose near Covent Garden last week was quite funny. Unlike some of your other prospects, she's clever and has some conversational skill. She's pretty enough. She's not a terrible candidate for a wife."

"Oh, not a terrible candidate? A ringing endorsement."

"You know what I mean."

Anthony crossed his arms. "I'm definitely not interested. And I thought if I made some kind of promise to my mother about marrying sometime in the distant future, she would leave me alone, but no. She's like a dog with a bone."

"So what is your strategy now? Humoring her but reporting back that every woman you meet is dull and ugly and unworthy of the Beresford title?"

That had been the strategy. "I suppose."

"Hard to make that argument with Lady Charlotte. I found her perfectly charming."

"Should *I* be jealous?"

"You say that in a way that implies *I* was jealous."

"You were. Why else would you have invited yourself to dinner and then stared at me all through the meal as if you thought to murder either me or Charlotte with just your eyes?"

Lark tutted and went about fiddling with his breeches. Anthony had already helped him out of his boots, at least. Presumably Lark could take off the rest of his clothing, but it looked like a struggle.

He stood and said, "Since you already dismissed your valet and are incapable of undressing yourself, I shall step into the role."

"It's not necessary." But he lifted his arms and let Anthony help him out of his breeches and stockings.

"Do *you* think I should get married?" Anthony asked. "Because sometimes, it sounds like you do."

"I most assuredly do not, but it seems inevitable." Lark grunted as Anthony succeeded in getting the fastenings of his breeches undone, and now seemed disgusted with the whole thing. He stepped away from Anthony and pulled them off, grunting the whole time. "And I suppose," he added, tossing his breeches over a chair, "I am unnerved by the fact that you and I are in love but can make no public show of it. I hated telling you to stop coming to the club so frequently, but I worry the wrong person will find out about us."

Anthony nodded. "There's a vote scheduled for next week on an anti-sodomy bill. I plan to vote against it. I don't care who knows. A man's business should be his own."

Lark rubbed his forehead. Anthony helped him out of what

was left of his clothing and then took off his own breeches and stockings.

"But," Anthony said, "I do agree that our lives should not be so…public. That anyone in this whole blasted city cares what either of us gets up to on our own time is the real travesty. If I could move through life without worrying about the scandal sheets, I'd be a lot happier."

Lark pulled off his shirt. "I'd propose we move to the country to live in obscurity, but you love the city too much."

"Too true. And I would miss my social malfeasance being reported in the papers, I admit. I suppose what I actually want is for society to acknowledge that there is nothing wrong with us."

"You'd have as much luck persuading the aristocracy to do manual labor."

"Hmm." Anthony took in the sight of his lover, *sans* clothing. They'd achieved an easy, casual regard for each other that often allowed them to just *be* comfortably. But Lark really was a handsome man. His dark hair had grown a bit long lately, just enough to cover the shells of his ears, and his eyes were just as piercing as they always were, but he also had a wonderfully fit body and all that smooth, pale skin… Anthony ran his hands over Lark's chest, his shoulders, the back of his neck, the ends of his hair. "We should go to bed."

Lark lowered his eyelids and shot Anthony a wry look. Then he kissed Anthony, so clearly they were thinking along the same lines. Anthony smiled into the kiss, reveling in it.

The gender of one's partner should not have signified. Anthony's love for Lark wasn't hurting anyone. Why should they not be able to be together? He didn't care about marriage. Marriage was an institution primarily meant to legitimize heirs. There would be no heirs for Anthony and Lark, so there was no need to marry. But they should be allowed to spend their lives together without familial pressure to do otherwise.

Anthony loved Lark. He parted his lips and deepened the kiss and put his arms around Lark's shoulders to hold him there. He pressed their bodies together, loving the contours of Lark's body against his own.

"I love you," Anthony whispered.

"I know." Lark sighed. "I love you, too. But this is doomed."

"Then come to bed and let's make the most of it."

Lark nipped at Anthony's lower lip. "All right."

IN ALL, PENNY and the Hastings ladies stayed for two weeks, and though Grace was sad to see them go—especially Penny—she was grateful for the silence and solitude she gained in their absence. Plus, she was itching to return to her pottery.

She was, however, beginning to feel like she'd kept an illness at bay through sheer force of will. Once her guests were gone, she'd spent more time vomiting than she cared to admit to anyone, although the household staff of course knew something was wrong. Grace talked them out of calling a doctor because she didn't think it was that serious. She just needed whatever it was to work its way through her body.

Still, when she resumed her pottery lessons with Catrin Davies, Catrin seemed to notice right away that something was off. "You look too pale, my dear."

"I'm all right."

"No, something is off with your coloring."

Grace sighed. "Should I be offended?"

"I'm merely making an observation." Catrin looked her over slowly. "You are ill."

"I lost my accounts this morning," Grace said. "It doesn't feel like anything serious. I've just felt a bit unsettled for the last couple of weeks. I thought at first it was something I ate, but perhaps it is a mild illness. Nothing rest won't cure."

"You've been ill for a fortnight and have not seen a doctor?" Catrin narrowed her gaze at Grace, and then something seemed to light up behind her eyes. "Oh," she said.

"What?"

"When was the last time you saw your husband?"

Grace didn't know what that had to do with anything, but she said, "About three months ago, I'd guess."

"That timing makes sense."

"What timing?"

"Do you truly not know?"

Grace just stared at Catrin, not understanding what Catrin was saying.

"I have two children," Catrin said.

Grace already knew that. Catrin talked about her children—a boy and a girl—all the time. She still didn't see what Catrin was getting at, unless…

"I went through the exact same thing with both of them. Right around the third month. When was the last time you had your courses?"

"Oh, it must have been…" But Grace slowly realized they hadn't come at all since she'd been in Wales. She hadn't really given it much thought. Her courses had always been irregular, skipping a month here or there was not unusual, but it truly had been three months since her wedding.

She clapped a hand over her mouth.

"Before your wedding?" Catrin supplied.

"But it can't… how can it…"

"You're tired all the time. Sometimes weird smells make you feel like you need to toss up everything you've eaten that day. You've gained a little weight, and not just from our fine Welsh cuisine."

"Yes, but—"

"You, my dear, may be increasing."

Just then, a wave of nausea hit Grace. She excused herself and ran into the back garden.

When she returned, she didn't feel any better, but Catrin had gone to the water pump in the kitchen and gotten Grace some water.

"Drink this."

"A baby? I'm to have a baby?"

"Did it really not occur to you after you and your husband...had marital relations."

"No," Grace said honestly. "I didn't think about it at all."

Catrin smiled. "Charmingly naive of you. Is not the whole point of consummating a marriage to an earl to make little earls?"

"I suppose, but we never talked about it. I assumed we'd have children eventually. But now?"

"You should see a doctor to confirm it. But yes, I think that is why you are feeling not quite yourself. All the signs are there."

A baby. Grace had logically known this was a possibility, but the way her mother had explained marital relations had made the process of conceiving a child sound so dry and dull—an indignity to be tolerated—and not like the beautiful intimacy Grace and Owen had shared. Mother had never talked about how it could feel to be with a man, how Owen made Grace's body sing, or how being with Owen had made Grace feel closer to him. Everything they'd done together had been thrilling and exciting, the opposite of dry and dull, and somehow it had just never occurred to Grace that in her time with Owen, they could have conceived a child.

And yet, as soon as Catrin had said it, Grace knew it was true.

"But I don't know anything about having a baby. What do I do? I can't have a baby," Grace said.

Catrin smiled. "Women have been having babies for thousands of years, my dear. You can do it, and I will help you. What are friends for, after all?"

"It hurts, doesn't it? It must be terribly painful."

"I'll be honest, a lot of it is terrible. I got over the initial sickness pretty quickly, but I was often very uncomfortable. And yes, when you push that baby out, it does hurt a great deal. But then the doctor places your child in your arms and you forget all about your pain."

Grace was dubious of that. And now she felt terrible.

"I have to..." Then Grace bolted for the garden again.

Chapter Thirteen

Dearest Grace,

Thank you for your continued descriptions of what is happening at home. I am glad renovations are proceeding apace.

I am sad to report that I feel obligated to continue to fight with my colleagues in Parliament for a new bill I am proposing to help laborers who are worried about being replaced by machines, which I believe will put an end to the rebellions. I hope my solution is one everyone finds satisfactory, although I do not have confidence that this will be the case. Parliament is disagreeable in that way.

It is unfortunate because I want nothing more than to run from London and my obligations here so that I might be in your arms sooner. My friends tell me I am acting like a besotted fool, and I suppose I am. Maybe the distance between us is making me grow fonder of you, or perhaps this friendship we have been forging with our correspondence has made me want to hear your voice, but whatever it is, I do miss you, and I want you to know that. Beresford said to me recently that you deserved someone who cared for you in a way that he could not, and I do hope that I am that person, even all the way in London. I think of you often. I hope to be at your side once we take care of our current government business.

Perhaps you miss me also. I understand if you do not, but I would be gratified to hear that you think of me sometimes in your next letter…

Once Grace had confirmation from her doctor that she was indeed increasing, and once she got over feeling like this was an existential crisis, Grace considered telling Owen about the baby.

But somehow, it felt easier not to.

For one thing, Catrin had been happy to answer her most invasive questions candidly, for which Grace was enormously grateful. Owen didn't need to know about the particulars of any of that. Grace worried that if he knew about it, he'd never want to lie with her again.

For another thing, Owen's last few letters had indicated that he was busy with government business. There were strikes and seditious pamphleteers and all sorts of things going on in London. And Grace knew, without needing to ask, that Owen would abandon all of it and run home to her the moment he knew they were to have a child. But the baby's arrival was still months away, and Owen's place was in London.

So Grace…didn't tell him.

She *did* think of him often. How could she not? She lived in his house, where his presence was everywhere, and his child was growing in her womb. And hearing Owen express that he missed her so explicitly did warm her heart. She often found herself yearning to speak to him as well, to touch him, to be held by him. She'd missed their physical intimacy acutely in the weeks after he'd left, and although that ache was not so strong anymore, she did sometimes wake up in the middle of the night, wishing he were there.

The one thing she could have done without, though, was everyone treating her like a porcelain doll the moment it became apparent that she was pregnant.

Gwen and Carys Williams came to visit on Grace's invite and brought her a hamper full of food they said would be good for the baby. They insisted on coming to the house instead of letting Grace come to them, and even though most of their advice sounded like old wives' tales, Grace was happy for the company. But when she started to move about the room, they insisted she sit down.

The servants jumped into action, constantly asking Grace if she felt all right. She usually answered yes, even if she didn't, because she wanted them to leave her alone.

There was no way to hide her condition. She had to get a few of her day dresses altered, and she gave up on wearing stays. Still, she felt vaguely uncomfortable all the time. And while it was improper for a woman in her condition to be out and about in public, she slipped a few coins to one of the carriage drivers to shuttle her back and forth to the cottage; she told Catrin she would continue to make pottery as long as she could reach her potter's wheel.

The wild part of all of it was that her designs were very much in demand. She'd received letters from her dealer in London saying that the months she'd taken off while she'd been in the process of moving to Wales meant that he now had a waitlist for the next Gerard Makepeace sculpture.

She was feeling inspired, though. She loved the sea and the view of it from her cottage, which she was starting to think of as *hers* and not *Owen's*. Caer Newydd was beautiful and welcome, but it was Owen's house. Because this cottage had been a blank slate, Grace had decorated it in the way she liked, and it felt like hers. And she mixed glazes in colors to match the sea, she put natural details into her work, she played around with firing techniques that imprinted the local plants on her work, and she created some of the best pieces she'd ever made in her little studio. She explained to Catrin that she was making art under an assumed name and selling her work in London, and so Catrin became her apprentice—learning to make bowls and dishes for her family in exchange for helping Grace pack up her work to ship to London.

But Owen didn't know about Gerard Makepeace, either, did he?

Grace felt bad about keeping things from her husband. She should tell him everything. And yet, she didn't.

She wasn't used to telling people things. She kept most of her inner life from her parents, who didn't seem to much care anyway. She was used to keeping her own company. She had never considered what it would mean to share her life with someone, as she was supposed to with her husband. The fact that he was such a great distance away made it easy to continue to keep her own company, except all the other people—Catrin, Morfudd, the Williams family, some of the folk in the little town around the cottage—made sure she was never lonely.

Grace wasn't at all used to it, but having these people there, this family of sorts, it was nice. She found she liked having people around to talk with about idle gossip, about the estate, about the pending birth of her child. Having this level of support was something she'd never experienced it before, but she was grateful for it.

And yet, despite all these people around her, she missed Owen even more. He was her actual family and he should have been a part of what she was building here in Wales.

And, well, she wanted him with her again.

Grace sat with Catrin at the pottery studio, all of this swirling in her mind. She was so distracted, in fact, that she put too much pressure on one side of the vase, and by the time the slip of clay under her fingers snared her attention, the whole shape was a lost cause. One side of the vase caved in and the force of the wheel sent it flying to the floor.

"Your head is in the clouds," Catrin said.

"It is. Apologies."

"What are you thinking about?"

"Whether I should tell my husband about the baby. I should, I know, but I don't want him to rush home right now."

"Why is that?"

"Because he's busy at Parliament, of course. There's no need to take him away from his work when the baby is still months away."

Catrin narrowed her eyes. "I suspect another reason."

Grace had no idea how to explain what she was feeling. She wasn't even sure she understood it. "This…changes things. When I was still living with my parents in London, all I wanted was to be free of them. To get away from the city and build a studio for my art and never have to worry about my father telling me the pottery was silly or my mother watching my every move for the slightest impropriety. And Owen gave me everything I'd ever wanted. He was not eager to marry, nor was I, so we made an agreement. He'd give me the freedom I craved here in Wales, and he'd go back to London."

"All right. And?"

"And now I regret the arrangement. I wish he were here."

"So why not ask him to come home?"

"His letters are filled with the things he's doing in London. He's very busy. So how can I ask him? I'm the one who sent him away."

Catrin nodded. "All right. So postpone telling him a little longer, but you *should* tell him. Give him enough time to get home when the time comes. Believe me, you'll be happier with him here."

Grace nodded. "A reasonable compromise." She rubbed her belly. "I feel somewhat better now, at least."

"Less tossing of accounts?"

"It's been a week since I had to."

"Well, that is some progress."

OWEN THREW HIMSELF into a chair next to the fireplace at his club and regretted many of his life choices.

He'd spent the day being lectured by older Lords about the way he should be performing his role in Parliament, and he resented all of it.

Fletcher was already sitting there, reading a newspaper. He

spared Owen a glance. "Challenging day?"

"The aristocracy is terrible."

"Indeed."

"How are things in your life?"

"Not bad," said Fletcher. "The weather is unbearably hot, but I went to a garden party thrown by a friend of Louisa's this afternoon, and though it was quite prolific with feminine giggles and ruffles and things, I had a good time despite myself. But I also felt the need to come here tonight to talk to some of my male friends. Drink some whiskey." He grunted and tapped his chest.

"Yes, of course. That's nice, though."

"Louisa wanted to introduce me to another friend of hers, a Miss Angelica Rathbone, who does live up to her name, because she is indeed quite angelic. Face like a porcelain doll."

Owen sat up, happy to have someone else's life to focus on for a change. "Oh? Do you have designs on Miss Rathbone?"

"No. She's beautiful, but she's only seventeen, and I think Tilton had an eye on her."

"Marriage is not so bad, you know."

"I suspect I will succumb to it eventually. But have you ever met a woman who is perfect on paper but for whom you feel nothing? Everything about Angelica Rathbone screams 'ideal wife candidate.' She's beautiful and clever and speaks with a voice like honey, and yet I felt no physical pull toward her."

"Is there anyone you are attracted to?"

Fletcher shrugged, which implied he did. But then he said, "No."

"I did have that experience once," Owen conceded. "Do you remember Octavia Laurence?"

Fletcher appeared to mentally search his memories. "Everleigh's daughter?"

"Yes. Beautiful girl, right? One of the smartest people I ever met. Studied mathematics for fun."

"Oh, yes, I remember her. Dark hair, on the thin side, very tall. Yes?"

"That's her. We spoke for nearly half an hour at a ball once, and I found her quite charming, so I called on her the next day and took her on a promenade around the park. But in the bright light of day, I realized that I felt nothing for her. She didn't, how shall I put this? She did not stir my loins."

Fletcher laughed. "Yes. Precisely. That is how I felt about Angelica Rathbone."

"Of course, I was having an affair with Miss Mooney at the time."

"Yes, your actress. So perhaps you were besotted with your lover that Octavia Laurence's virginal purity did not signify."

"Perhaps. That is, Elsa Mooney was a bit of a distraction, but Grace was similarly the picture of virginal purity, and I was instantly attracted to her."

"And not still bedding Miss Mooney."

"True. Right, my point was, perhaps you really do harbor some feelings, physical or otherwise, for another woman and thus do not feel the pull toward Miss Rathbone."

"But there's no one in my life to whom I have that pull. I am not currently having any affairs."

Owen suspected the object of Fletcher's desire was his dear old friend and frequent social companion, Lady Louisa, but he let it go because Hugh and Lark arrived then.

"What are we discussing?" Lark asked as he sat.

"Fletcher's lack of attraction to Angelica Rathbone."

Lark wrinkled his nose. "Really? She's beautiful."

Fletcher rolled his eyes. "As I was explaining to Owen, she is the sort of woman whom I should like, all things being equal, but I just don't feel a pull toward her, for unfathomable reasons."

Hugh nodded. "Several of the women my mother threw at me before my nuptials were like that. The heart wants what it wants."

"All of you are cliched sops," Lark said.

"Surely you have someone you *should* have been attracted to but weren't," Fletcher said to Lark.

Lark blew air through his teeth. "Well, all right. You won't like this example, though."

"Tell us," said Owen.

"Lady Wolverhampton had a tea party last Season in which she displayed some of her new art acquisitions, which included a painting of a young man from some young French artist I've never heard of. The artist *and* his model, with whom I'm fairly certain the painter was having an affair, were both at the party. Lady Wolverhampton gestured at the portrait of the young model and went on and on about his ethereal beauty, and it was true, he was something of an Adonis. He looked like… Who is that fellow who is obsessed with collecting marbles?"

Owen had no idea where this was going. "Lord Elgin?"

"Yes! Elgin. Elgin has, in his collection, a replica of a sculpture from Italy. Michelangelo's David. That was who this young man looked like. Improbably muscled, curly blond hair, the most perfect face I ever saw. It was like he existed to attract me specifically."

Owen decided to slide past the inappropriateness of the attraction and said instead, "This was last Season? You were with Beresford at the time, though, yes?"

"Yes, that's true."

Owen looked at Fletcher. "More evidence to support my hypothesis."

"What is your hypothesis?" asked Lark.

"Owen thinks I'm not attracted to Miss Rathbone because I am attracted to someone else. But it's not true. It's just one of those things." Fletcher's voice rose in pitch as he spoke, clearly irritated now.

"He stole those marbles, you know," Hugh said.

"What are you talking about?" said Fletcher.

"Elgin. He stole the marbles from the Parthenon. He claimed he was going to preserve them because the weather was eroding the original structure, but I don't believe he paid Greece anything, and most of what arrived in England was just…pieces.

Very few complete statues. I went to see them and he told me the whole saga. I don't remember the details, but the marble itself is brittle, and then the boat he was shipping them on sank, and it sounds like not everything made it to England in the condition Elgin found it in Greece."

"What do you think the purpose of bringing the marbles to England would be?" Owen asked.

Hugh shrugged. "So Elgin can say he has a bit of the Parthenon in his ballroom? I know not."

"I'm just saying, he would have done less damage if he'd decided to do the preservation work in Greece."

"He wrote a whole pamphlet defending his actions," Lark said. "And then the British government purchased them last year for an astonishing sum."

"What is the British government doing with them?" asked Fletcher.

"They're putting them in the British Museum," said Owen. "I voted in favor of buying them in Parliament."

Everyone turned to look at Owen.

"What? I don't disagree that Elgin probably stole the marbles, but they're here. Might as well put them in a place where people can see and learn from them. And given all the turmoil in Greece right now, they are probably safer here for now anyway."

"I've never been to the museum," Fletcher said.

Owen laughed. "Really? Aren't you a patron of the arts?"

"Contemporary arts, certainly. The British Museum is all stuffy old Greek marbles and artifacts from long dead Saxon kings, no?"

"Philistine," said Lark. "It's worth going. I know it is forever under construction, but there is some valuable art there."

"And the Rosetta Stone," said Owen. "It's the stone they used to finally translate Egyptian hieroglyphics."

"Right, of course," said Fletcher. "Boys, you all are like brothers to me, and thus you should know by now that while I do patronize the arts, I am hardly an expert. And the only reason I go to the opera as often as I do is because Lady Louisa often asks for my escort."

Owen made eye contact with Lark and raised an eyebrow. Lark nodded.

Fletcher sighed. "I hate all of you." Then he pointed at Owen. "Can't we go back to mocking Owen for being besotted with his wife."

"I am not…" But Owen couldn't finish the sentence. It was true. He was besotted.

"I do not see why this is a reason for mockery," said Hugh. "The poor man has been alone for an indeterminate amount of time. I'm sure it is a struggle."

"The letters are nice," Owen admitted. "She's a better writer than I am."

Beresford interrupted him then, brandishing a bottle of whiskey and five glasses held carefully in one hand. Without saying a word, he put all five glasses on the center of the table and poured a finger into each.

"Drink up, gents," Beresford said. "I nicked this whiskey from my cousin Stephen's plentiful cabinets. Best drink it before he notices."

"You are incorrigible," said Lark.

"Perhaps, but this is very good whiskey."

Owen reached for the glass closest to him and took a sip. It was indeed smooth.

Beresford pulled over a chair and settled into it. "Now, what were we talking about?"

"Nothing," said Fletcher.

"Oh, good. Did you hear the latest about Lord Edgerton?"

Owen mostly tuned out Beresford's tale of gossip and woe, preferring instead to sip whiskey and think about Grace.

Chapter Fourteen

Dearest Owen,

I am as ever enjoying your little cottage by the sea. The weather here has been lovely, and I adore the sea breeze as I know you must. I find it inspiring to be here, so you need not worry about me. I've been so productive at my pottery wheel that I recently sold some pieces to a little shop in Penmaenmawr. It's not much money, but it was enough to buy a new chair for the cottage in which I can sit and watch the sea.

You have seemed distressed in your last few letters, bemoaning the fate of your various works in Parliament, and for that, I am sorry. I wish I could help in some way. But I do understand if you need to spend additional time in London. I suppose it is more than we had originally planned. Be assured, I am enjoying my time here and do not want you to worry about me.

I do miss you, though. I almost wish I had something more substantive to tell you beyond chairs and vases, but that is taking up most of my life at the moment. Your work seems so important, and so I do not wish to pull you away from it, but instead I wait patiently for your return at your earliest convenience. I'm eager to show you what I've done with the cottage. I think you would like it. But of course, it can wait.

In the meantime, I shall soldier on. Morfudd and I bought a new rug for the castle, and she has a keen interest in doing something interesting with the courtyard, perhaps making it a space for performances. This seems a farfetched idea to me, but a part of me wants to see if Morfudd can follow through with her plans. It might be interesting to bring a bit of culture to Caernarfon. Can you imagine the local folk crowding into the courtyard for a bit of Shakespeare? It seems fantastical to me, but...

Owen told himself that he liked beautiful things, and that was why he was in a shop in London that sold fine goods with which to decorate one's home. When Owen had expressed interested in Gerard Makepeace, Anthony had directed him to this shop.

When he walked in, he was instantly overwhelmed. Well-lit shelves held trinkets and vases and fine dishes and glasses. Paintings hung from every available bit of wall space. Even though Owen had no doubt everything here was well made and expensive, there was something gaudy about having so much of it in crammed into a few square feet.

"Can I be of some assistance, my lord?" the shopkeeper asked.

"I wondered if you had any pieces by Gerard Makepeace. You see, the Marquess of Beresford has a piece that I thought was quite lovely, and I wondered if—"

"You are in luck, my lord. We had a bit of a delay in new pieces. I believe Mr. Makepeace went on holiday for a couple of months and then moved somewhere a great distance from here. I can't recall where. Scotland, perhaps. But it is of no consequence, because we just received three new pieces, and they are his best work yet, I believe."

Owen let the shopkeeper escort him to three pillars in one corner of the store, on which stood three elaborate vases. One of them was tall and narrow, with violets painted on it. The style of painting could be similar to the vase Grace had sent him, but Owen was not enough of an expert to know. Another of the vases was wide and had handles at its sides that were made to look like ivy vines. The third had a mouth that was painted and shaped to look like a lily.

"These are striking," Owen said. "Do you mind if I take a

closer look?"

The shopkeeper glanced at Owen's hands, which were gloved. "Please," he said in a way that indicated he was nervous Owen would destroy one of them.

Owen carefully picked up the one with ivy handles. He looked inside, then he turned it over to see the mark at the bottom.

"Ah, yes. Check for authenticity. That is, I can assure you, these are genuine Makepeace vases. I received a letter from Mr. Makepeace himself when these arrived, but I understand the need to check."

Owen thought the shopkeeper rather resented Owen checking, but Owen did spot the mark on the bottom.

GM. Gerard Makepeace. Grace Midwood.

But surely it couldn't be.

"I'm afraid I don't know much about pottery," Owen said, "aside from the fact that my wife dabbles in making her own pieces. She made me a lovely vase recently, although not nearly as lovely as these." That was a lie. Owen loved the piece Grace had sent him more than any other piece of art in his house. "What would you say are the distinctive qualities of a Makepeace vase?"

"No two are alike, for one. But also, he always makes these rounded bodies, like this, you see?" The shopkeeper pointed his pinky finger along the side of one of the vases. "And then he puts a little twist near the mouth. That is one of his signatures. Overall, though, the main trait is that they always look graceful, like this one does. I believe he's changed his glaze formula recently, too, because the white on these is brighter than in some of his older pieces."

Owen put the vase in his hands back on its pedestal. He realized that the vase in his home had that same signature twist near the mouth. Was it possible that his wife did not just dabble in pottery but was, in fact, so talented that her work was coveted by the wealthiest men of Britain? The evidence was not inconclusive, but there was enough for Owen to think his suspicion was correct.

"Tell me, for how much would a piece like this sell?"

When the shopkeeper told Owen, he felt his jaw go slack. Was it possible his wife was also independently wealthy? If she made money from pottery, where did she keep it? And then, if she had enough money from this endeavor to live on, why marry him?

Before he had some kind of mental episode, he thanked the shopkeeper for his time and promised to return at a later date. He then opted to walk home instead of hiring a hackney, so he could contemplate what all this meant. If it was true, he didn't love that Grace had kept it from him, although if she were operating with a male pseudonym, he supposed he could understand why. But he was trustworthy, was he not? Why could she not confide in him?

Of course, he did not know if any of it was true. It could be a coincidence that the GT and GM marks looked so similar, that Grace's initials before she married were GM, and that she also produced pottery at a fast enough clip to sell a few pieces to a shop in Penmaenmawr—if that was even true—and ship a few pieces to this shop in London. Not to mention, Mr. Makepeace's holiday would have correlated to Grace's move to Wales.

He wondered if he should ask her directly in his next letter, but that seemed aggressive. And maybe he *hadn't* earned her trust. After all, they'd barely known each other when they married, they'd only spent a few weeks together after the wedding, and the agreement they'd made allowed Grace her independence.

So maybe he was wrong to feel offended if she was indeed keeping a secret. She didn't owe him anything. He, in fact, had told her repeatedly that she didn't.

On the other hand, he thought their letters had brought them closer together and she could trust him now. But perhaps he was wrong.

Why did that make him feel so terrible?

CATRIN HELPED GRACE pack two vases into a crate, careful to shove as much straw and crumbled newspaper inside it as possible to ensure the vases stayed whole in transit.

"Explain to me again why you haven't told your husband you're this famous artist," Catrin said as Grace fetched a hammer and nails to seal the crate.

Why hadn't she? "I feel silly about it now."

"It's all right. Just tell me what you are thinking."

Grace sighed. "At first, I didn't completely trust him with the secret. I barely knew him when we married. I didn't know if he'd think it inappropriate for a woman to be an artist or earn her own money, and I didn't know if he'd forbid me from doing it. But then when we arrived in Wales, he was so sweet, and allowed me to use the cottage to make my art. But I still wonder sometimes if he would find it objectionable."

"Perhaps," said Catrin.

"And even if he's fine with all of it, he'd wonder why I withheld for so long, and now it's been months, so I feel like I can't say anything. If I confess I've held secrets from him, he'll be angry I withheld them."

Catrin raised an eyebrow. "What other secrets are you keeping?"

"I...nothing." She still hadn't told him about the baby, though. She had no real justification or it. "We made an agreement when we married that he would allow me independence. I wanted to live in the country and make my own friends and make art without anyone telling me what I could or should do with my time. That's all I ever wanted. If I could have done that without marrying, I would have, but my parents never would have allowed it. My husband offered me the greatest gift he could have, which is that he would let me live here while he is away on business in London and that I might conduct my affairs as I see fit.

This is how I see fit."

She placed a nail at the corner of the crate and hammered it into place.

"Do not take out your aggressions on that nail," said Catrin. "I did not mean to anger you. I just wanted to inquire as to why you were keeping things from your husband. I do not blame you, I am merely curious. What you just said may be true, but circumstances have changed somewhat now that you have a baby on the way. Not to mention, you've said you and the earl have grown closer as you've exchanged letters these last few months. Surely your feelings have changed somewhat."

Suddenly a little dizzy, Grace placed the hammer and nails on top of the box and sat in a nearby chair. "They have changed, I suppose. And I do wish he were here sometimes. But he's been gone so long now, I think I'd forget his face if there weren't a portrait of him hanging in my home. And his business in Parliament has been challenging. His letters often tell me he's struggling. He's so busy in London that I think if I asked him to come, he wouldn't."

"Surely, that is not true. You are his wife. You're about to be the mother of his child."

He still did not know about the second thing, and the truth was that Grace suspected if she wrote and told him he had a child on the way, he would drop everything and come to Wales. She didn't want that. She wanted to be able to work on her own at the pottery studio until she grew too big to reach the pottery wheel. She didn't need him fussing over her. She wanted her independence.

Right?

"I do miss him," Grace said, "but it's better this way. And surely this is something I should tell him face to face, rather than in a letter."

"If you insist." Catrin tutted and then picked up the hammer and pounded in the nail. Then she said, "I suppose I don't understand because I've never lived apart from my husband, and I suppose I'm not an aristocrat."

"I'm not much of an aristocrat."

"No, but things are done differently. My husband and I share a bedroom, and our house is spacious enough to fit us all, but I can hear my children cry at night if they need me. And Gareth and I, well, we knew each other as children because we both grew up in this village, no more than a stone's throw from each other. So in truth, I've never been separated from my husband. But yours must be in London regularly, and I understand it is not uncommon for aristocrats in arranged marriages to lead somewhat separate lives."

"Yes," Grace said, although she wondered what it would be like to have Owen close, to be able to hear their children cry at night. As it was, the nursery was upstairs from the earl's bedroom, and it was expected she'd hire nurses, nannies, and governesses to take care of this baby and any other children they'd have.

Because that was how things were done.

Although, one advantage to independence was that she could do things the way she wanted them done.

"Are you feeling all right?" Catrin asked.

"Just a little dizzy," Grace allowed.

Catrin nodded. "That can happen. Here, I'll finish this and wait for the mail coach. You should head home and eat something."

"Oh, I'm all right, I'll—"

"I insist. We finished all the food you were keeping here yesterday, remember? Go home. Eat. Take care of yourself and that baby. I can do this."

Grace understood the wisdom of that. She pushed herself out of the chair and went to tell the footman to bring her carriage round.

"Thank you for your help, Catrin."

Catrin waved her hand, as if it were of no consequence. "What are friends for? But you should consider telling your husband everything. I believe he deserves to know."

Chapter Fifteen

ANTHONY HAD BEEN feigning drunkenness and counting cards for the entire game, so when at last it ended and he won all the money in the pot, he had to pretend like this was just luck and not something he'd been working toward the whole game. Several of his opponents groaned or threw their cards on the table in disgust.

As the men left, Anthony finished raking his winnings into a sack he'd carried for this purpose. A moment later, Lark approached. "You knew Rutherford had the seven of diamonds."

"I did."

"You're not drunk, are you?"

"Haven't had a drop of alcohol all night." He pointed to the glass near him. "That is just a bit of juice." And bless Rutherford's green-tinted glasses; the tumbler of juice looked like it held whiskey.

"You're quite the actor."

"Were you watching?" Anthony scooped the last of the coins into the sack and then looked up at Lark, who wore a pained expression.

"I lost ten pounds to Dain, and refused to bet any more because I know he cheats, so I had a little time waiting for you to finish." He sighed. "The room is clearing out. I suppose we must rejoin the ball."

The Rutherfords had decided to throw "a small gathering" for whoever was still in town now that the Season was long over. Although many had decamped for their country homes, enough aristocrats remained in town for this to be not so much a small gathering as a ball. The one saving grace was that there were not many unmarried women about.

After Anthony stepped outside to find one of his footmen to secure his winnings, he rejoined Lark in the ballroom. It was late and nearly everyone at the ball seemed deep in their cups. Lark himself drank what looked like brandy and glared at the dancing crowd.

"We could make our excuses," said Anthony. "This ball has already thinned out a bit."

"I almost enjoyed myself this evening. There wasn't the pressure to pretend I'm willing to make a match with some young lady."

Anthony was exhausted by the argument they'd been having for weeks about each of their relative willingness to get married. He opted not to respond to Lark's comment. Instead, he watched the dancers, currently fumbling their way through a very drunk waltz. The wine had been flowing like a waterfall all evening. And although Anthony had abstained so he could keep his wits about him in the card room, part of him wanted to be drunk enough to have the courage to dance with Lark.

"I suppose we should leave," said Lark.

But Anthony plucked a glass of wine from a passing tray. "If everyone else here is drunk, and if everyone thinks *I'm* drunk, maybe I should just indulge myself." He took a big gulp.

Lark rolled his eyes. "I have better wine at home."

A compelling point. Anthony drank the rest quickly and motioned toward the door.

They stumbled outside, where Anthony's carriage was suddenly nowhere to be seen. A Rutherford footman offered to see about fetching it. As they walked forward, Lark, who was *definitely* drunk, tripped on something invisible on the walkway. Anthony reached out and grabbed him before he tumbled to the ground.

"This is why you lose at cards," Anthony observed.

Lark hung on Anthony's arm and gave him a moony look. "You're very handsome, you know."

Anthony grinned. "I do know."

Someone, likely another drunk reveler, stepped out of the shadows and into Anthony's peripheral vision. Anthony pushed Lark into a standing position, but Lark seemed disinclined to let go of Anthony's arm.

Anthony glanced at the man and saw it was Samuel Gordon, the third son of the Marquess of Barstow. Gordon was a weasel, but he had the ear of some powerful people.

"Nice night," Anthony observed. "I hope you enjoyed the ball."

"I did, I did," said Gordon. "Did Waring drink a little too much?"

"I'm afraid so."

Gordon stepped forward. "You should know, you aren't as clever as you think."

What the devil did that mean? "Likely true, but I don't see the significance."

"Be careful, Beresford."

He looked like he was about to say something else, but Anthony's carriage finally returned. Anthony tugged Lark toward the carriage and said, probably louder than he needed to, "I will see that Waring gets home. Toodle-loo, Gordon."

When they got to Lark's house, Lark had sobered up somewhat and led Anthony into the parlor and poured them each a glass of wine, but Anthony didn't need it now. He felt on edge.

"Gordon is onto us," Lark said.

"Or he thinks he is. Let him present evidence."

"But Anthony—"

"Hush. I do not want to speak of it tonight." Lark's staff had been dismissed, they were quite alone, and so Anthony said, "All I wanted to do tonight was dance with you."

Lark looked somewhat alarmed by that. "Dance with *me*?"

"While I'm certain the very notion offends all of your training and sensibilities, it is not so absurd. Husbands and wives dance together all the time. Why should I not desire to dance with the person I love."

"I don't know how to dance with a man."

"Sure you do. You have to face other men in country dances sometimes."

Anthony approached Lark slowly. He took Lark into his arms.

"There's no music," Lark said.

So Anthony hummed the tune of a waltz he knew and then he whisked Lark around the room. Lark laughed but went along with it, following as if he were the woman in the pair. It *was* funny and awkward, but it was nice, too.

Anthony slowed it down, drawing out the pace of the song he was humming, and Lark slowed with him. Anthony met Lark's gaze, and they stared at each other as they moved in a slow circle. Then Anthony trailed his fingers along Lark's arm and all but came to a stop.

Being together like this was a nice reminder of why he liked Lark so much. The man was beautiful, for one thing. Straight dark hair, combed forward but unfashionably long enough to dangle over his eyes. An angular face with dark eyes. A fit body. But more than that, Lark was willing to humor Anthony's whims. He liked spending time with Anthony, which many of his fellow peers didn't; Anthony knew people found him annoying or ridiculous, and Lark probably had at some point, too, but not anymore. Lark listened to him. Lark took him seriously.

They'd been sharing a bed for more than a year, which was longer than any affair of Anthony's had lasted. That had to mean something. He never tired of Lark.

They'd been tossing *I love you* at each other for months, but sometimes Anthony wondered if they simply did it out of habit. But it was true, wasn't it? Anthony was in love with this man. That was why he didn't want to marry a woman. If it wasn't for

Lark, he probably could have gone along with the farce, but he wasn't ready to let Lark go, and he didn't think he ever would.

"I do love you, you know."

Lark nodded in acknowledgement and put his hands on Anthony's chest. "Of course I love you, too. I never say that without meaning it." He sighed. "I don't want to let you go. I can't imagine what life would be like if I have to go to another party and have to watch you swindling our friends out of their money or dancing with your wife. My heart would shatter into a million pieces, I think."

"Let us not dwell on that potential future now. I still have time to…."

"Time to what? Wriggle out of your destiny? Until Gordon tells the wrong person?"

"Maybe. Maybe not. But forget about all that now. Let us just be together."

Lark leaned forward and pressed his forehead into Anthony's shoulder. He lifted it again and said, "I'm sorry for telling you to stay away from the club. That was stupid of me. I think instead, we should spend every minute together possible."

"You were trying not to get hanged," Anthony pointed it out.

"I missed you."

"Lark, my love, we see each other nearly every night."

"Yes, but that is often for…bedsport. I love just…speaking with you. You're the only man of the *ton* who is a bigger gossip than I am. And I like talking with you and puzzling out my friends' problems with you. And I think my friends may actually like you. They always ask after you when you aren't there."

"So my exile is over officially? I don't have to bribe my way in with my cousin's good whiskey?"

Lark ran his hands up Anthony's chest and leaned close. "It's over." Then he kissed Anthony.

They'd kissed hundreds of times. They'd been inside each other's bodies. But something about this kiss felt charged in a new way. Anthony parted his lips and let Lark in.

They kissed for what felt like a long time, but it wasn't a prelude to anything. It was…an expression of affection.

Anthony understood that it was because Lark still thought Anthony would get married, but rather than pushing him away, Lark had decided they should make the most of what they had before that inevitable day. Anthony liked the idea, although he did still intend to figure out a way *not* to get married.

He put his arms around Lark, happy for the press of Lark's body against his own.

They swayed with each other for a long moment, Anthony humming the waltz again.

"Even though my exile is over, I want you to know, I will continue nicking whiskey from Cousin Stephen. He's a right toad, that man. He deserves to have his good liquor stolen."

Lark laughed. "You want more wine or do you want go to bed?"

"Let's go to bed."

Chapter Sixteen

Dearest Owen,

I do wish at times that you could see what I've made of your little cottage, because it is everything I've dreamed of. With my friend Catrin and her husband's help, we have built a kiln outside that is the perfect place to fire my work. I've decorated the inside of the cottage in a way that feels comfortable and homey. I adore this place and I'm grateful that you gave me permission to furnish it as I desired, because I think it might be my favorite place.

But I miss you. I think about you constantly. I feel your presence everywhere in Caer Newydd. I hear your voice in the accents of your neighbors. I loved your last letter dearly, loved hearing stories about your friends and what you are up to at Parliament, and I could almost imagine that you were sitting with me at our dining table and regaling me with these tales yourself.

I know you're busy with everything in London, and that is where you should be. I do miss you, but I want to reassure you that I am as happy as can be here. Catrin has made a fine apprentice and a dear friend. Morfudd makes me laugh whenever she comes for a meal. Gwen and Carys Williams and I get together regularly for meals—Gwen is an excellent cook. I have found the people here to be lovely and friendly and eager to teach me Welsh words.

You asked me recently to tell you I think of you, and I do, daily, hourly, perhaps every minute some days. I do like hearing about what you are up to in London and sometimes I wish I could be there with you to support you, because it sounds like you are quite troubled by what you must do.

I miss you, but I imagine I will see you soon. When your Parliament session ends, I hope you will consider coming to see me and the rest of your family....

P.S. We've worked out that you and Catrin's husband had the same great-grandfather! Catrin and I joke that, in point of fact, we are cousins.

Owen felt a pang as he finished reading the letter. He missed Grace, of course, but he missed Wales as well. Her last few letters had been full of stories about the people she'd been meeting. Some of them were ones Owen knew well and missed, too, some of them were new friends of Grace's, but if her letters were anything to go by, she was thriving there, and Owen was sad to be missing it.

His gut told him to go to Wales, with all possible haste. He'd ride through the night if he had to. But his duties and obligations kept him in London.

So, at the end of the day, as a waiter at the club poured him a generous serving of gin—might as well cut to the chase—Owen felt like he was losing on all fronts. He missed his wife, he missed his homeland, and he'd failed to get any of his bills through Parliament, which was the main reason he'd chosen to be here instead of where he wanted to be.

"Clear liquor," Fletcher said, joining Owen by the fireplace in the club. "Has everything truly gone horribly wrong?"

"I believe so, yes."

"Maybe I should have some of that, too, except I am meeting Lady Louisa for the opera in an hour."

"Which opera?" Owen asked, mostly as a formality. Fletcher attended the opera about once a month, and Owen rarely did, if he could help it.

"*The Magic Flute.* It's her favorite. The tenor is some chap from Italy who is drawing attention on the Continent. And…you do not give a whit about opera."

"I don't, no, but I appreciate that you do."

"Mostly for Louisa. She needed someone to accompany her and I had no other engagements this evening. Unless you wish me to cancel so that I can help you?"

"No, that's all right. Enjoy the opera."

"But you are determined to be in your cups."

"My bill got laughed out of Lords today."

"The one about the roads or the one about the Luddites?"

Owen was taken aback that Fletcher actually listened to him and knew the bills he was pursuing. He sighed. "Well, both, but more crucially, the Luddites. Why take an approach that could help the people when you could instead just send Wellington's army to shoot them all."

"Wait, is that true?"

Owen sighed. "I do not know if the intent is for the troops to shoot the rebels. They may just seek to capture them. But yes, tomorrow we shall be voting on whether to send troops, and most of my colleagues support the idea."

"Seems like a tragedy to send the army Wellington won with at Waterloo to suppress a few angry artisans."

"My feelings exactly, but my feelings do not matter. So I've just spent several months that I could have spent getting to know my new wife pursuing bills here that are doomed to fail. I've wasted my time, and I'm frustrated by it. Thus I am drinking."

"Well deserved," said Fletcher. He lifted his glass of wine and gestured at Owen with it.

Beresford, of all people, walked in then. He dropped into one of the chairs and said, "Lord save me from meddlesome women."

"You could…just not get married," Fletcher said, probably recognizing that whatever meddlesome woman Beresford was mad about was trying to get him into a church to troth to a potential wife.

"I certainly am trying."

"Can we…be of assistance to you?" Owen asked. "Because my plan for this evening is to get rip-roaring drunk."

"That's an excellent plan." Beresford snapped his fingers at a waiter. "Whiskey." When the waiter left to fetch Beresford's drink, he asked, "Why are you getting drunk?"

"Government business and a wife miles away."

Beresford nodded. "I heard your bill got scuttled. I suppose now that we've run Napoleon out of Europe, the army needed something to do."

"That's one way to put it," said Fletcher.

"Listen, I'm sorry," said Beresford. "For what it's worth, I agree with you that sending troops is excessive and that we should probably do something to help the rebels, but the rich folk in Lords will never see the world that way. You're too much of a do-gooder."

"Well, look who's here…"

Hugh and Lark arrived together. Lark was wearing something fashionable and slightly ridiculous. His waistcoat was bright green, though obscured by his dark blue coat, and his breeches were tight enough to look painted on.

Owen opened his mouth to ask what he was wearing, but thought it would be rude.

Apparently everyone else was staring, though.

"The waistcoat is too much, isn't it?" Lark said, fingering the edge of it.

"That color is quite becoming on you," said Beresford. "Did you dress up for me?"

"Perish the thought. Hugh and I just came from a garden party. The less said about it, the better."

"Profoundly dull," Hugh agreed. "A fundraiser for parks in London, so a good cause, but the crowd left something to be desired."

"The gray-haired set?" asked Beresford.

Lark tapped his nose.

"So we're all having a terrible day," said Fletcher. "Well, I'm not, actually. I spent a perfectly pleasant afternoon working with my father on some plans to extend our estate in Cornwall. And now that the rest of you are here, I must be off. But please keep an eye on Owen, who has dived right into the clear liquor."

"Gin is a poor man's drink," said Beresford with disgust. "How can you stand the taste of it?"

"I prefer it to whiskey, in fact," Owen said, "but I only indulge when my day seems especially disastrous."

"Parliament?" Hugh asked.

"Indeed."

Fletcher left, and Hugh and Lark took the two empty chairs. Once they had drinks in hand, and after Owen recounted what had happened in Parliament that day, they toasted to a terrible day.

"All those months wasted," Owen said, his brain swimming in gin. "I never expected to miss her this much, but I do, and it's my own damn fault because I was idealistic enough to think I could affect change in this godforsaken country."

"Your wife?" asked Lark.

"Aye. I'm fed up with London. You gents are my dearest friends, but I'd toss you all in the Thames if it would get me home faster."

"I can't imagine being separated from Adele for that long," said Hugh.

"Should I leave for Wales straight from the vote tomorrow or what?"

"No," said Lark. "You promised you would attend the charity ball my mother is hosting next week. I need reinforcements."

Owen let out a breath. "Right. Of course I will be there. I am in no condition to leave for Wales right now anyway."

This was true. He needed to get his servants and his belongings in order. It would take him at least a week to pack up his London house for a long-term vacancy. Not to mention, he should write to Grace to warn her he was coming before he left. He'd love to be able to leave immediately, but there was a lot to arrange. So he was stuck in London for at least another fortnight.

He leaned back into his chair. "Another round?" he asked.

IN OWEN'S LATEST letter, he'd asked about Gerard Makepeace, because apparently the Marquess of Beresford had seen the vase she'd made for Owen and remarked that it looked like Makepeace's work.

It was probably time to come clean. Grace almost wondered if Owen was fishing for information. Had Beresford said something that made him suspect?

She wanted to tell him everything, but then she received a newspaper from London—they often arrived a few days late, but she liked keeping abreast of the news in England—and there was an article about the rebellion Owen had written to her about. It mentioned the bill he was pushing in Parliament. She admired Owen's kindness and desire to find a solution that did not involve the rebels being treated harshly.

Things had changed—Grace knew that. She knew that the original arrangement had been a product of her ignorance of Owen and of marriage, and now that she knew and understood him better, she wanted him here with her. But she was reluctant to ask him to do that, not sure if his own feelings mirrored hers. She'd wanted independence, but now she regretted asking for it.

She'd lucked into marrying a handsome, kind, considerate man, one who made her feel things she'd never felt before, and that had changed everything. She didn't want her independence anymore. She wanted her husband. And she knew she should write him and tell him to come home with all possible haste.

In fact, she even wrote such a letter. She wrote out all of it—the baby, her *nom de sculpture*—in a missive, telling Owen to come home at once because he was about to be a father. She weighed whether or not to mail it, nervous suddenly that such a plea would be unwelcome. She reasoned she still had a few more weeks to decide.

However, the choice to do so was swiftly taken out of her hands.

Catrin had explained the basics of childbirth, but Grace was still not prepared. When she felt the first pang, she dismissed it, assuming it was like a flutter or a kick, the sorts of things she'd been feeling for months now. But then came another. And another. And soon, Grace was anxiously pacing up and down the hall outside her bedroom, trying to decide if it was time to summon a doctor. Then her maid, Mary, found her with a puddle at her feet, and said, "Aye, my lady, you should be in bed."

The doctor arrived within the hour.

Grace felt like she was in good hands, between the doctor, the midwife who arrived with him, and Mary—who had a brood of her own children she worked to support. But as the pain increased, so did her panic. She'd thought about what it would be like to give birth constantly for the last six weeks, but now that she had to push this baby out of her body, it seemed like an impossible task.

She wouldn't remember much after the fact. The pain became so intense, she felt herself floating out of her body. It would have been easy to let go, but she was determined to do this, and to be a good mother, so she fought to stay present and follow the doctor's instructions.

It was a struggle. The doctor speculated that the baby was big and healthy, which was a good thing, of course, but made labor more of a challenge. Catrin had told Grace that birthing a baby would hurt, so she assumed this pain was part of that, but she couldn't help wailing, "It hurts too much. I don't think I can do this."

"You can, my lady. Stay with me. Hold Mary's hand if you need to."

She wanted Owen. He would hold her and encourage her. Instead, because of her own blasted decisions, she was quite alone.

But just when the pain became more than she could bear, the doctor yelled, "Push, my lady. Push."

She screamed as she pushed. She couldn't shake the mental image—something that had appeared her nightmares for weeks—of this baby tearing her body apart. The pain was acute, more than anything she'd ever borne before.

Then she heard it. It started softly, but then it became a full-on wail. The baby was here—and he was crying.

"It's a boy!" the midwife said. "Ten fingers and ten toes!"

The doctor did some things Grace couldn't see, and the baby continued to wail. Grace strained to see the child, but the edges of her vision started to go blurry and dark.

"Doctor…" she murmured. "Something is…"

But before she could say anything more, everything went black.

Chapter Seventeen

G RACE'S LETTERS USUALLY arrived on Wednesdays like clockwork, and one being a day or two late didn't necessarily *mean* anything. His majesty's post was not always reliable. Weather in Wales could have slowed it down.

So he tried to shove the delay aside as he walked into the club Friday night.

But the truth was that he hated that he hadn't received a letter. He was worried, in point of fact. Had something happened? Was it just the post or was there something wrong? Had a roof caved in? Was Grace ill? Had she been injured?

He did his best to convince himself it was just a post delay and found his friends near their usual spot ear the fireplace. It was an unusually cold night, so the fire was roaring. Fletcher sat in one of the big chairs, staring into his whiskey.

Owen plopped into a chair. "Is everything all right?"

"Oh, I'm overreacting."

"Join the club. To what are you overreacting?"

"Lady Louisa called on me this afternoon to announce that—"

Fletcher closed his mouth abruptly as Lark and Hugh arrived and took the other two chairs near the fireplace.

"Did we interrupt something?" asked Hugh.

"It's nothing," said Fletcher.

"It's something," said Owen, knowing his friend. Fletcher was clearly upset about something related to Lady Louisa. Fletcher would swear he loved Louisa like a sister, but Owen was near certain he had romantic feelings for her. So Owen decided to egg him on. "Fletcher was just saying that Lady Louisa called on him this afternoon to announce something."

Lark's eyebrows shot up. He loved gossip. "Announce what?"

Fletcher sighed. "The Duke of Rotherfield is formally courting her."

"Rotherfield?" said Lark. "Well, that is a surprise."

"In what way?" asked Fletcher.

Lark shook his head. "Oh, just...he's young and handsome and I assumed he'd enjoy the bachelor life for a few more years before committing to marriage. And you know I adore Louisa, but she's practically a spinster."

This was a comment on Louisa's age. She was a few years younger than Fletcher, but she was old enough to be considered on the shelf. She didn't really have that reputation, because she was charming and beautiful, and frankly it defied all logic and reason that she was still in the marriage market. It wasn't a surprise that Rotherfield wanted her. Owen had known Louisa for years and genuinely liked her, so Rotherfield must have, too.

"She is receptive, I assume," said Hugh.

"It's a very smart match," said Lark. "They'd be an attractive couple."

"I should be happy for her," said Fletcher. "But something about it bothers me."

Owen just raised an eyebrow. But Lark said with a smirk, "Because he's better-looking than you are?"

Fletcher rolled his eyes. "No, it's merely that... Well, what do we know about Rotherfield? As a man, I mean. A pretty face does not signify he is of good character. What if, for example, he is a cruel husband or a disinterested father?"

Hugh nodded thoughtfully. "I will admit, I do not know Rotherfield well. He is younger than we are, correct? I believe he was at Eton, but several years behind us."

"Yes," Lark said.

"I've met him a few times," Owen supplied. "He appears at Lords every now and again. I do not know much about his political leanings, but he has always been polite when we've spoken."

"I've never heard anything bad about him," Lark, the gossip-monger, replied.

"I just want her to be happy," Fletcher said. "She says she is fond of him. But something about Rotherfield rubs me in the wrong way."

"Jealousy," Lark suggested.

Fletcher balked. "I'm not jealous of Rotherfield. I have no romantic designs on Louisa. She's like a sister to me. I want her to have a good marriage and I want her to be happy, that is all. It seems odd to me that she would agree to court Rotherfield given that she barely knows him."

Owen didn't believe Fletcher, but he nodded. "Perhaps she would like to get to know him. Is that not the purpose of courtship?"

"I suppose," Fletcher said reluctantly.

"And perhaps she is feeling some familial pressure to not be placed permanently on the shelf," Owen added.

"I imagine so. And I recognize that there is no rational reason for me to be so bothered by this turn of events. Louisa is free to make her own choices, of course. I just do not understand why this is making me feel so bad."

Owen glanced at Lark, who subtly shook his head.

"I'll survive," Fletcher said, shaking it off. "How are you gents doing?"

"Anthony is in Kent, attending to some family business," said Lark. "So I am a bit at loose ends."

It was said as a statement of fact, and Owen could not readily detect how Lark felt about it. Was Lark relieved to be rid of Anthony's constant presence for a bit, or was he lonely. Owen found he was often lonely without Grace in his bed, that sometimes, he even ached with it, but he didn't want to imprint those feelings on Lark.

"My mother has been a persistent presence at our house, despite now having a house of her own," Hugh said. "Adele is feeling frustrated."

"Do Adele and your mother still not get along?" Owen asked.

"They normally tolerate each other. I believe Mother's constant presence is driving us all mad, though. And I cannot figure out why she calls so incessantly. I just spent a lot of money building her a new house and yet, I feel like I see her more now than when she lived with us."

"Have you asked why she calls so often?" said Lark.

"She insists she just wants to spend time her grandchild. Mostly, she pesters me about when we will have another."

"Ah," said Lark. "And will you have another child?"

"I do not know. Adele was so ill her entire confinement, I am loathe to put her through that again."

Owen found his mind wandering to Grace again. Would they have children? That would be part of the plan, wouldn't it? Was not the point of marrying to pass on the earldom to his son? He should probably mention as much to Grace in his next letter. Discuss it with her when he next visited. Certainly the conception of an heir itself would be a delightful way to spend time, although Owen would feel terrible leaving Grace alone in her confinement.

What a pickle he'd put himself in. Could it be that Owen was fond of his wife?

"What are you thinking about so hard?" Fletcher asked Owen.

"Oh. I haven't heard from Grace in a bit, is all. Probably just some problem with the post. She is a very reliable correspondent, you see. But her usual letter is a few days late. I am overreacting, obviously."

"You miss her," said Hugh.

"I do. I look forward to her letters every week. She is funny and thoughtful and tells me stories about life in Wales. It was a bit of an adjustment for her, I suppose. She has been overseeing renovations at the seaside cottage I bought, and she always has something clever to say." Owen sighed. "I do enjoy her letters. I wish I could see her sometimes, but the journey to Wales is too long to make spontaneously. The delay caused me to worry that something had happened to Grace, but I'm sure I am being irrational. Something as simple as a thunderstorm could delay the post."

"Indeed," said Lark. "I received a letter from my aunt in Shropshire today, and the date was more than a fortnight ago. I believe there was a big storm along the Welsh border."

"That must be it, then." Owen let out a breath. That was, of course, the simplest explanation. Posted letters went on walkabout all the time. Really, the miracle was that Grace's letters had arrived so regularly the last few months.

Somehow, this did not soothe the nagging feeling Owen felt in his gut.

"Maybe I should just go to Wales," he said. "The various votes in Parliament are over. Prinny will probably close the current session soon. And if no one is going to listen to me anyway, what good am I even doing?"

"If you feel you need to," said Hugh.

Owen nodded. "I think I do."

GRACE REGAINED CONSCIOUSNESS shortly after she'd lost it. The midwife explained that it was a difficult labor—the earl's new heir was a large baby—and that Grace had lost a lot of blood, but she was all right, and the baby was healthy, and that was all that really mattered to Grace.

It was a long recovery, and Grace could barely move for a few days, but once she felt well enough to sit up and be out of bed for more than a few minutes at a time, she had her maid dress her for the day. Once in a crisp, muslin day dress, she already felt more like herself. She was sore, but the pain was easing. The doctor had provided a list of things she should eat to restore some of the blood she had lost, which didn't make logical sense to Grace, but she followed his instructions to the letter.

She'd named the baby Dafydd Gruffudd Thomas, using a few Welsh names she'd heard from the locals. She assumed Owen would appreciate that. Once she was out of bed, she spent hours sitting beside his cradle and just staring at him. She couldn't believe that she'd made this little person. He sometimes screamed like a banshee when he was awake, but he slept peacefully, and Grace felt she could look at his face for days on end and still not see all of it. He had big blue eyes and soft baby features, but Grace thought something about his face reminded her of her father. And he had black hair and bright eyes like Owen's.

Grace loved this little person more than anything she'd ever loved anyone.

She'd opted to feed him herself instead of hiring a wet nurse. Some of the staff seemed judgmental about this, but Catrin came to Caer Newydd with a salve for Grace's aching nipples and helped Grace when she began to feel frustrated with the feeding process. And maybe it was improper for an aristocratic woman to feed and raise her own child, but Grace couldn't imagine surrendering care for her little son to anyone else. Catrin supported this decision and offered advice whenever Grace had a question. Gwen Williams chimed in with her own advice when she visited, as she'd reared a brood of her own and did not seem to think it odd that Grace wanted to be so near her child all the time.

Morfudd came to see the baby and declared that he looked just like some Thomas ancestor, and applauded Grace on her choice of names. Morfudd also brought little presents for the baby and she'd come across some little outfits that had belonged to Owen when he'd been a boy. Grace found it all quite darling and was grateful for Morfudd's company.

When at last Grace felt well enough to sit at a desk, she wrote letters to announce the birth to her parents and Penelope, but for some reason, she struggled with what to say to Owen. *I'm sorry I didn't mention this sooner? You have a son now?* She still had the unposted letter where she'd confessed everything, and now she went through three drafts before she settled on what she wanted to say, composing a heartfelt letter full of remorse about Dafydd. She intended to send them both. Then she took the letters downstairs to tell Iain, one of the footmen, to post it for her.

He looked at the letter and saw its destination, he said, "My lady, you may want to wait to post this."

"Why is that?"

"We've just received word that the earl is on his way to Wales. If you post this now, it will arrive in London after he arrives here."

Oh. Oh, no. Owen was headed here? Already?

How could she explain why she'd kept so much from him?

"Do you know when he left? When he is set to arrive?"

"The missive we just received suggested he'd be here in three days' time."

Grace nodded and thanked Iain. That gave her three days to figure out what she'd say.

Chapter Eighteen

OWEN'S FIRST GOAL was making certain that Grace was all right.

He hadn't thought this through entirely when he'd decided to leave London, but he'd had plenty of time to think along the way. If his fellow Lords were going to send troops to put down a rebellion rather than do anything to solve the cause of the rebellion, well, it was out of his hands. If the members of Parliament were going to treat him as an idealistic fool, then he didn't need to be there.

But he did need to be with his wife, because two weeks had gone by with no letters at all. In the eight months since he'd left Wales, he'd received a letter every week.

Once he saw her with his own eyes and verified that she was of sound mind and body, he would ask her about her pottery, and GM. Well, maybe not right away, but at dinner, they would discuss it. He spent most of the carriage ride concocting a polite way to bring up the questions he wanted answered.

It seemed a small problem in the scheme of things. She didn't owe him much, and he'd told her that before he'd returned to London. They intended to live separate lives. If his suspicions were accurate, he was disappointed that she hadn't told him, but he understood her reasoning. But the truth was that he wanted her to trust him, to care about him the way he was beginning to care about her.

Or, hell, the way he'd come to care for her in the weeks after their wedding. And he didn't think it was entirely sexual.

The thing was, the letters had changed everything. When he'd first committed to marrying Grace, they hadn't known each other, and it was easy to agree to live separate lives. But now that they did know each other—body, mind, and spirit, from Owen's perspective—he wanted to spend time with her. So he'd made plans to spend at least a month in Wales, exploring the intellectual connection they'd developed over their letters and to verify his hunch that the two of them could easily fall in love and have a true marriage.

He made the journey in four days, hastily writing letters to his various friends and colleagues in London and posting them along the way to explain his sudden absence. It was a lot of time in a coach, or on a horse when he got tired of just sitting, and he made his stops as short as possible. The members of his staff who had come along on this trip kept looking at him like he was crazy, but he had this burning need to get to Wales as quickly as possible.

At long last, his carriage rumbled up the drive at Caer Newydd. They should have known to expect him today, and a few staff members were standing in front of the house to receive him.

He alighted from the carriage and was met by Driscoll, the butler. He was conspicuously not greeted by Grace.

"Is the countess home?" Owen asked.

"She is, my lord. She has been a bit unwell, so she declined to step outside today, but you can find her in the parlor."

"Thank you."

"I will see to your things."

Owen didn't much care about his luggage. Grace was alive, at least, although he wondered what Davis meant by *unwell*. He wanted to run but held himself back. Instead, he walked straight to the parlor, knowing he probably smelled like horse and was covered in dust from the road. He just needed to set eyes on her as soon as possible.

Grace was in the process of standing when he walked into the parlor. God, she was a sight for sore eyes. She wore a simple muslin gown and her hair fell in loose waves around her shoulders, although she some hair pinned away from her face. It was clear she was not ready for visitors, but then, he was her husband. And if the staff knew to expect him, she must have, too.

"Owen," she said.

Something in him melted. He crossed the room and took her into his arms. "Grace. My goodness. I am very glad to see you."

"And I you." She let out a heavy sigh and put her arms around him.

They held each other like that for a long time. Owen stroked her hair. He was relieved to find her in one piece, and gratified that she was just as beautiful as he remembered, but the fear that she was still unwell tugged at him. He stepped back so he could look at her face more closely. She was a little pale but did not look sick. "Are you all right?"

"I am fine, my lord."

"Let us dispense with formalities, Grace. I have been worried for weeks. Your letters always arrive at a dependable interval and I had grown to look forward to them. But when I didn't receive any letters for two weeks in a row, I grew concerned. And I've been wanting to see you for months, if I'm to be honest, but business kept me in London. But that is not important, because you did not write me, and then Driscoll mentioned that you are unwell. What happened?"

"Oh. Yes, I was quite unable to write to you, and I apologize for that. I really should have, but by the time I felt strong enough to write a letter, we got word that you were on your way here so it hardly seemed worth it to… Oh, Owen, I have much to tell you."

"You were ill?"

"In a manner of speaking, yes. I had a bit of a scare. And I am still recovering. But I knew you were coming today, so I put the effort into being ready to greet you. I apologize for my appearance, but the last few weeks have been challenging."

"Do not trouble yourself on my account. I don't need to see you in fancy clothing to know how beautiful you are. I admit, I feared the worst, that some disease had claimed you and I would never see you again. You were ill in a manner of speaking? Were you injured?"

"Yes, you could say that. I will explain."

"No, wait. Let me just look at you for a moment."

She really was lovely. A flush came over her cheeks as she looked back at him with her sparkling blue eyes, and even dressed simply, she was gorgeous.

"I was so worried," he murmured. He put his hands on her face, needing to feel that she was still warm and alive.

"I missed you," she said.

He could wait no longer. He kissed her.

She put her hands on his shoulders and parted her lips and Owen dove in, needing not just to taste her again but to drink her up. He'd been starving for her, and terrified for weeks, and now she was here in his arms again, and she was alive and by the look of it, mostly well. She tasted like heaven, and she sighed into his mouth, as if she'd been waiting for this for as long as he had, like this kiss was for both of them like a cold drink on a hot day. Owen was happy and relieved and enormously glad he'd decided to come back to Wales.

"I am very glad to see you," she said, pulling away slightly. "But there is something I must tell you."

"All right. Tell me."

She opened her mouth and closed it again. "It's probably easier if I show you."

GRACE *WAS* ENORMOUSLY happy to see Owen. And she was glad

that he seemed so happy to see her, that he'd been worried about her when she hadn't been able to write. His presence here, his eagerness to see her, that all gave her hope. But she knew she was about to destroy all of that.

She led Owen upstairs, encountering Mary on the way. "How is Dafydd?" Grace asked.

"Still sleeping, my lady," Mary replied. "Did you need something?"

"No, Mary. I am taking the earl to our rooms now. You are dismissed unless I ring for you."

Mary curtsied. "Yes, my lady."

"Who is Dafydd?" Owen asked.

How could she ever explain? "Please have some patience with me," Grace said instead of explaining. "I should have written you sooner. I didn't because I knew you were busy in London and I didn't want to make you feel like you had to rush home. When I did finally write to tell you about everything, well, something interrupted, and when I went to post the letter, I got word you were already on your way here. Truly, I wanted to tell you about everything before you arrived home, but I ran out of time, and I do not have the words for how much I regret that." She didn't know what else to say. She hoped that the sight of Dafydd would make Owen understand, although she feared he wouldn't. Everything had seemed so abstract and unreal until Owen was standing before her, in the flesh.

He looked confused. "What is going on?"

Grace couldn't read Owen's tone. He didn't seem angry as such, but he was starting to act a little frustrated.

They arrived at the entrance of her bedchamber. "I've moved some furniture."

"I told you that you could."

"Yes, but the arrangement is…unorthodox. The staff think I've lost my marbles."

"Have you?"

"I do not believe so. It's just that this house is so big and…"

She knew she could postpone the inevitable no longer. "I understand that traditionally, the nursery is on the third floor, but I could not bear to be so far from him."

Owen's eyes grew wide. "The nursery?"

"Owen, you have a son."

That appeared to break something in him. He stared at her in disbelief for a long moment. "I…what?"

"It was a difficult labor and I have struggled a bit with recovery, but I am getting better by the day, and he's so perfect. I could not bear to be apart from him much, so I turned the lady's chamber into a nursery."

He closed his eyes and then stared at her again. "A son?"

"I had a baby three weeks ago, Owen. I know this must come as a shock. I knew you were busy in London and was reluctant to urge you to return home, but… I was wrong, Owen. It was a mistake not to tell you as soon as I knew myself."

"There's a baby?"

"He's asleep in here." She pointed to the door.

"Can I see him?"

"Of course." She held a finger up to her lips and opened the door.

She felt terrible, like she'd swallowed a rock and it was sitting in her stomach. Owen deserved to know about his son, and sooner than now. Her excuse, that he'd been busy with Parliament, felt weak now. If only she'd gotten that letter in the mail the day she wrote it! Likely Owen would not have made it to Wales sooner, since the baby had come early, but at least she wouldn't be surprising him like this.

Once the shock wore off, he would be upset with her, and she would have to live with that.

He followed her over to the crib, which she'd had the staff put at the foot of the bed. She'd slept in here with Dafydd the first few nights after his birth, but then she'd worried that if she made noise in the night she would wake him, so she moved to Owen's bed in the adjacent room but left the connecting doors open so that she could hear Dafydd if he cried.

Their son was asleep, but his lips were pursed and he made a sucking motion.

Owen looked into the crib and stood perfectly still for a long moment, just staring.

Grace couldn't tell if there was much family resemblance. Dafydd had a head of dark hair and a chin dimple like Owen's, but otherwise he mostly looked like a baby to Grace. He *was* beautiful, though, and he was *hers* and she was fiercely protective of him, to the point where everyone thought she was mad.

"My son," Owen whispered.

"Dafydd Gruffud."

Owen put a hand over his mouth. "That is perfect."

By Grace's calculation, Dafydd had been asleep for nearly three hours and was about due to wake up, but she didn't want to disturb him. Catrin's advice had been to rest whenever the baby was resting, which had been sound so far.

But, perhaps sensing his parents were staring at him, Dafydd stirred.

Remarkably, he did not cry. He looked up at Grace and moved his arms around. She wondered what he was thinking, if his little baby brain even understood.

She reached into the crib and scooped him up.

"Hello, baby," she said to him. She rocked him in his arms a little. "Do you want to meet your papa?" She looked up at Owen. "Do you want to hold him?"

"Can I? I've never held a baby before."

"A lot of it comes by instinct. Just make sure you hold his head carefully. Like this." She held up Dafydd to show Owen how to hold him.

Owen held his arms out, so Grace placed the baby in them.

Dafydd just stared at his father for a long moment.

"I can't believe it," Owen said.

"He's very handsome, don't you think? Just like his papa."

"Yes. A very handsome boy. And everything is all right with

him? He has all his fingers and toes?"

"Yes. He's perfect, Owen. That is, he does not do much at this stage of life. He mostly cries, sleeps, eats, and fills his nappies. But every day I look at him and I'm amazed."

As if understanding that he was not fulfilling his assignment, Dafydd began to cry.

"What do I do?" Owen asked.

Grace took the baby back. She rocked and soothed him and he began to calm back down.

"Did you just need your mum?" she asked Dafydd.

"Is there a nurse? Or a nanny?" Owen asked.

"No. I have interviewed a few candidates, but haven't found one I like yet. I've been feeding him myself."

"That is unorthodox."

"So everyone says. I will hire a nanny, once I find one I trust. In the meantime, I am his mother, and I should be able to take care of him."

"Of course."

Dafydd calmed and drifted back to sleep. Grace placed him carefully back into his crib.

"You should know, though," Grace said. "The labor was quite difficult. I lost consciousness for a while, due to lack of blood."

Owen's mouth fell open. "That is... Thank God you are all right now."

Grace walked toward the master's bedroom and through the room that connected them. Owen followed.

"He was born here," Grace said. "I had to replace the mattress and bedding."

"Oh. Oh, Grace. I'm so sorry that I was not here."

"I didn't tell you. I should have told you."

"Have you been abed these last three weeks?"

"Not entirely, but a lot of the time. My friends and the staff have been helping. I sent them away today because I knew you were coming and I wanted to see you alone."

"This Catrin woman you wrote me about?"

"She has several children of her own. She helped me a great deal when Dafydd was first born. And Morfudd and Gwen Williams have been here too to look after him so I could sleep. And Mary, my maid, she's helped a great deal, too. You should give her a raise."

"I will," said Owen. "You've been taking care of Dafydd by yourself?"

She nodded. "I will hire a nurse. It's just hard. I don't know how noblewomen leave their children in nurseries on distant floors, to be taken care of by strangers and then just go back to their lives like nothing significant has changed. I love him so much, Owen. I struggle to be apart from him."

Owen put an arm around her and kissed the top of her head. "You should raise him however you see fit. But if you are still recovering, you should perhaps get some help. I can afford to hire help."

"I'm so sorry, Owen."

"I know. And I am quite shocked, so I may have more to say on this later, but… I am just glad you are all right. That you both are."

"I can sleep in my own room tonight so that you can have the bed."

"It's all right. If you are sleeping here and do not mind a large earl taking up part of the bed, there is no need to sleep elsewhere."

"I do not mind, but I cannot… That is, I am still recovering and a bit sore, so I won't be able to…"

"It is all right. I will make no demands of you."

That was a relief. "I am glad to see you," she said.

Chapter Nineteen

OF ALL THINGS, a baby was not among the things Owen suspected.

He hated himself a little for immediately wondering about the boy's parentage. But he'd done the math, and it made sense for Dafydd to have been conceived when Owen and Grace had first arrived in Wales. Also, the poor boy looked like Owen's uncle Edmund, so it was hard to deny a family resemblance. The dark hair, the chin cleft, those were distinct Thomas traits.

And now he had a son. He didn't think this would ever stop being startling news.

Dafydd Gruffudd Thomas was a fitting Welsh name for a Welsh boy. Technically, he was Baron Conwy, the courtesy title of the eldest son of the Earl of Caernarfon, but Owen would wait to break that news until a time when Grace looked less exhausted.

They had dinner together, and Grace struggled to hold up her end of the conversation, because she couldn't seem to stay awake. Owen made a note to ride out tomorrow to speak to the doctor to find out how Grace's recovery was going, although maybe Grace didn't want him to do that. There were a hundred things he wanted to do to adjust to the news, but he didn't know if any of them were appropriate, and suddenly he found himself at an impasse.

He felt like he'd arrived back at a strange house.

Grace had, of course, made some changes. She'd rearranged the furniture in both bedrooms. She'd taken down old art and put up new. She'd replaced the sofas in the lounge and bought new chairs for the parlor. But that was all cosmetic.

He was a different person. He was a father now. He had this little family that he was responsible for. And he was determined to do right by them. He knew nothing about babies, so he'd have to learn quickly, but he could defer to Grace on that. She seemed to know what to do with Dafydd.

And under all that…he was deeply hurt that she hadn't told him.

He would have come, had she asked. If she'd told him she was expecting, he would have gotten in a carriage immediately and come to her. He wished he could have been here for the birth, so he could have been here for Grace when she struggled. So he could have taken care of his son. Forget Parliament; this was more important. And she seemed to know that, meaning she'd deliberately withheld this information. She wrote to him weekly, after all. Had it truly never occurred to her to mention it? That seemed impossible.

He sent Grace to bed when it was clear that she wasn't so much eating as dozing off. She put up a mild protest, but seemed relieved when he told her to go to sleep.

After dinner, he tracked down Mary. "May I ask you a few questions?"

"Of course, my lord."

"I'm worried about the countess. She said her labor was difficult. Were you here for it?"

"I was, my lord."

"Tell me what happened."

"Well, my lord, I do not know exactly, but there was a lot of blood. Some blood is normal, but this was more than with my own children. The countess was in some distress. Shortly after Master Dafydd was born, she lost consciousness, and it took quite a while to revive her. She was weak. She needed a few stitches."

"Oh, goodness."

"She came round, but we were quite worried. The doctor told her to rest as much as possible and for us to make sure she was eating. So I've been seeing to her meals. But she rises at all times of the night to comfort the baby, and she seems very tired a lot of the time."

"She needs some help, would you agree?"

"She's interviewed five different candidates for nurse and found them all wanting. But yes, I would say she could use some help. She gets better each day, and she is putting on a strong face, but she's still very tired." Mary looked up and met Owen's gaze. "I am glad you are here, my lord. I think she needs you."

"She did not tell me."

"Did not tell you what?"

"That we were to have a baby. I did not know until I arrived here. I hope you know, I would have come—"

"I have no doubt, my lord. The countess kept saying she didn't want to take you away from Parliament business, and I imagine she thought she was doing what she thought was best. Perhaps she did not know how much she would need you until the baby came. These last three weeks have been difficult, my lord."

"I hope they get better, starting now."

Owen went to the kitchen next and asked the cook for a tray he could bring up to Grace to make sure she ate a little more when she woke up. The sun had barely set, but his journey here had been grueling and he was tired, too.

He found her sound asleep in their bed. And it was *their* bed. He placed the tray on the side table and then adjusted the blankets around her. She looked peaceful and beautiful and his chest hurt when he thought of the pain she must have gone through. He, of course, knew the mechanics of how babies were born, but he'd never had to think much about it before. He hadn't known it would be so difficult on a mother, although looking at how big Dafydd was and Grace's small frame, he shouldn't have been surprised that it had been such a struggle.

Why hadn't she told him?

The question burned, and he didn't know what to do with the pain, because he didn't want to put it on Grace. She'd suffered enough. But he'd thought they'd grown close enough to be honest with each other, and yet there was a lot that Grace had withheld from him. Her art, the baby—what else?

Owen went to his dressing room, where his valet had already hung all his clothes. He'd changed for dinner, mostly to get out of his traveling clothes, but he'd dismissed his valet because he just wanted to be alone with Grace.

And their son. Owen pulled on a nightshirt and then peeked into Grace's bedchamber. Dafydd was asleep in the crib. Owen made himself leave so he didn't wake the boy, but he wanted to just sit and stare at him. He didn't think he'd ever get enough of looking at his son.

He pulled on a dressing gown and walked into his bedroom. He thought about walking to the library to fetch something to read until he felt asleep, but then Dafydd began to cry.

Grace woke up with a jolt. She looked around and spotted Owen.

"Oh."

"I was about to follow you to dreamland," he said. "Do you want me to fetch him?" He gestured toward the other room.

"Oh. Yes, that would be nice. Can you bring him here?"

Owen went back into the other bedchamber and picked up the writing child. He did seem quite upset.

"This is no way for a gentleman to behave," Owen said, rocking him gently. "Your poor mother needs her sleep, and little boys should always respect their mothers."

Owen brought the crying baby to Grace, who held her arms out. While Owen had been in the adjacent room, Grace had undone the buttons of her nightgown. She took the baby now and brought him to her breast.

Owen was fairly certain his own mother had not fed him this

way, as most aristocratic women didn't, but he marveled that Grace was doing it. As she fed Dafydd, he climbed into bed beside her and looked over her shoulder at the baby.

"I brought you some food," he said softly. "You didn't eat much at dinner and I thought you might get hungry. Mary said the doctor said you needed to eat in order to recover. It's not much. Some cured meat, a little cheese, some bread."

"That sounds lovely. Thank you, Owen."

"I want to help you. You've said these last weeks have been difficult. Please tell me if there is anything I can do."

"I will," she said.

"Does that hurt?" He gestured to Dafydd.

"Not much. My skin is a little irritated, but Catrin gave me a salve that helps." She looked up at Owen. "He's a healthy boy. He likes to eat. The doctor said he was a large baby, which I suppose explains what happened."

"I wish it had been less hard on you. Were you sick throughout your confinement? My friend Hugh's wife felt unwell through much of hers."

"No. Well, yes, at first. I got dizzy and nauseous. But then it was all right. It was very strange. I could feel him move around in me. I liked that part. And I was not much confined. I walked around the property. I went to the cottage until my belly was too big to reach my pottery wheel."

Owen kissed her temple. "You astonish me." It was true. He couldn't believe the delicate woman he'd married had done all that.

When Grace had finished feeding Dafydd, and he'd drifted back to sleep, Owen carried the boy back to his crib and settled him in. When he returned to the bedroom, Grace was eating the food he'd brought up.

"Thank you for this," she said.

"I can find somewhere else to sleep if this is too much for you."

"It is fine. I did miss you, Owen. And having someone to

fetch the baby for me is a big help. I'm so tired."

"No wonder. You made a person."

She smiled at that. "I am glad to see you, but as soon as I finish this, I am going back to sleep."

Owen hung his dressing gown on the hook next to the bed and slid under the sheets with her. He wanted to hold her but didn't want to bother any of her injuries. Instead, he stayed on his side of the bed and watched her.

"If you need something," Owen said softly, "you'll tell me, right?"

"I will try," she said, which wasn't much of a promise.

GRACE KNEW OWEN was upset.

And she knew it was her fault.

After the first day of his return, perhaps after the initial euphoria of seeing each other again had passed, Owen had acted cool toward Grace. He was kind and polite, but he hadn't really touched her or said much.

On the fourth day, Catrin called. Owen was out touring the estate with his man of business and was not in the house when Catrin arrived, so Grace invited her friend to sit in the parlor with her.

"I've made a terrible hash of things," Grace told her after they were served tea.

"Oh, sweetness. What happened?"

"The earl is here. Well, not here in the house right now. He is off on an errand. But he is here in Wales. And the letter I wrote to tell him about the baby didn't make it into the post before he returned. I believe he is angry with me about it, but he's being very odd. He has not yelled or criticized me. Instead he is just…well, ignoring me."

"You've shocked him."

"Yes, and I've apologized several times. But I fear he may not forgive me."

"But you want him to."

"Yes. I regret not telling him about the baby more than I regret anything I've ever done in my life. I was so happy when he arrived home. I've missed him. But now that he's here, he barely looks at me. Which perhaps I deserve. But I want to fix it."

"You must speak with him. Confess how you feel. Grovel a little. He may come around."

Grace wasn't sure he would.

"You are actually fond of your husband," Catrin said. It wasn't a question.

"I am. We've been exchanging letters for months. He's clever and passionate about his work. That was why I put off telling him about Dafydd. I didn't want to take him away from his responsibilities. What he was doing seemed important."

But was that really true? Grace had been telling herself that for months. But she also had to admit that she wanted her independence. And if Owen came back because of the baby, that would change.

After all, she'd been the one who insisted on moving to Wales and staying here, she was the one who wanted to live in the country and have independence. She'd wanted to make her pottery, she'd wanted to leave London. That had been the *plan*, the reason she'd agreed to marry Owen.

Only none of this had gone the way she'd expected. She'd become used to being alone when she still lived with her parents. Her sister was much younger than she was and they barely interacted. Her father was never home and Grace thanked God daily that her mother considered herself too aristocratic to bother spending time with her children. Grace had assumed that being alone was what she wanted, in part because it was what she'd always known.

But spending time in Wales had corrected that misunderstanding. She had friends here, a surrogate family, people who checked on her to make sure she was all right, who kept her company when she was struggling and brought her treats and made her laugh just because she they were friends.

On top of that, she'd grown to actually like Owen. And the more they corresponded, the more she missed him and wanted him to be here in Wales with her.

That was the opposite of what they'd agreed to.

He'd told her that he felt the same way. Maybe she'd have to remind him why he liked her to begin with.

"Can I ask you a personal question?" Grace asked.

"Anything, dear."

"How long after you had each of your children did you wait before you...had marital relations again."

"Using your feminine wiles, eh?" Catrin winked.

"I am considering it." Not that Grace thought it would solve the problem, but she did want to lie with Owen again and she thought it might help bring them closer together. Assuming he ever spoke to her again.

"About a month, I believe. But in your case? You should wait until you feel fully healed. The births of my children were not nearly so...violent. If I were you, I would ask your doctor."

Grace's face flooded with heat. "I could not possibly tell my doctor I want to...you know...with my husband."

"Why not? Is not the purpose of marriage to make heirs, especially if one has a title to pass on? The doctor will understand. He knows what married people do."

Grace let out a breath. This was bothersome. She did not think she could broach the topic of...marital relations...with the doctor, nor did she feel fully healed. She wasn't sore anymore, but she still felt weak and fragile, something she absolutely loathed. One of the things she liked about her independence was that no one ever treated her like she was stupid or breakable. The people she surrounded herself with here in Wales all treated her like a peer, like someone who was strong and knew her own mind, and Grace appreciated that. But for the last few months,

Grace had felt not at all like herself, and she didn't know how to get her strength back.

Catrin frowned at her. "I know this situation with your husband troubles you, but it is also worth considering… That is, I have heard of cases in which women who have just had babies feel unbearably sad or fretful. I believe it is quite normal."

Grace shook her head. She wasn't sad, exactly, just…not herself. "Did you experience that?"

"No, but that does not mean there is anything wrong with you if you do."

Grace took a deep breath. "I love my son. He makes me happy. I think once I make things right with my husband, I will feel a lot better. I just need to figure out how to do that."

Catrin nodded. "Have a frank conversation. Apologize."

"Yes."

Grace changed the subject to pottery, and Catrin told a story about something one of her sons got into the other day, but Grace was only half listening.

Then Owen came home.

Grace could hear the commotion when Owen entered the house, and his voice drifted down the hall as he spoke with Driscoll or whoever had greeted him at the door. Driscoll must have directed him down the hall, because suddenly Owen was in the doorway.

Catrin shot to her feet, so Grace stood as well.

Formally, she said, "My lord, let me present my friend, Catrin Davies. Catrin, may I introduce you to my husband, the Earl of Caernarfon."

Owen strode into the room. "We need not be so formal. I usually go by Caernarfon or Owen."

"I go by Catrin, if that was not clear."

As he was clearly trained, he took Catrin's hand and kissed her knuckles. "It is nice to finally meet you. Grace has spoken of you a great deal."

"All good things, I hope."

"Yes, of course. She speaks highly of you. I appreciate that you've been a friend to her while I've been London."

"It has been my pleasure."

"Well. I merely wanted to drop in to say hello. I have some things to attend to. I shall leave you ladies to your tea. Are you staying for dinner, Catrin?"

"No, I must attend to my own brood."

"Of course. Well, I'll be off. Enjoy yourselves."

"Thank you, Owen," said Grace.

He nodded and left.

Grace sat back down and took a fortifying sip of tea.

"Well," said Catrin, retaking her own seat. "I can certainly see why you'd want to resume marital relations."

"Catrin!"

"He's very handsome, your husband. He has some charm."

"You sound surprised."

"I suppose I expected someone older. I met the previous earl a time or two, and he was elderly when he passed, so I assumed his son would be older, but he is not much older than you are."

"No."

"Men do tend to take their time getting ready for marriage, whereas we ladies are often pushed out of our homes before we turn twenty."

"Yes, well. I was a bit on the shelf because of a betrothal that was never going to end in marriage."

"Yes, you've told me this story. And look where you are now!"

"With a husband who can barely stand to look at me."

"I think he will come around. Give him some time."

"You just met him. You cannot possibly know how this will go."

Catrin shrugged. "I have a good feeling about him."

After Catrin left, Grace climbed the stairs to check on Dafydd. She was surprised to find the door to her bedchamber open ajar. She opened it slightly farther so she could see what was happening.

Owen sat on the bed with Dafydd in his lap. The two of them were looking intently at each other, and Owen was speaking so softly, Grace couldn't hear him.

She felt her heart squeeze. Here was Owen interacting with his son, which most aristocratic fathers would not have done. Grace was moved that Owen would take the time. Tears stung her eyes, as they had so often since Dafydd's birth. Her midwife had told her to expect this, but she still hated how little control she had over her emotions.

She must have made a sound, because Owen's head suddenly jerked toward her.

"Grace," he said softly.

"Sorry, I did not mean to interrupt. Catrin just left and I wanted to check on Dafydd."

"I was just—"

"There's no need to explain." She walked into the room. "You should spend time with him. Talk to him. I love that you are doing that."

Owen's expression softened. "Are you crying?"

She wiped at her eyes. "I do a lot of crying these days. I feel sometimes like my body is not my own again yet."

Owen cradled the baby in his arms. "I cannot imagine what that must have been like." He looked down at Dafydd. "He is a good-looking little man, I can say that much."

"He must feel safe with you." She gestured at Dafydd's face. He was struggling to keep his eyes open as he snuggled against his father's chest.

"I want him to feel safe with me. I was trying to get him used to the sound of my voice. I do not know how much babies understand."

"I likely know little more about babies than you do. A lot of the time, I am just guessing. But I think familiarity probably helps. If he recognizes your face and understands you will not harm him, he will learn to trust you. But I am just guessing."

"But you had three weeks more than I did. You should give yourself more credit. You likely understand more than you think"

There was no animosity in his voice, but Grace knew he was still upset.

"We should talk," she said.

"Yes, but not right now. Let us not disturb him."

She nodded and sat next to Owen on the bed.

She wanted to tell him everything. How much she regretted not being completely honest with him. How much the distance he put between them was killing her. How much she wanted the magic of their honeymoon back, the promise of that kiss he had given her when he'd first arrived home. She wanted to give him time to decide how he felt about everything, but she wanted him back, too.

But not right now.

"I think I may need to lay down for a little before dinner," she said, standing back up. "He's asleep now. If you leave him in the crib, I will hear him if he wakes up."

"All right. I'll put him in there in a few minutes. I just want to hold him a little longer."

"Take your time." Grace smiled at him. She was suddenly very tired. She left the room before she started crying again.

Chapter Twenty

ABOUT A WEEK after Owen returned home, as they had dinner, Grace asked him when he planned to return to London.

"I have not given it much thought yet. I had thought to stay here at least a month, but I have no specific need to go back."

That was something. At least he was not in a hurry to leave.

"I think we need to talk."

Owen nodded. "I've never found myself in a situation like this. That is, I have quarreled with my family before, but I am having a hard time deciding what to do here."

She considered asking him to clarify, but of course she knew. Still, she said, "We are not exactly fighting."

"No, I suppose not. There has been no shouting or exchanging of course words. But I find I am… I don't know how to express what I am feeling. Disappointed. Sad. Angry."

"I know."

"I don't know how to act around you, Grace. I thought I understood something about our relationship. But you kept things from me and now I feel like I hardly know you. I don't understand anything."

She nodded, because of course she knew that. "I am genuinely sorry. I should have told you about everything sooner. I regret that I didn't. I thought… This is not an excuse, but I thought I had more time. And from the beginning I wanted to be independent."

"Independent. So had I not come home, I might never have known about Dafydd."

"No. I wrote a letter. It didn't get it posted in time. The baby came early."

Owen frowned. "Independence is one thing, Grace. We had an agreement. You wanted privacy and distance from London and I gave you that. But I also thought we were growing closer through our letters. I told you everything that was happening with me in London. About what my friends were doing, about what I was working on in Parliament. I left little out. I thought you were communicating with me using the same level of honesty. I thought we were beginning to truly get to know each other through our letters. But it turns out you withheld some very large things from me."

"Yes."

"He's *my* son, too."

"Of course, Owen."

"Many noble marriages are mere formalities."

"I didn't think *ours* was. We… I enjoyed our honeymoon, and our letters back and forth."

"Yes. I have never been anything but completely honest with you. But there's so much you didn't tell me in those letters. I thought I understood our relationship, but it was all lies."

"I *never* lied to you, Owen."

Owen looked directly at her. "But what I knew two weeks ago about my relationship with you… That was not true. And a lie by omission is still a lie. And this was such a big thing. I hope you know, I would have been at your side as soon as feasibly possible had I known. I thought we cared about each other, but you didn't care enough to tell me."

Grace knew exactly why he was upset. She didn't need him to explain it to her. "I wanted to tell you. I wrote a letter to tell you everything, but the baby came early and then you arrived home before I could post it."

"That doesn't do me much good now." Owen looked down

at his plate. He hadn't really eaten anything so much as pushed his food around. "Are you Gerard Makepeace?"

That was not what she expected to say. She was so surprised she dropped her fork. "How did you—?"

"Answer the question, Grace."

"Yes." But she had no earthly idea how Owen would have known that. "I meant to tell you that, too."

"But you didn't." Owen gave up pretending to eat and put his fork down. "It was Beresford and that vase you sent me. He saw it and thought it was a Makepeace, and at first I thought that was ridiculous, but I looked into it. I went to the shop in London that sells your work, and there were definite similarities between those pieces and the one you sent me. The mark on the bottom, the initials GM? Gerard Makepeace. Grace Midwood. Your scheme only works because most people don't assume a woman is capable of the kind of art you make, which is a foolish assumption because those vases are beautiful. And I can understand why you didn't tell me. I'm not knowledgeable about art, so if it had not been for Beresford, I never would have even guessed. And a male artist is taken more seriously. I have no doubt that, if your dealer in London knew you were a woman, he wouldn't be selling your pottery. And, as you say, you wanted your independence."

"I still should have told you. I know that."

He nodded. "I spent the entire trip here intending to confront you about Makepeace and the vases and intending to forgive you. When we parted all those months ago, I didn't feel we owed each other much. You asked for your independence and I gave it to you. Hell, I gave you permission to redecorate my houses. And you did a marvelous job! This… I understand why you kept up the ruse. You want to be taken seriously as an artist. You didn't know if you could trust me at first."

"Yes," Grace said hesitantly.

"Yes. The thing is, I thought we were growing closer. I thought we were sharing secrets in our letters. I told you things I haven't told my friends. But you didn't tell me about Dafydd or the pottery and now I find myself wondering what else you haven't told me."

"Those are all my secrets." Grace could not have felt worse. Owen was, of course, completely correct. There was no reason he should believe her. "I promise they are."

"I want to believe you, but I don't know how I can trust you now. Not when you've withheld so much." Owen dropped his head and rubbed his forehead. Then he looked up at her. "The worst part about this is that I thought we had something that we clearly don't. I rushed home because I was worried about you, because I've come to care about you a great deal, but I suppose that was one-sided."

"Owen, it—"

"I already know what you will say, and I want to believe it, but I don't right now. I don't know how you can earn my trust back, but I think you must if this is going to be anything but a marriage in name only."

Then he stood and left the room.

Grace cried, because of course she did. But she had no idea how to fix this. Owen was upset and it was her fault. He was right, they had grown closer through their letters, but she'd made a terrible mistake in withholding things from him. How could she ever convince him to trust her again?

Chapter Twenty-One

A NTHONY FOUND LARK at home, in his study, reading from a stack of letters he'd received in the last week.

Lark motioned for Anthony to sit without looking away from what he was reading.

"You summoned me," Anthony said, opting not to take a seat. "I am here at your request and yet you leave me waiting."

Lark held up the letter he'd been reading. "Apologies, but this was interesting. We've solved one mystery. Caernarfon has become a father."

"What?"

"You'll recall that he was distraught he had not received a letter from his wife in a fortnight and so ran off to Wales to make sure she was still alive. According to his letter, she's fine, but gave birth and had a difficult labor from which she needed time to recover, so she was unable to write him. He seems a little peeved that she did not tell him she was expecting. But now he has a son with some Welsh name I do not know how to say. Duh-fidd?"

"More like Da-vith, I think. The Welsh form of David."

"Hmm. Well, anyway, that's two of my friends who have families now."

"To be fair, Caernarfon started a family the moment he got married. Once you are responsible for someone other than yourself, you have a family."

Lark tilted his head. "That is an interesting definition."

Anthony shrugged and sat in the wingback chair near Lark's desk. The truth, though, was that he had given this a lot of thought. In a way, he was responsible for Lark's happiness and well-being, which made Lark his family. They'd never stand in front of a priest and promise to obey each other. They'd never have children together, nor did Anthony want to raise children. But that didn't mean they couldn't be a family together. Perhaps, instead of a child, they could acquire a dog. Or five.

"Not that I am not delighted to see you, but your note said it was important. What is happening?"

"You don't find it odd that Caernarfon's wife didn't tell him he had a son? Or that one was on the way?"

"Larkin. You are stalling."

"Something happened."

A deep sense of foreboding settled over Anthony. Something about Lark's face told him it was bad. "What happened?"

"Samuel Gordon."

Anthony swore.

"It's good news and bad news," Lark said. "Gordon approached me a few nights ago. He threatened to expose us."

Anthony sat forward. "What? How? And where were you?"

"At the club, with Hugh and Fletcher. I got up to use the necessary and he cornered me."

"What does he think he knows?"

Lark let out a breath. "He *thought* he knew that you and I were having an affair. He threatened to take it to a scandal sheet if I did not pay him a very large sum of money."

"Did you pay it?"

"I didn't have to."

Anthony tilted his head. "Why? What happened to—"

"He was hit by a carriage yesterday."

"He...what?"

Lark sighed and set the letter from Owen aside. "Obviously I don't wish Samuel Gordon ill."

A lie, Anthony knew. "Obviously."

"I was prepared to pay him, although I was reluctant to do so because I didn't think this would make him go away. He would just continue to extort me. But I thought paying him would buy us some time until we could come up with a more permanent solution. But Fate took care of that for me."

"He was hit by a carriage?"

"Got rip-roaring drunk last night, stumbled into the street, met his end."

"So he's dead."

"Alas, yes. It was in the *Times* this morning. You didn't read it?"

Anthony waved his hand. "I didn't read the paper today."

"The thing is, I don't think Gordon was the only one who knew about us."

"How did he find out? Did he tell you when he confronted you before meeting his untimely end?"

"Not specifically, but he implied he'd seen us somewhere."

"That doesn't narrow it down much."

"Anthony."

"Around the club?"

"Probably one of the times you pulled me into the coat closet."

Anthony sighed. It was true, they had not been the most discreet, especially at the club. They'd fooled around in that coat closet more than once. If someone had walked in when they'd been too occupied by what they were doing to notice, the information might have gotten out. "Do you think others know?"

"That is why I called you here."

"You think they do?"

"I don't honestly know. But if Gordon knew, it's not completely out of the realm of possibility that others do as well."

Anthony feared where this was going. "Have you heard something?"

"No. But Anthony, the Season is nearly upon us."

"Yes."

Lark frowned. "I don't want to have this conversation."

"I gathered."

"The thing is, you promised your mother you'd find a wife by the end of this Season."

This again. "I did."

"And I'm sure a year ago, the end of this Season seemed impossibly far away, but here it is, and I just think…"

Anthony's stomach sank. He knew exactly what Lark was going to say. "Don't say it."

"Anthony."

"I made a promise I never intended to keep to my mother."

"No. You made a promise you intended to keep but didn't want to follow through on." Lark frowned. "Anthony, I love you, but one of your chief flaws is that you never think things through. You never think long-term. You like instant gratification. Which means you and I have been postponing the inevitable because it feels good and we're fond of each other. But you have an obligation to follow through with the promise you made to your mother, no matter how loath you are to do it. And we are on the verge of getting caught."

"You want to end our affair."

"I don't *want* to. I just think it's the best course of action to secure our futures. You and I both knew this couldn't last forever. It's bad enough that we'll have to find wives eventually. I know you imagined you'd put in a token effort to court a few women and then find all of the young misses of the *ton* to be wanting. I know that was your plan. And I know you think that you and I could just keep carrying on forever, as if the Samuel Gordons of the world finding out about us wouldn't put both of our necks at the wrong end of a noose."

"You have no intention of marrying, though."

"I don't know what I want anymore. Perhaps my friends settling down has made me more circumspect. Marriage has not been a priority for me, but unlike you, I do find women appealing, and I could do right by a wife, if needed."

"Yes, but isn't that all the more reason for me not to go through with it? I have no interest in women. I'm not even sure I could father the grandchildren my mother so desperately craves." Anthony felt desperate to persuade Lark, and he'd been rehearsing his argument for weeks knowing this conversation was coming. He'd hoped that Lark's love for him would postpone this situation or make Lark set it aside, but here they were.

"You must try," Lark said.

"But why? Why should I not lead the life I want? Why should I put some woman in the untenable position of being the wife of a man who cannot love her? This is the whole reason I did not marry the Countess of Caernarfon. She was saved by Caernarfon and her own wit and beauty, but as beautiful as she is, I never desired her. I'm not built that way. I don't know how to be a husband and father, nor do I want to be. I've never wanted children. I should not have made the promise to my mother. I will find a way to get out of it. Just…please, Lark. I love you. Don't leave me."

"I have to." Lark's voice was watery with emotion. "I have to let you go. It's too dangerous for us to stay together. For both our sakes, I believe at least one of us must marry. That may have to be me. I don't like it, but what choice do we have?"

"We have a choice!" Anthony shouted. He stood up. "There's always a choice. I've been selfish insisting we stay in London. I'd rather give up the city than give up you. You want to find a house in the country where we can live together and raise sheep or dogs or horses or whatever you want? We should do that. This cannot possibly mean the end of us."

Lark stood as well. "I do appreciate that you are not insisting you can marry and still see me, because you don't want to do that to your future wife. You're a good man, Anthony. Which is how I know you will ultimately do the right thing. You know as well as I do how impossible our relationship is."

Anthony did know. He knew he was blessed that their friends accepted them but he resented that he and Lark had to keep their relationship a secret otherwise. He knew Lark was right that they'd be hanged if another Samuel Gordon discovered them, and he knew he'd been trying his luck with Lark in public. His title and his status only got him so far, especially since he knew much of the *ton* thought he was frivolous. Lark had a better reputation, was well respected, and did not deserve to have Anthony bring him down.

"I don't want to end this," Anthony said.

"I know," Lark said, taking a step toward him. "When we first started fooling around, I never expected to feel this way."

"Why did we start this, then?"

"Because I thought you were unspeakably beautiful. I still think that. And I loved gossiping with you. Discovering that you have hidden depths, that you have an essential goodness to you, that was a pleasant surprise. Spending time with you has made my life better. But we can't carry on as we have. You made a promise."

"Did I not make a promise to you?"

"No. How could you? We cannot marry each other. We cannot stand at the front of a church and promise to love each other forever. We had almost two years together, and I am grateful for that time. I had no notion this would last so long. But we both know it has to end."

Lark stood about a foot away from Anthony now, so Anthony closed the distance between them by putting his hands on Lark's beautiful face and then pressing their lips together. Lark returned the kiss, closing his eyes and sinking into Anthony. He put a hand on Anthony's arm.

Lark pulled away. He was openly crying now. "This will only get harder, the longer we postpone the end."

"So don't end it."

"Anthony."

Anthony dropped his forehead to touch Lark's. "I know." He did know, and it ripped him apart. He wanted to stay with Lark more than he wanted his next breath, but he knew Lark was right, that they couldn't keep carrying on as they were.

He hugged Lark close. If this had to end, then Anthony would get his fill now. He would hold Lark for the last time, and he would make it mean something.

"Being with you has changed my life," Anthony said. "I did not know I was capable of loving anyone as much as I love you."

"You'll find love again."

"I doubt it."

"I want you to live. It would kill me if they hanged you. And you don't want to disappoint your mother. It's safer for us both if you follow through with your promise."

"I will miss you tremendously."

Lark sniffed. "I will miss you as well. But this is for the best. I know it doesn't seem that way, but—"

"I hate it when you're right."

Lark laughed softly, but it sounded like a sob. "Precisely. Lean into that hatred. It may be the only way to get through this."

"What do we do if we run into each other at the club?"

"We say hello. We are polite to each other. But we cannot be together the way we were."

Anthony hugged Lark again. "I will be miserable without you."

"I shall feel the same, but I cannot find a way out of this."

Anthony kissed Lark again, then gently withdrew. "All right. I will follow your wishes for now. But this is not over, Larkin Woodville. Our story cannot end this way."

"I don't see how else it can end."

Anthony felt tears sting his eyes, too. He rubbed at them. "Then good-bye for now, Lark. But not good-bye forever."

Anthony had to take himself out of Lark's house. Lark squeezed his hand, but then he let go, and Anthony knew this was the end of the conversation.

For now. As he walked out of Lark's house and rubbed at his face so it didn't look like he'd been upset, he vowed to find a way to balance all of the parts of his life. He had no idea how to be with Lark and also adhere to his mother's wishes. Those two things were completely incompatible, but Anthony would figure out a way to make it all work. He had to.

Chapter Twenty-Two

GRACE'S REMORSE WAS palpable.

It had Owen tangled in knots. At night, they still shared a bed—although it wasn't unusual to find Grace asleep in the adjacent room, next to the baby, in the morning—but they avoided each other during the day. Partly, Grace was tired and wanted to stay near the baby, and partly, Owen had a lot of business away from the house, especially now that Grace was less able to run the estate. But there was a distance between them that Owen didn't like and didn't know how to close, an impasse Owen couldn't figure out his way through.

On a warm morning, toward the end of the summer, they had breakfast together in the morning room, and Grace handed him a couple of envelopes.

"What are these?" Owen asked.

"The letters I wrote you that I could not post before Dafydd was born. I want you to read them."

Owen stared at the envelopes. Each had his address in London neatly printed on them. "I will," he said.

"The doctor is coming today to see about my recovery," Grace said.

"Good." Owen slid the letters into the inside pocket of his jacket. "I will read these later."

"All right."

Owen polished off his breakfast and left the room.

He decided to make himself scarce while Grace visited with her doctor. He had no particular business today, so he got on his horse, Glyndwr, and decided to ride out to the castle. On the way, he mulled over this tangle. On the one hand, he knew Grace was sorry. On the other, he didn't know how he could trust her again. And he couldn't figure out a way back from that.

After securing his horse in the stables near the castle, he found Morfudd overseeing some work on the exterior, where some old stones looked to be crumbling.

"Ah, Owen. What a pleasure to see you! I heard a rumor you had returned to our ancestral homeland."

"I apologize for not coming to see you sooner," he said, leaning over to give Morfudd a kiss on the cheek. "My wife did an admirable job with the estate in my absence, but I had some odds and ends to attend to. And, as I'm sure you know, she has not been feeling well."

"I'm sure you also spent some time with that adorable baby."

"Yes, that as well."

"I was about to stop for luncheon. Would you care to eat with me?"

"I'd love to."

When she worked on the castle, Morfudd often stayed in rooms in a squat, three-story building across the street from the castle that had been owned by her late husband. The first floor was taken up by a shop from which Morfudd sold trinkets to castle visitors. She led Owen to her flat above the shop and then went about putting some water on to boil. "I'll make tea," she announced.

"All right."

"Are you hungry?"

"I suppose a little. You promised luncheon." Although, truth be told, Owen hadn't eaten much lately. He'd felt sick to his stomach since he and Grace had talked a few nights before, since he realized he didn't trust her anymore. That was the crux of their current woes.

Morfudd produced a loaf of bread and some salty butter, and she also offered a bit of ham and some pickled vegetables. "I've got some tea cakes I stole from your kitchen when I came by to check on your wife yesterday. Shame you were not there."

"I was meeting with the Williams men to discuss some mundane matters related to shearing. I enjoy Arthur's company, but I enjoy yours more." He smiled.

Morfudd grinned. But then she seemed to take in his overall countenance. "I take it you and your wife are at odds about something."

Owen sighed. He wouldn't disclose Grace's secret identity, but he did say, "Did you know she did not tell me about the baby? I found out when I arrived in Wales."

"And this bothers you."

"Grace and I exchanged letters weekly. I read every one at least twice. Could she not have at least mentioned her condition?"

"What brought you back to Wales? Grace and I have been handling most of the estate business, so it wasn't that."

"The Parliament session was nearing its end, but honestly, the haste was because she stopped writing."

"The birth was very hard on her. Did you know that?"

He nodded. "Yes, I was told."

Morfudd reached across the table and put her hand on Owen's. "Truly, it was more than just hard on her. I arrived at the house shortly after the baby was born. She was in a bad way. We thought we'd lost her. I've never seen so much blood."

"Oh, God." Owen hadn't known it had been that bad. He'd gathered she'd bled a lot if she'd had to replace the mattress and bedding, but he hadn't known she'd nearly died.

"Thankfully, she survived. And she dotes on that boy. I know your mother had all the maternal instincts of a stone, but Grace took to motherhood quickly, and she loves that little baby deeply. I don't know why she didn't tell you he was on the way, but I think she's been punished enough."

"That's not how this works. She wasn't meant to do penance.

She lied by omission, and her not trusting me with that information is deeply hurtful. So how can I trust her back?"

"What are you really upset about?"

"Is that she lied not enough? It wasn't just the baby. There were other things she didn't tell me about. They aren't my secrets to share, but they were things I found out about on my own and not because Grace told me."

"Look, my marriage was short, sadly. And George and I had time to court and get to know each other before we married, so we weren't strangers. Obviously I never had children. And I've had no notion to remarry. I enjoy my friends and my castle and I'm perfectly content in my life. So I don't know what it is like to be in a marriage like yours. But I'm guessing that you are upset because you care about her, and thus you view her sins of omission as a betrayal."

"Yes," said Owen.

"And thus your relationship is not what you expected."

"That is exactly it."

"But, and I know you know this, but let me remind you: you have not been here. You drove your wife out here, deposited her in your great house, and then went back to London."

"It's what she wanted."

"And you would do whatever your wife wanted."

"Yes. Within reason."

Morfudd leveled her gaze at him. "Have you asked her what she wants now?"

"She *lied* to me."

The tea kettle started to whistle. Morfudd got up to turn it off. She poured tea for herself and Owen. "So you have not yet gotten past feeling betrayed."

"How else should I feel? Yes, I was in London, but I thought we'd grown close. All those letters. They were precious to me. And I came home because I was worried about her, but I was also hoping to have this happy reunion, and while I find Dafydd to daily be a delightful surprise, I can't seem to reconcile the fact that she didn't tell me about him. Not once did she mention it."

Except she had, hadn't she? Owen suddenly remembered the letters in his pocket. He reached into his jacket and pulled them out.

"What are those?" Morfudd asked.

"Letters Grace meant to post but didn't because the baby came early." Owen turned them over in his hands. "She gave them to me this morning."

"You should read them."

Morfudd busied herself with preparing luncheon while Owen read the letters.

The first one said everything: they were to have a baby, due around the end of August, which was now. The baby *had* come early, Owen had already done the math on that. This letter was dated at the end of July, so Grace must have thought she'd be giving Owen just enough time to get back to Wales. The letter also confessed that she was Gerard Makepeace. She said at the end that all of this was news she would have liked to tell him in person, and she hoped they could discuss when he came home.

The second letter was dated a week after Dafydd's birth, and it was informing Owen that he had a son and that Grace greatly regretted her earlier letter had not made it into the post with enough time to summon Owen home for the birth.

From all this, Owen inferred that Grace had put off telling him as long as she could so that she did not take him from his business in London—perhaps because she knew he'd drop everything and rush home as soon as she told him about the baby—but suddenly the baby's birth was almost upon her. If only she'd gotten that first letter in the mail sooner.

When he finished reading, Morfudd was staring at him expectantly.

He grunted. "I wish I'd been here when she went through labor. I don't know if I could have helped, but maybe I could have offered some comfort. By her delay in informing me that the baby was on the way, she didn't let me make my own choice about whether to come."

Morfudd nodded. "So she was wrong. I understand why you are angry. I suppose the question is, what will you do about it? Has she apologized?"

"Several times, yes."

"But you are still angry."

Angry was the wrong word. Hurt was closer. And the letters helped soothe it somewhat. It was clear that she intended to tell him. "I am upset."

"What did she say in the letters?"

"She told me about the baby and some other things. She had been reading my letters and knew I was doing some difficult work in Parliament. She didn't want to force me away from that, wanted me to have my moment to do something meaningful, so she postponed telling me about the baby as long as she felt necessary. And, of course, that was too long, it turned out, because the baby came early."

"Was it important? Your business in Parliament?"

"I thought so at the time, but it wasn't more important than my family. And it came to nothing anyway."

"What happened?"

Owen gave her a brief summary of the situation with the compromise road bill and the Luddites and how Owen wanted to act, but how no one else in Parliament seemed interested.

He concluded, "As we so often do, we sent troops instead."

"That is the English way."

"But I am not English."

"No. Perish the thought."

Owen sighed. "I worked hard for months and got nowhere. And because of it, I missed the birth of my son."

"Ah, here it is. You're mad at yourself as well."

"Perhaps I should not have stayed away so long."

"Perhaps." Morfudd frowned at him. "So you blame yourself, at least a little."

"I thought I was doing what she wanted."

"Maybe what she wanted changed."

"But how was I to know that? How are we supposed to have a marriage if we don't talk to each other? If she wanted me here, she should have said something. I cannot read her mind." He shook his head. "I missed her desperately when I was in London. I would have taken any excuse to come back to Wales, but I didn't, because I thought my absence was what she wanted."

"Maybe that feels bad, too. You want to be with her, not apart from her."

"Yes."

"But now you are *not* with her because you are cross with her."

"Well…yes."

"You are married and you have a son, so it is in your best interest to figure out how to be together. You should have a frank conversation with her about what you both want. I don't know if that will resolve the fact that you don't completely trust her right now, but you could also give her the chance to prove she is trustworthy."

The letters had helped with that, but he was still unsure. "How do I do that?"

"Give it time. Speak with her in person and not via letter. Stay here in Wales until you have a better understanding of what is going on in your marriage."

"For someone who is not currently married, you are wise."

Morfudd preened. "I know. I am a keen observer of people. Look, Owen, your wife is lovely. She is friendly and kind and I adore her. I've been teaching her Welsh, you know. I helped her pick out the boy's name because she wanted to give him a hearty Welsh name. She made a mistake, and I know it's not a small thing and I know you need time to figure out how to forgive her, but do not carry a grudge forever. She's good for you and will make you happy if you can find understanding."

Morfudd was probably right. Divorce was not an option, nor was it what Owen wanted. What he wanted was Grace, and not to feel the way he currently felt about everything.

"How long do you intend to stay in Wales?" Morfudd asked.

"I do not know. I received a letter yesterday that Parliament has been sent off on recess officially, so there is nothing pressing for me in London right now."

"Aside from the start of the Season."

"That is not as important as fixing what I have here."

Morfudd smiled. "Yes. That's the spirit. You'll be all right, my dear Owen. Talk to your wife. Do not make assumptions. See what she wants. Maybe you can yet find happiness in each other, if that's what you both want."

"Well. Thank you for talking this through with me." He took a deep breath and broke off a piece of bread. A block of Morfudd's homemade salty butter sat there, and it was indulgent, but he spread a healthy amount on his piece of bread. "Well, enough baring my soul. Update me on the castle now. How are improvements proceeding?"

Morfudd grinned and began regaling him with tales of the castle renovation.

OWEN ARRIVED BACK at the house in time to see the doctor leaving. He dismounted from his horse as a groom ran up to take Glyndwr back to the stables, so Owen met the doctor in the drive, in front of the house.

He knew Dr. Jones, because he'd seen to his father near the end of his life. He liked the man immensely and had always known him to be kind and knowledgeable.

"I am pleased to report, my lord, that the countess is healing well," Dr. Jones reported. "She will be all but fully healed in another week or so, I believe."

"Oh. That is good news. Everyone has been vague with me when discussing my lady's...situation."

Dr. Jones nodded. "Then I shall be candid with you. The baby was a big, healthy boy, which we like to see, but a baby that large can…how shall I put this?"

"I am an adult, Dr. Jones."

"There was some tearing. She required stitches."

Oh, God. "Is this why she bled so much?"

"Yes. It's not unusual, I'm afraid. She lost a great deal of blood, and her recovery has been slow, although much better in the last few weeks. I imagine having you back home has been a help."

Owen doubted that. He hadn't been very warm toward her.

"But she is nearly healed now, you say?"

"If you are anxious to bed your wife, I would wait another week or two, but I am satisfied with her progress otherwise. She still tires easily and is at times overly emotional by her own admission, but that is all normal and she'll be perfectly fine with a little more time."

"It's not that I'm anxious."

Dr. Jones smiled. "It's very common for husbands to ask. But trust your wife. She knows her body. She'll tell you when she's ready again."

Well, then. Owen and Grace had done naught but sleep in their bed since he'd arrived back from London. Owen hadn't known what to do. He didn't want to pursue physical relations when they felt so estranged, plus she seemed so exhausted all the time. "She insists on taking care of the baby herself. I imagine that is a factor in her fatigue."

"Is that why she has yet to hire a nurse?"

"She says she interviewed a few and found them wanting."

Dr. Jones nodded. "If you are still looking for a nurse, I do have an excellent candidate in mind. The children she currently minds are old enough for school and she mentioned to me the other day that she is about to start looking for a new post. She is exceedingly patient and kind, like an aunt to many in the community. Too old to be a wet nurse, but that does not appear to be something the countess wants help with."

"No, I do not believe so. It would please me to talk to your candidate."

"Indeed. I'll arrange something."

"Thank you, doctor."

Dr. Jones shook Owen's hand. "It is good to see you, my lord. Come to Wales more often."

"Yes. I have been in London too long."

Owen saw Dr. Jones to the end of the drive and then walked into the house.

"Where is the countess?" Owen asked as Driscoll helped him out of his coat.

"Her bedchamber, my lord."

As Owen climbed the stairs, he reflected on the fact that Grace had been sad since he'd arrived home. It was something he'd noticed but not really internalized. On their honeymoon, she'd had an easy smile and seemed to be made partly of sunshine. That light had dimmed, and Owen was likely the cause of it. He wanted to trust her, but she'd been through a lot, too.

He found her lying on their bed, staring at the wall but not asleep. When she noticed him walk in, she sat up abruptly.

"Don't get up on my account," he said, walking into the room. "Are you tired?"

"A bit, but I'm all right. The doctor just left."

"Yes, I ran into him outside." Owen walked toward the bed. "We should probably talk."

The expression on Grace's face was earnest and heartbreaking. She looked exhausted and dispirited. He believed that her remorse was genuine. He'd never get to witness the birth of his son. But maybe he could forgive her for that if they could build a life together. If that was what she wanted.

He realized he already had forgiven her for her vase-making alter ego. She made beautiful things and wanted to sell them. There was no shame in that. He was in awe of her talent, in fact.

He sat beside her on the bed. Softly, he said, "I do not mean to further plague you. I merely want to explain myself. The reason I was so upset is that I want to be with you, Grace. I do. But I want to be able to trust you, too."

She settled into a sitting position on the bed. "I understand."

He wasn't sure she did. "I read your letters."

"Did you?"

"I admit, I am as frustrated with you as I am with myself. We both made mistakes. I spent time in London and got nowhere with my Parliament work, and I feel foolish for being so idealistic, for failing, when I could have been here with you and avoided the whole ordeal. I *should* have been here with you."

"I understand why—"

"We both made mistakes—that is what I am trying to say. Perhaps we should be fair about that."

"All right." Grace looked confused.

"Let me ask you something." He paused to think about how to phrase it. "When I was in London, I missed you, and I came back here thinking, as long as you were okay, I would propose having a real marriage and not just an arrangement. But only if that's what you wanted."

Grace's face crumbled. She pressed her face into her hands. "I'm sorry. I cry so much lately."

"It's all right."

"No. You…you came here and I shocked you. And I don't know what I thought I wanted anymore, because all I know now is that there's distance between us, and even though you have every right to be angry with me, I hate that distance."

He wanted to take her into his arms, but he stayed in place. He wanted to be sure they understood each other before they went any further.

The truth was, he missed her. He was upset, yes, but he could find a way to forgive her if there was some promise of a future together. They'd either stay married and lead separate lives, or they'd find a way to be together.

"It's been hard for me," Owen said. "I felt betrayed. I felt like

I misunderstood the entire nature of our relationship. And I know you regret what happened. You don't need to apologize again. And I know I've been hard on you since I came home. I had to figure out what I wanted and what I needed, and I had to adjust to this new…situation. I apologize for putting distance between us. I felt I needed to in order to… understand what is happening now. None of this is what I expected when I came home."

"If I could do it over again, I would do things differently. You weren't wrong, Owen. I looked forward to your letters every week, too. I missed you a great deal when you were gone. I thought that I wanted independence, but that was before we spent time together, before you sent m all those wonderful letters. You shared your life with me, and I appreciate that so much, I truly do. But it's hard for me to share myself because I have spent my entire life hiding it from my disapproving parents. But I don't like the way things are between us, Owen. I want to close the distance."

Owen understood that. Yes, there'd been sexual attraction between them, but they'd connected during their honeymoon, before they'd ever exchanged a letter. And then, like a fool, he'd left.

"If we forgave each other, what would you want our future to be? And please be honest with me."

She wiped her eyes and then looked up at him. "I want us to be together. I want us to raise Dafydd together. I want you to be a part of Dafydd's life, because he deserves to have a father who cares about him, who accepts him. I mean…well, he's only a month old, I don't know what he deserves or not yet, I suppose, but I love him so much, and I want you to love him, too. That's what I want."

"Would you come with me to London if I needed to return?"

"If you were going to be away for months, then yes. This last week has been so hard because I'm so happy to have you home, but you're not really here. And…" She started to cry again. "It's been so hard. I don't remember his birth. I started to feel faint, and I suppose I passed out. And I couldn't get out of bed for a few days. I am so grateful for everyone's help, but you weren't here, and you should have been. But you weren't, because of me, and I will never forgive myself for it. I didn't understand my own feelings until he was here and you were here and I'm so sorry…"

Owen lost his nerve and pulled her into his arms. She put her arms around him and pressed her face into his shoulder. He stroked her hair.

"Grace. I forgive you. I came here wanting to have a marriage, and that is still what I want. I want to be with you and I want to raise Dafydd, and I will drag both of you all over this bloody island if that's what it takes for us to be together. I am so sorry, Grace. I am sorry this has been so difficult for you. I am sorry I wasn't more understanding. I'm sorry if I made everything worse. It was never my intention to make you feel bad. I was stunned by it all, I suppose."

She was crying too hard to speak, so Owen held her. He didn't know that they'd spent enough time together to fall in love, but the last year had changed him, that was for certain. He'd never thought he truly wanted a wife or a son, but now he couldn't imagine living without them.

She sat up and pulled away slightly. "Can we…well, not start over, but can we move forward?"

"Yes."

They looked at each other for a long moment. Grace had apparently taken to wearing her hair loose around her shoulders, and Owen loved her shiny blond locks. He ran his fingers through one that rested on her shoulder. Then he cupped her cheek and kissed her.

He thought about his lonely nights London, about the glorious nights of their honeymoon, about everything he imagined they'd do together in the future. He thought about what Morfudd said.

He pulled away. "It was never my intention to punish you. I know things have been difficult. I just needed to work out my own feelings. But I think that, if we are to move forward, we must talk to each other. We must say what we feel and think. We must always be honest and tell the whole truth. I swear to you, Grace, that though I am a flawed man, I will always be fully honest with you. If you swear the same, then I think we can have a very good marriage."

"I promise, Owen."

He believed her. He kissed her again. And was like coming home. Grace put her arms around him and Owen held her close. This was an embrace, an understanding, a promise.

Then Grace pulled back. "Owen, I… I hope you know, I want to be able to…that is, I am in no rush to have more children, but I—"

"No need to worry about that now."

"I would like to lie with you again. But I meant to say, I need a little more time."

"That is all right. I will wait for you to be ready. I am not in a rush."

Grace balked. "Do you not want me?"

Oh. Perhaps he'd been too hasty in telling her he would wait. "Of course I want you. All I thought about when I was in London was being with you again. At least I can say that, when Dafydd was conceived, you and I were enjoying each other. I would of course love to do that again very soon. I merely meant, I do not wish to push you into doing anything you are not ready for."

"The worst part about all of this is that you are a kind-hearted man, Owen Thomas, and I will spend the rest of my life trying to be worthy of you."

"You are worthy, Grace." He kissed her again, but somewhere in the distance, he heard the baby cry. "Oh, perhaps he is feeling left out."

Grace let out a watery laugh. "Impeccable timing."

"What do you suppose he wants? Is it mealtime? Does he need a fresh nappy?"

"It's likely one of those."

"Do you see how quickly I learn?"

Grace laughed and pushed herself off the bed. "I shall fetch him."

"I shall help, then."

Chapter Twenty-Three

Mrs. Roberts, the nurse Dr. Jones recommended, turned out to be a woman of about fifty years who was one of the sweetest, kindest people Owen had ever met. She instantly put Grace at ease, too, which is what made the decision to hire her relatively easy. Once Mrs. Roberts made it clear to Grace that she didn't judge her for taking care of her own son—apparently the other nurse candidates had found this choice bizarre, which had made Grace self-conscious—Grace seemed much more enthusiastic about hiring her.

Thus Grace felt all right leaving Dafydd with Mrs. Roberts while she and Owen rode out to the cottage.

Grace hadn't been there since Dafydd's birth, but she'd told Owen she was eager to have him see it. She wanted his opinion on the changes and improvements she'd made.

It had been an odd week. Owen felt like he and Grace were finding their way back to each other, emotionally, but they hadn't come back together physically. As each night passed, the ache Owen felt being unable to touch his wife became more acute. But he was also terrified of hurting her, and she'd said she didn't feel ready yet, so Owen kept his hands to himself. He supposed there were other sorts of intimacy, but he was waiting for a cue from Grace.

In the carriage to the cottage, he put an arm around her and kissed the top of her head.

"Sometimes," Grace said, "I can't tell how well we know each other. We've spent all of six weeks in each other's presence. That's so little time."

"Yes, but we wrote those letters."

She sat up a little so she could look at him. "Do you suppose that means we know each other well now?"

Owen considered the question. "I imagine that, as we grow older, we will continue to discover new things about each other. I look forward to that, in fact."

Grace nodded slowly. "Yes. I suppose that is true. And I promised to be honest with you." She let out a breath. "I found suppliers for my pottery locally, and I'm working with a shop in Penmaenmawr that is both selling some of my vases and shipping them to London."

Owen understood that this was Grace's attempt to be completely honest about her work, and he appreciated it. "All right. I didn't realize there were places locally from which you could acquire supplies."

"There are potteries in the region. Small ones. It's not like Staffordshire." At what must have been Owen's blank expression, Grace added, "Stoke and a number of other towns in Staffordshire are where most British pottery is made. The dishes in your house? If you look at the stamp on the bottom of each plate, it says they were made in Staffordshire."

"Oh. I suppose I never gave that much thought."

"As I'm sure you're aware, the Welsh like to do things their own way, so there are a few small manufacturers in the region. They have clay available for purchase as well."

"I am glad you are able to find everything you need," Owen said. "I love the vase you sent me. As I may have mentioned, I put it in a place of honor in the dining room. It's beautiful and you are enormously talented."

"Thank you."

"I'll keep your secret, as long as you no longer keep secrets from me."

"I won't ever again."

"I believe you."

"I did spend some money on the cottage, although I buy my pottery supplies with my own money from the sales of my work."

"That's all right. I told you to furnish it."

"I sometimes spend a full day at the cottage. Any food I left behind will have rotted in the many weeks I've been away, but I was keeping some there. There's a kiln in the backyard. And I furnished the bedroom. I wanted a bed. Before I grew too large to operate the wheel, I sometimes got tired and needed to nap. Making a baby is hard work."

"Indeed, it must be!"

"Hopefully you will not think I've wasted your money."

"Impossible. I've seen the ledgers. You did spend money, but you were also more frugal than I expected you to be."

"I suppose that is good news."

They arrived at the cottage. Owen wasn't entirely sure what to expect. The main room was styled as a sitting room, with three large chairs and a low table. The pottery studio was in the sunny room overlooking the sea, at the back of the house. There were several cabinets and shelves lined with finished objects.

"I was teaching some of the locals how to make pottery, but Catrin was my only regular student. The bowls on that shelf? Those are hers. I don't think I have much else finished here. I stopped being able to make vases some months ago and sold what I had to the store in Penmaenmawr."

"How long does it take you to make one of those vases?"

"The whole process takes a few days. Usually I sketch it out first, then I need a couple of hours to shape a vase on the wheel, then I leave it overnight to dry. The next day, I do the detail work and fix any errors and let it dry again. The day after that, I apply glaze, which can be time consuming if I decide to paint a design instead of glazing everything white. Then I set up the kiln and bake the clay. Usually by then, the item is finished, but sometimes

I do some additional painting."

"So it's an involved process. I had no idea."

"I'll show you how sometime."

Owen shook his head. "I've no talent for anything artistic. But I'd love to watch you."

Grace had to smile at that. "My favorite part is the sea. If we stepped outside, we could smell it."

"I know. It's why I bought the cottage."

"I hope you do not mind that I have taken it over."

Owen looked around. "I do not. It feels...homey. Lived in. You've made the space useful. That's true of the estate, too. So many nobles feel their homes must be perfect all the time, but I think that makes the home feel like a museum and not a space where people live, with all their messiness."

Grace smiled. "I agree. My parents' home was always spotless. I sometimes felt as if I couldn't touch anything."

"You must tend to this place yourself."

"I do try. It's...it's a sanctuary, for me."

"It's yours," Owen said.

"Yes, I suppose it is. But it's yours, too. I wanted to bring you here to show it to you."

Owen understood that it was technically true that he owned the cottage, but this was clearly Grace's space. He also understood, therefore, that it was a gift that she was showing it to him. "It's lovely," he told her.

"Thank you. Let me show you the other rooms."

There weren't many, but Owen let Grace take her on a tour of what was there. The pottery studio. The small kitchen in which all remaining food had indeed rotted. And finally the bedroom. The bedroom was fully furnished, with a proper bed, several chests of drawers, and a trunk. This room also felt homey.

"This is nice," Owen said, then moved toward the door, figuring they'd leave soon.

Grace stopped him by putting a hand on his chest. "Owen. Would you lie down with me here?"

"Do you mean—?"

"Yes." She took both of his hands in hers. "I suppose I don't actually know where our son was conceived, but I'd like to think it was here, on that old lumpy mattress. I think this little cottage by the sea has some magic."

Owen leaned down and kissed her. "I don't want to hurt you," he said.

"I don't believe you will, but I will stop you if it becomes an issue."

Owen took in her face and how earnest she looked. She was asking them to come back together as a married couple, and he wanted to. She looked wonderful today, her blond hair pinned up, her simple dress doing nothing to diminish her beauty.

He kissed her. Warmth spread through his body. He'd been waiting for weeks to do this, months really, when all those nights lying next to her had not been enough. His hunger came alive as he kissed her, and her hands on his shoulders, on his back, told him she was just as eager.

He took her face in his hands and looked into her eyes. He cherished this woman. He longed for this woman. He thought about her constantly. And she was *his*. "I love you," he said. "I don't believe I've ever said that to you before, but it's true."

She smiled. Something in her seemed to melt a little bit. "Oh. Owen. I love you, too. Please come to bed with me."

She pulled him over, leaving no question about what she wanted. She wasn't wearing much under her dress—a shift, but no stays—and he'd dressed simply that day, too, in just trousers, a shirt, and a jacket, so they were able to make quick work of their clothes. It was the first time he'd seen her body since returning home. It had changed, undoubtedly. But he loved that, too, because she'd had his child.

"I was nervous about this," she said, gesturing toward her belly. "I feared you'd find me ugly."

"I could never. You are the most beautiful woman I have ever laid eyes on." He splayed his hand over her belly. "Your body has changed, but that makes you more beautiful to me."

Grace kissed him. She pulled away slightly. "You look entirely the same," she said with a laugh.

"Yes, well, women have the harder time of it, I suppose."

He moved his hand up to cup her breast. He loved the feel of it against his palm. Her breath hitched as he touched her, as he got his hands on her the way he'd wanted to for months. They kissed, and she moaned against his lips.

She ran her hands through his hair. Lord, he'd missed this. Just the simple act of being with someone, but with this woman specifically, the one who had his whole heart and who he would never leave behind again.

And when at last he slid inside her, it was like coming home.

They made love and he met her gaze, their eyes and hearts connecting as they moved together, and Owen knew he'd remember this moment for years to come. He treasured it and treasured her and realized he'd completely forgiven her.

They'd both made mistakes. Now they'd get it right.

He felt her quake around him, and she shook and clutched at his shoulders. He rode through it until his own climax was nearly upon him. It was a close thing, but he had enough presence of mind to pull out. No new babies, at least not yet.

But who knew what the future would bring?

As he lay down beside her and pulled her into his arm, he thought to himself that he wanted a future, and that he wanted some it to be mysterious, but he wanted to experience all of it with Grace.

"Did you coax me out here today just for this?" he asked her softly, stroking the soft skin of her back.

"No, but it was a pleasant diversion."

He chuckled. "A pleasant diversion? Is that all?"

She slapped his shoulder playfully. "It was very good and you know it. Don't look so smug." She lifted her head and smiled down at him. "Do you really love me?"

"I really do. And when I get called back to London, as I inevitably will one of these days, I want you and Dafydd to come with me. We will be back, of course, as I would not want to separate you from your art. Or, hell, we can buy a potter's wheel for my house in London. You can spend all of my money on it if you want to. I don't care, as long as you are with me."

She leaned down and kissed him. "I agree. Let us not separate unless necessary ever again."

"You have a deal."

Her stomach grumbled and she groaned. "We should probably get back so that we can eat dinner. And I want to check on Dafydd. This is the longest I've been apart from him since he was born."

"Of course, of course. We shall leave in a few minutes. Although I assure you he is quite safe with Mrs. Roberts."

"I know. I do truly believe that. But it is difficult to be parted."

"Then we shall return posthaste. But only after I hold you for a few more minutes."

She looked like she wanted to argue with him, but then she smiled. "Well, all right. If you insist."

Epilogue

GRACE WAS NOT happy about returning to the Rutherford Ball, exactly, but the annual fete was indeed probably the best place to reenter society. There were plenty of people here—including her parents, unfortunately—so it was easy to get lost in the crowd, but plenty of people she knew asked after her and her health.

She found herself sipping lemonade with Penny, much as she had a little over a year ago just before the kiss that had sealed her fate. She couldn't say she regretted any of it.

Penny said, "I intend to let Beckwith dance with me as soon as he tears himself away from the card room."

"Indeed. I had forgotten how handsome he is."

"Yes. We rode in Hyde Park yesterday and it was a delight. Raced each other a bit. I had the *best* time. I do think a proposal will occur soon, although I don't want to count on it."

"He'd be a fool not to offer for you. You are beautiful and clever."

"Yes, thank you. I hope you are right."

Beckwith did indeed appear at Penny's side a few minutes later. He held out his arm for her.

That left Grace alone, so she went to go look for her husband. Likely he was also playing cards. When she escaped the ballroom, into the hallway, she found Anthony leaning against a wall, nursing a snifter of whiskey.

"Hello, my lord," she said.

He looked up and smiled at her sadly. "Hello, my lady. It is good to see you. You look lovely tonight." He lifted her hand to his lips and kissed her knuckles.

"You seem to be drowning in melancholy. Or whiskey perhaps. Is something wrong?"

He sighed and went back to leaning on the wall. "Oh, everything is wrong. I'm to be married."

"Are congratulations not in order?"

Anthony looked up and down the hallway, likely verifying that they were alone. Softly, he said, "Waring has left me. Ended our relationship about a month ago. And I promised my mother I'd marry by the end of this Season, so I have just become betrothed to a virtual stranger and we are to be married in a few months."

"Oh. Oh, Anthony. I am sorry to hear about Waring. Is that why you are so sad?"

"I suppose it is obvious, isn't it?"

"You are drinking alone in the hallway at one of the largest balls of the Season."

"My mother thought it would be good to be seen with my fiancée."

"And who is she, if I might ask?"

"Matilda Clairborne."

"Oh. She is lovely, at least. I don't know her well, but I've met her a few times and always found her to be friendly and clever."

"Yes, that is something. Unlike many of the other chits my other threw at me, Miss Clairborne and I do seem to be able to hold a conversation."

"Anthony." Grace tutted. "Such low standards."

"I do not wish to marry at all, if you must know. What I want is to be with Lark again."

"Lark? Oh, The Earl of Waring. I had forgotten his Christian name was Larkin."

"I suppose I am getting to be pretty deep in my cups if I have become so informal." He sighed and set the glass on a nearby end table.

"I am sorry, Anthony. I know you are a good man. You deserve happiness as much as anyone else. I am sorry that it is apparently not in the cards."

"I shall persevere." He smiled ruefully. "Well, my dear, I understand you have produced an heir for Caernarfon. Congratulations are in order."

"It is not so formal as all that. We have a son, yes. I brought him with us to London. You could come by and see him, if you'd like."

"You brought an infant to London?"

"My husband was called back to Parliament. He refused to be parted from me, and I refused to be parted with my son, so yes, we all came to London. The carriage ride was among the worst I have ever taken because I worried that he'd be injured if we hit bumpy road, although I will admit that the rocking of the carriage often just lulled him to sleep. And we did manage to startle a few of the proprietors at the coaching inns Caernarfon usually stays at as we traveled along the way. But Dafydd, my son, is very cute and could charm the paint off a wall, so truly, it was not so bad. I'm afraid I have become one of those mothers who is quite protective of her child."

Anthony smiled. "How very gauche of you."

Grace laughed because she understood he was joking. "I know. But Caernarfon is letting me do things my way, even if it is unorthodox. Although he did also talk me into hiring a nurse. Mrs. Roberts rode with us from Wales and is currently watching the boy like a hawk. We fear he may start crawling soon."

"Babies do such things, I've heard."

"Yes. But seriously, you should call on us. I know Caernarfon and Waring are close friends, but *you* are my friend."

Anthony nodded. "Thank you, I appreciate that. I don't care much for babies, as you must know, but I will make an exception for you if he really is as cute as you say."

"Even more so."

"Although perhaps I might wait until Parliament is in session. I do not think your husband cares much for me."

"I think you're wrong about that, but whatever you are comfortable with. Or bring your fiancée to dinner sometime."

Anthony frowned.

"Is Waring here?" Grace whispered.

"No. We seem to be avoiding each other. I no longer go to my club for fear of running into him, and he has not been coming to social engagements unless he knows for certain I will not be there."

"Tragic."

"Yes, well. Welcome to my life this Season."

"Truly, I would like for you to come visit our home. Do not be a stranger to us. All right?"

"I promise."

"What exactly are you promising to my wife?" Owen asked, suddenly appearing. He held out an arm for Grace, so she slid hers around his.

"Your wife has invited me to dinner. I hope you do not find this objectionable."

"I do not," Owen said. "You are Grace's childhood friend, after all."

"I suppose you do not find me threatening."

Owen frowned at that. "Look, Beresford, things are awkward right now. I've known Waring since we were boys at Eton. He is one of my oldest friends, and he is no happier about your present situation than you are. But I swore an oath to give Grace whatever she wants, and if what she wants is to have you over for dinner, then I am amenable to it."

"This is the oath you swore?" Grace asked.

"Have I ever denied you anything?"

She laughed. "I suppose not."

"Listen, old man, I heard about your engagement. I hope you

are eventually as happy as Grace and I are." Owen leaned over and patted Anthony's arm.

"Unlikely under the circumstances, but I appreciate the sentiment."

"And now, if you do not mind, I should like to dance with my wife."

"Of course. Do not let me keep you. My misery is company enough."

Owen tilted his head and made a puzzled expression, as if he could not tell if Anthony was joking. Grace couldn't tell, either. "Will you truly be all right?" she asked.

"Oh, I shall. For the sake of my mother, if no one else, I should find my betrothed and take a turn around the dance floor. But go ahead. I am right behind you."

"All right."

Grace let Owen lead her back into the ballroom. It was a crush, and the air was hot inside, but it was not too bad amongst the other dancers. A slow waltz was playing, and most of the other couples on the floor were married, so Owen apparently felt little compunction about pulling Grace close as they danced.

"So, you were talking to Beresford."

"He is my friend, Owen. And he is very sad."

"I know. I have spoken with Waring at length since we returned, and he is just as unhappy. I don't know Beresford well, but I am sorry about what happened to them. I feel I should have some loyalty to my old friend, but if you want to have Beresford and his fiancée to dinner, I will not object."

"Thank you."

"And I trust you not to run off with Beresford."

Grace laughed. "Is that because you trust me or because you trust Beresford would never run off with a woman?"

"Both."

Grace laughed and hugged her husband. "Enough about Beresford. This is our first real night out in the social scene of London as a married couple. Let us show these people that the gossip is wrong and our marriage was not a mere convenience."

Owen spun her around as the music picked up in tempo and led her around the floor. She laughed with him as they danced. When the music slowed again, Grace said, "Show off."

"You asked for it." He smiled. "Let us take one more turn about the floor and go home to our son, all right?"

"I thought you would never ask. I like being out and social again, but this ball is overwhelming."

Owen smiled. "I love you."

"I love you, too. Now dance with me."

THE END

About the Author

Kate McMurray writes romance novels. She likes creating stories that are brainy, funny, and of course sexy, with regular guy characters and urban sensibilities. She advocates for romance stories by and for everyone. When she's not writing, she edits textbooks, watches baseball, plays violin, crafts things out of yarn, and wears a lot of cute dresses. She lives in Brooklyn, NY, with a bossy cat and too many books.

Instagram / Threads: @katemcmurraygram